Cayman pulled down the latch and the door slid open. Wind swirled around the gap, and Kross leaned forward into the gale. He leveled his guns at the cycle rider. Bannickburn could see the rider's eyes widen behind his wraparound shades. Their pursuer had a gun of his own, but he'd been aiming at the tires. He couldn't swing it around in time.

Kross fired both guns. One bullet caught the rider in the shoulder. A moist splotch appeared on his thick black jersey, making him drop his gun. The second shattered his sunglasses and buried itself in his face.

The front wheel of the cycle bucked and the back end flipped in the air. The lifeless rider was catapulted forward, flying at least fifteen meters before skidding on the pavement. His motorcycle followed him, sending up a shower of sparks as it dragged along the ground, eventually hitting its former rider and rolling over him before both came to a stop.

"Close it," Kross said. Cayman and Alex heaved forward, pushing the door closed. Kross wore a satisfied smirk. "One down. They'll be a little more careful about sneaking up on that side."

A HARD LESSON

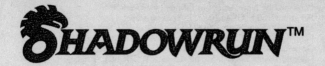

DROPS OF CORRUPTION

A Shadowrun™ Novel

JASON M. HARDY

A ROC BOOK

ROC
Published by New American Library, a division of
Penguin Group (USA) Inc., 375 Hudson Street,
New York, New York 10014, USA
Penguin Group (Canada), 90 Eglinton Avenue East, Suite 700, Toronto,
Ontario M4P 2Y3, Canada (a division of Pearson Penguin Canada Inc.)
Penguin Books Ltd., 80 Strand, London WC2R 0RL, England
Penguin Ireland, 25 St. Stephen's Green, Dublin 2,
Ireland (a division of Penguin Books Ltd.)
Penguin Group (Australia), 250 Camberwell Road, Camberwell, Victoria 3124,
Australia (a division of Pearson Australia Group Pty. Ltd.)
Penguin Books India Pvt. Ltd., 11 Community Centre, Panchsheel Park,
New Delhi - 110 017, India
Penguin Group (NZ), cnr Airborne and Rosedale Roads, Albany,
Auckland 1310, New Zealand (a division of Pearson New Zealand Ltd.)
Penguin Books (South Africa) (Pty.) Ltd., 24 Sturdee Avenue,
Rosebank, Johannesburg 2196, South Africa

Penguin Books Ltd., Registered Offices:
80 Strand, London WC2R 0RL, England

First published by Roc, an imprint of New American Library,
a division of Penguin Group (USA) Inc.

First Printing, May 2006
10 9 8 7 6 5 4 3 2 1

Copyright © WizKids Inc., 2006
All rights reserved

ROC REGISTERED TRADEMARK—MARCA REGISTRADA

Printed in the United States of America

PUBLISHER'S NOTE
This is a work of fiction. Names, characters, places, and incidents either are
the product of the author's imagination or are used fictitiously, and any resem-
blance to actual persons, living or dead, business establishments, events, or
locales is entirely coincidental.

The publisher does not have any control over and does not assume any
responsibility for author or third-party Web sites or their content.

For my mother, because I owe her one,
and because this is the exact opposite of the kind
of book she normally reads.

TRANS-POLAR
ALEUT

ATHABASKAN
COUNCIL

SALISH-
SHIDHE
COUNCIL

QUÉBEC

ALGONKIAN-MANITOU
COUNCIL

Seattle

TÍR
TAIRNGIRE

SIOUX
NATION

UNITED CANADIAN
AND AMERICAN
STATES (U.C.A.S.)

UTE
NATION

Denver

CALIFORNIA
FREE STATE

PUEBLO
CORPORATE
COUNCIL

CONFEDERATED
AMERICAN STATES

AZTLAN

CARIBBEAN LEAGUE

NORTH AMERICA
AS OF 2060

Copyright 2005, WizKids, Inc.

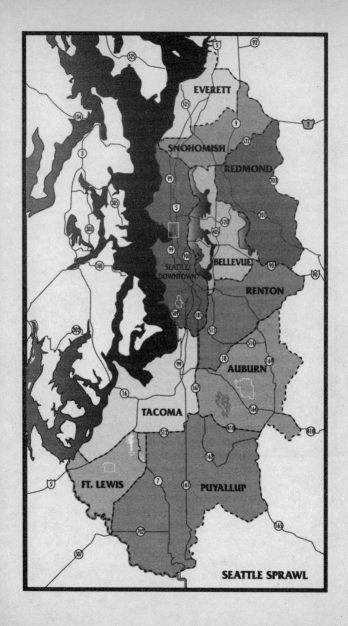

SEATTLE SPRAWL

1

The crowd never parted for Quinn Bailey. He knew
people who could make others veer out of their way
with a glance, or with a heavy stride. But he was too
short, too light, too friendly looking to intimidate people.
He had learned to work with his appearance, sliding between people, bobbing and weaving around the shifting
mass on the casino floor.

He smiled at everyone. In return, he got hostile stares,
puzzled glances, downcast eyes, and, on rare occasions,
smiles. Bailey grinned and nodded at them all, enjoying
the sight of them losing money.

He loved gambling. Not the gaming part of it—he
never played because he always lost. What he loved was
the concept of it, the whole idea of putting up a neon
sign and having hundreds, thousands of people lining up
to give you money, and all you have to do to keep them
happy is give some of the cash back to one of them.
It's the perfect business—you don't have to manufacture
anything, you don't have to sell anything, you just have
to rearrange the distribution of cash among a large
group of people and make sure you keep a big pile for
yourself.

A few meters away bells rang, lights flashed, and a
bourbon-scraped throat let out a raspy whoop. Dozens
of coins clinked into a metal cup. Most of them were

tokens good only for another pull on the machine or some other bet inside the casino, but it was a win, and a hundred jealous eyes watched the gleeful man scoop coins out of the cup. Then they turned back to the machines in front of them and gave their levers a vengeful pull.

There was no one at these machines whom Bailey wanted to see. If he was going to get anything done tonight, it would be at the tables. The people who were simply hoping luck would go their way didn't have much to offer him, but those working their opponents, or developing a system to beat the house, or even those just trying to drink their friends under the table had a chance of being useful. No guarantee—not by a long shot—but at least a chance.

But then there was an obstruction, like a boulder with a blue blazer. Bailey took a step to his right, and the rock moved with him. Then it spoke.

"How are you this evening, Mr. Bailey?"

Bailey sighed to himself. "Fine. Wonderful, in fact, and thanks for asking. But I believe I just saw my Aunt Gertie near the baccarat tables, and she's not supposed to gamble with her pill money, so if you'll excuse me . . ."

The security guard was not amused. The expression on his flat face did not flicker.

"I've been asked to remind you that the Gates Casino is open to almost anyone in the metropolitan area. It's a policy we're proud of."

"And well you should be," Bailey said.

"But, of course, we need to protect ourselves. Which means there are some people—people management thinks are potentially dangerous—whom we don't admit. For the protection of the casino."

"These people sound like trouble. I feel much safer knowing that you don't admit them. Thank you. Keep up the good work!"

"I've been told to tell you you're not on that list. Yet. But some people you know are on that list. And if you keep coming here, and we know you keep associating with the people we're concerned about, we may have no choice but to put you on that list."

"Well, that sounds dire indeed. I'll do everything in my power to prevent you from making such a drastic move."

"The management is quite serious about preserving casino security."

"I have no doubt." Bailey knew where this conversation needed to go, so he steamrolled the guard's attempts to say anything else. "Which is why the management has never, ever had anything to do with anyone of a questionable nature. Especially for, I don't know, the purposes of cleaning up some soiled money. The thing is, I'm serious about what I do, and the people with whom I associate are serious about what they do. We're all serious people. Look, I can even make a serious face. See?" Bailey furrowed his brow and made his mouth a horizontal line. "So you do what you have to do, and I'll do what I have to do, and your bosses will do what they have to do, and if what they have to do makes me mad enough, well, then, I'll just have to shoot them, but we're not to that point yet, so why worry about it? Let's all just enjoy our evening, shall we?"

Bailey wanted to think his display of wit and logic persuaded the security guard, but the more likely explanation was that, having delivered his message, the guard no longer cared to deal with Bailey. The boulder moved aside, and Bailey continued on his way.

The rows of slot machines gave way to felt-covered tables, and the pace of the action changed. Rather than bleeding their money away coin by coin, the gamblers at the tables paused, pondered, deliberated, placed a series of small bets, won a few, until the moment came when they placed a large bet and a more skilled gambler (either another patron or the house itself) relieved them of their money, and in an instant they lost two or three times as much as the slot machine gamers spent in an entire night. Bailey made a mental note of the gamblers with the largest stacks of chips in front of them, so that he could to talk to some of them later when they were away from the tables.

He saw at least three more security guards watching him closely as he flowed through the crowd, and he felt bad that he wasn't really giving them anything to see. Maybe he should lift a few chips from someone, or slip a knife in someone's back, or run back to the slot machines, find a little old lady, and punch her in the face. Preserving one's reputation sometimes required effort.

However, while getting thrown out of a casino (or bar or any other establishment) had its fun side, business had to get taken care of first. If all went well, maybe he could start a fight in an hour or two.

Beyond the gaming tables a broad archway flashed red and purple. The room on the other side was dim, though with plenty of black light—Bailey could see some of the ultraviolet tattoos on the faces of the patrons from here. Beyond that archway were the finest virtual reality rigs money could buy. Beyond *that* were the famed back rooms of the casino, the ones that management swore up and down didn't exist until you paid them enough money and promised to be discreet. In those rooms, just about anyone with a halfway decent datajack could experience any sensation the world had to offer.

Bailey didn't plan to go within twenty meters of the archway. The young corp drones who typically hung out there were useless to him, and the addicts in the simsense rooms were even worse. At least, he thought, the rooms kept many of the people he wanted to avoid concentrated in one place.

Ahead of him, at last, was one of the casino's half-dozen bars. Half the crowd was energized, on their first few drinks of the evening, steeling themselves for a night at the tables. The other half had just returned from the tables, where their alcohol-dulled nerves had helped them lose their entire night's stake, and all they had left to do was drive themselves the rest of the way to sullen intoxication.

He scanned the tables. He saw two of his men right

off the bat—Shivers and Boone, both with full tables, following their instructions perfectly. Bailey noticed that when he gave orders that involved drinking, they were obeyed far more often than orders involving, say, orks.

He approached Boone's table first, sauntering over, plotting a course a little to Boone's right, watching the bar, waiting to be noticed.

". . . I don't know *how* many drugs he was strung out on, but he couldn't even move his legs, while his upper body was just, you know, *whirling*, throwing random punches at anything he could reach, then scratching at the floor, clawing himself forward a half meter, then looking for someone else to hit. When no one else was in range, he'd give *himself* a few punches in the gut. I mean, he was *gone*, and—hey, is that Bailey? Quinn! Over here!"

Bailey, assuming an expression of surprise, turned to Boone. "Cal? Hey, good to see you. What's going on?"

They went through a process Bailey had been through a hundred times. Boone introduced Bailey to his friends. Bailey ordered a round of drinks for everyone. Bailey talked for a minute or two, then slowly pulled back from the conversation and just listened and watched.

He watched the body language of Boone's friends, checked to see how confidently they held themselves, how hungry they were for attention, how well they held their liquor. He listened, too, but what they said was usually less important than how they carried themselves. Still, he could often identify the suck-ups and the wallflowers in as little as a sentence or two, so paying attention to the words could be helpful.

Most of the time, Bailey didn't come away from these conversations with much of anything. Sometimes he found a two-bit thug who might be useful as muscle on some future job, but most of the time it was just wannabes and hangers-on, two groups Bailey had little use for. This table was no different—he was sure Boone had tried to put a credible group together, but good talent was hard to find. And Boone hadn't found any.

It took Bailey about thirty minutes to make his final judgments about the group, and another five to smoothly extricate himself from the conversation. Then he was on his way to Shivers' table.

Unlike Boone's table, the first sign at Shivers' was encouraging. Shivers was sitting back in his chair, one hand on his drink, the other hanging loosely over the chair's back, not trying to impress anyone with war stories. His thin lips shaped a grin barely this side of a sneer, a wavy lock of his light red hair dropping down near his left eye. The five people sharing the table with him spoke loudly and laughed even louder—Bailey had heard them several times when he was at Boone's table. As he approached, a casino floor manager was walking away, shaking her head. She'd undoubtedly delivered the fourth or fifth request of the evening for the group to keep it down, and for the fourth or fifth time she hadn't been well received.

Bailey hoped they weren't already too far gone for him to make a good evaluation.

Shivers didn't bother to put on a show of noticing Bailey like Boone had. He'd spotted Bailey the moment he walked away from Boone's table, and waved him over when he got within a few meters.

"Evening, Jimmy," Bailey said.

"Quinn," Shivers answered with a slow nod. "Win anything?"

"Not playing."

"Drinking?"

"Just water."

Shivers cocked an eyebrow.

"Still have some work to do before the night is over," Bailey said. "Need to stay sharp for a little while longer."

"Pity."

Bailey shrugged.

"Join us?" Shivers asked.

"If you have room."

Shivers motioned toward two of his companions, who

slid their chairs away from each other. "Always room for one more," he said.

Bailey sat down and went to work. He dismissed the kid next to Shivers almost immediately. A decker, with a gaping jack on the right side of his head. He had shaved all his hair and painted a red-and-white target on his scalp, with the jack in the bulls'-eye. His eyes looked dull, meaning either he'd had some work done on them or he was using as well as drinking tonight. He talked high and fast, slinging around thick slang. He might have some skills, but he was too eager, too anxious for a fight. Bailey had enough hotheads to deal with already.

He couldn't accept or dismiss the others as quickly, so he settled himself in to listen.

"It's a pit. It's a fraggin' coal pit," said one of Shivers' friends, a rotund man with a black-and-white striped goatee.

"It's not!" insisted a red-haired woman to Bailey's right. "The mine's all run out, these days. It's just a quiet village—lovely, really."

"If there's no mining, that means it's a ghost town. No money. Slagheap."

"There was going to be a story here, wasn't there?" interrupted an older man, an elf with bushy brown sideburns nearly down to his chin. "You can teach each other geography later."

The woman smiled at the elf, while the rotund man just shrugged. But they listened to him. Bailey took note.

"As I was saying," the woman said, "I was in Standburn, where I grew up, visiting some of my old mates. They told me some corp had been sniffing around, thinking there may be coal or something else still left in the ground, might buy up the whole fraggin' town. We run through the usual options—buying up as much land as we can, so we can make a profit selling to the corp, burning the whole town down to leave the corp with nothing—then we get creative."

The others around the table nodded.

"We don't want bleedin' corp money, and we'd like to avoid burning down our village unless it's truly necessary. We think for a time about what we want, and the first thing we want is the corp out of our town, always and forever. Not likely that'll happen, though, is it? So we move to the next best option—make them nervous."

"What corp was it?" said a muscular man with a metal plate over the left side of his scalp.

"McKinney Mining," the woman said, and everyone around the table immediately nodded in recognition.

"Bastards, all of them," the muscular man said. His Scottish burr grew thicker around the words.

"True. Which is why we decided to do what we did. Simple hex was all—smoke cloud spell with a special trigger set into the mine, waiting for the first steam shovel to hit. The tricky bit was getting the cloud just right. Ordinary smoke wouldn't do it."

The older elf saw it right away. "Gas," he said. "You wanted a gas cloud."

The woman grinned. "Dead right. Best-case scenario, they blow themselves up. Worst case, they kill a canary and then get all panicked for a time. Either one is fine by us."

"How did it work in the end?" the muscular man asked.

"McKinney bought the whole town, moved everyone out, and started digging." The woman grinned wickedly. "Then they blew the entire bleeding town apart."

Most of the table laughed. The elf and the rotund man, though, looked skeptical.

"You created enough gas with a smoke cloud to blow up an entire town?" the rotund man asked.

"Small village," the woman replied.

"I don't care how blessed *small* the village is. Most spells of that sort can't even blow up a single *building*, much less level a whole town."

"Just because *you* can't do it isn't reason enough to say *anyone* can't do it," the woman insisted.

"Fine. Fine. You and your mining-town friends were

the most powerful mages in Europe. Bloody amazing that you wasted your time and talents on pranks, when you easily could have been ruling any of several small nations.''

The argument was off and running. The others at the table chose sides, based more on whom they were sitting next to rather than any logic from one side or the other. They had strong liquor in their veins, they were in a bar, and they couldn't see any reason in the world not to get into a good fight.

All except the elf. Bailey had been watching him since the end of the woman's story, and it was clear the elf recognized the conclusion for the complete and utter bulldrek it was. But he didn't say anything, didn't get into the argument that his large companion was eager to rush into. He didn't seem to see much point in this particular fight.

Good judgment and discretion were things Bailey often found immensely useful. The elf was clearly the person to watch at this table.

He leaned over to Shivers, who yelled an occasional remark into the fray supporting the woman, but was otherwise staying out of the argument.

"You don't honestly believe her story, do you?" Bailey asked.

"Doesn't matter," Shivers said flatly. "She'll appreciate my support."

Bailey looked back at the tight black outfit the woman was wearing, trying to discern the curves of her form in the dim light of the bar. From what he could perceive, all the lines and angles seemed to be well placed.

"And how appreciative will she be?" Bailey said.

The left corner of Shivers' mouth twitched. On him, that passed for a smile. "Very."

Bailey nodded his approval. "Fine, then. So I know why she's here tonight."

Another mouth twitch. "I didn't bring her here for you."

"Clearly. But what about the elf?"

"Bannickburn."

"Right. What's his story?"

"Don't know much," Shivers said. "Originally from the Scotsprawl, hasn't been here long. Seems a little rootless. Not sure why he came, what he's up to."

"Probably came running from something, then," Bailey said. "Him and half of the rest of this city." *Probably a little desperate*, Bailey thought. *That's another thing I can use.*

"Did you bring him here for me?" Bailey asked aloud.

Shivers snorted. "Hate to say it, but evenings I'm mostly doing things for myself. Even the nights when you've given me homework. I brought him because he's a friend. But you can look him over all you want."

"Kind of you." He ignored, like he always did, any attempts by Shivers to get a rise out of him. Shivers reflexively rebelled against anyone who attempted to exert authority over him, and Bailey, like the parent of a teenage child, had learned to let certain things go.

He returned his attention to the larger conversation, sitting back in his chair and waiting for the right moment. When dealing with a Scotsman in a bar, he liked to stick with the sterotype; there was one sure opening to get on his subject's good side, and he was certain the moment for it would arrive shortly.

Bannickburn finished his drink, then glanced at the bottom of the cup, swirling the ice around, apparently hoping to catch a glimpse of a few drops of alcohol he might have missed. When he looked up, Bailey could read the disappointment in his face.

Bailey let a few more moments pass, allowing an additional touch of thirst to build in Bannickburn's throat. Then he stood, his own empty glass in his right hand.

"Need another?"

The elf crooked the left side of his mouth. "Wouldn't say no to it."

"What are you drinking?"

"Bourbon and tequila."

"At the same time?"

Bannickburn nodded.

"Be right back."

Bourbon and tequila, Bailey thought. If he wanted to have any sort of lucid conversation with this man, he'd have to talk fast.

2

It looked like Bel Red Road, but the signs were a mess, and so was Bannickburn's vision. He squinted, then opened his eyes wide, then squinted again. It started with a "B," ended with a "d," and had a capital letter in the middle. Had to be Bel Red. About damn time— seemed like he'd been wandering for half an hour.

Bannickburn prided himself on his ability to walk firm and straight no matter how much he'd had to drink. While he managed to look sober to anyone who watched him take five or ten steps, someone who decided to follow him for half a block or more would quickly notice that he didn't seem to have any idea where he was going. He often made 180-degree turns when he came to a street, walking back over a block he had just traveled, or he'd make consecutive right turns and walk in large circles. As a result, journeys home after drinking took a good five to ten times their normal duration.

He didn't mind. He wanted to be out on the streets. He wanted to be seen, especially by the people out at this time of night—this time of morning, rather. He wanted them to *see*, to have just some idea who he was.

He walked down the road he hoped was Bel Red. He guessed he was walking northeast. He passed gutter punks with whiskey stains on their ripped jackets, needle-haired gangers, and a considerable number of his fellow drunks. He also passed a handful of visitors drawn to Touristville for the chance to gape at the rougher elements Bannickburn had passed.

Bannickburn looked down his nose at everyone he saw, especially the ones who looked like they thought they were tough, daring anyone to challenge him about anything. *Do you know what I've seen?* he thought as he looked at each one of them. *Do you know who I've fought? Do you know who I've killed? Who are you next to them? Who are you next to me?*

He felt good. He felt very, very good—better than he'd felt since he'd come to this city, the mightiest rodent's nest in the Western hemisphere if not the world. His self-doubt, that unfamiliar feeling that had grown to cover his soul like a blanket, had dropped away around the time Bailey brought him his sixth drink.

Ah, Bailey. He was a good lad. He'd spent most of the night quenching Bannickburn's thirst and feeding his ego. He'd asked a little about Bannickburn's background, and though of course the elf didn't tell him everything about who he was—who he used to be—he'd let enough out that Bailey had asked to hear some war stories, and Bannickburn was ready with some of his best ones. Soon the whole table was hanging on his every word, laughing when they were supposed to laugh, gasping when they were supposed to gasp. They were entertained and impressed, exactly as they should be. Even Jimmy, a good Irish lad himself, was involved—more energetic than Bannickburn had seen him, maybe even impressed.

That by itself, though, wouldn't have been enough to put him in the mood he was in. It was what Bailey did next. The conversation moved on to other topics, as it tends to do, but Bailey moved closer to Bannickburn and talked to him in lowered tones. He talked about the unpleasant subject that Bannickburn generally tried to avoid thinking about, let alone discussing—the present. Bailey was interested in what he was doing, asking who he was working for, assuming not only that he was em-

ployable but that several parties might actually be com-
peting for his services. Bannickburn felt the world
shifting beneath him as Bailey talked. No longer was he
buried under all of it—he actually found his way on top
of it, or at least on top of a small piece of it.

The gambling helped, too. After Bailey ballooned his
confidence, Bannickburn had drifted to the blackjack tables for a while (he wasn't sober enough to play anything
that required more concentration, but he wasn't about
to flush his money down the slot machines). The cards
had fallen on him like manna from heaven, building up
to a pair of fours that he'd split, hitting one to twenty
and the other to twenty-one. He wasn't walking home
with a lot of extra nuyen in his pocket since he didn't
have much of a stake to start with, but the few hundred
he had won should buy some nice luxuries for him and
Jackie. He should probably buy her a good dinner.

Taken together, the camaraderie, the winnings, the
hero-worship he felt from Shivers and his friends all
added to one feeling—power. He felt powerful. Not the
kind of power he was used to, but these days some
power, *any* power, was a novelty. It didn't flow through
his entire body like it used to, but he at least could feel
it in his fingertips. It was something.

All the businesses on this stretch of road in Touristville had closed long ago, and the plate glass windows
revealed the blinking lights of numerous state-of-the-art
alarm systems. The apartments above these brick store-
fronts were all dark. He was on the edge of the Barrens,
close enough to the pits to attract plenty of criminals
but close enough to money and the infrastructure of civi-
lization to allow for some measure of security and safety.
Some of Seattle's wealthier criminals preferred to live
here, as it gave them good access to the Barrens, while
also allowing Matrix hookups and other facets of the
good life. Most of the bleeding-edge stuff here belonged
to them.

This block was empty of pedestrians. No one for Bannickburn to stare down. He tried to walk faster to get to a more populous area, but he felt himself swaying back and forth a little, and had to slow down.

A chopper turned the corner, engine grumbling, waiting to be kicked up a notch or six. Two Lone Star guards, all bright and shiny in mirrored sunglasses and polished helmets, did everything in their power to intimidate wrongdoers by their mere presence. The one in back fixed his eyes—or at least his lenses—on Bannickburn while the driver in front kept scanning the rest of the block.

Bannickburn drew himself to his full height and fell back on an old trick he had learned long ago—he looked for his own reflection in the sunglasses. It gave his stare a certain intensity and directness.

The Lone Star patrolman didn't back down. But he didn't stop, either. Bannickburn was clearly in violation of curfew, but the patrol didn't stop. They knew, Bannickburn thought, that it wasn't worth pulling in someone who looked as tough as Bannickburn for something as minor as a curfew violation, especially not in a neighborhood as iffy as Touristville.

Either that, or Bannickburn was too small of a fish for them to bother with. They cruised by.

Bannickburn shouted after them, an unintelligible slur of a word that he hoped conveyed defiance. Whatever he said was lost in the noise of the engine as it gunned to life, hurling the guards forward to something more important than a lone drunk.

He glanced behind him a few times on the off chance that the guards had turned around and come back. He had known so many ways to deal with them, once. He wouldn't have worried about two street cops any more than he would have worried about a couple of flies.

But in this damn city he had to worry. Sure, there were guns—he'd always had to worry about guns. Now, though, he had to worry about stupid things, like one of them landing a punch. A punch! A security guard—a street punk with a uniform—could lay him out with his hands! The prospect was more humiliating than Bannickburn could bear.

Not tonight, though. No one could touch him tonight. He had power again. Nothing like what he used to have, but more than he'd possessed since he'd set foot on this continent.

He entered the warehouse basement with a flourish. "I'm back," he announced.

Jackie was plugged in. Her physical eyes saw him, but didn't register anything about his appearance. "That's nice," she said absently.

"No, girl, you don't understand. I'm back. *Back!* I'm me again."

"Great. Who were you before tonight?"

"Some helpless, no-name slag. A nothing. But that's over now, and good riddance to it all."

He sat in the chair with the torn velvet upholstery, and put his feet up on the crate that served as an ottoman. Perhaps, he thought, that's what he should do with his winnings from the night—invest in a new chair for Jackie's lair. A throne to fit his new mood.

Jackie removed the plug from the side of her head, idly rubbed her short blond hair, and swiveled to face Bannickburn. Her sharp features and dark eyes made him smile.

"So what happened?" she asked. "Find some royal blood in your past?"

"Pfft," Bannickburn said with a hand wave. "That sort of information mining is your department. No, nothing really *happened*. It's just a feeling. I went through a period of adjustment, and now I've adjusted. I'm ready to rise to conquer."

"Drek, what were you doing tonight? Sitting in a corner snorting a kilo of bliss?"

"There's nothing artificial about this, my dear girl," Bannickburn said, affronted. "This is a natural reaction to the night's events. I had a lovely time at the blackjack tables, was vastly entertaining to my fine Celtic friends, and met a new man who seems to be a person of influence and who was quite taken with me. A fine night all in all."

"Great. You won a few nuyen and told some funny stories. So now you're king of the world."

Jackie was very lucky, Bannickburn thought, that the considerable quantity of alcohol he had swallowed had fuzzed up his emotions. If it hadn't, he might be taking some offense at her efforts to darken his mood. He decided that he could best preserve his good nature by changing the subject. He let his eyes wander around the dark cellar.

"I was thinking of purchasing something for you," he said. "A piece of furniture. A chair, perhaps. Bring the place up a level."

He had said something wrong. He didn't know what, but Jackie's eyes were suddenly horizontal slits. Muscles at the edge of her mouth clenched and unclenched. He knew she was preparing to say something, but was waiting until she had it worded just right in her head.

"You're saying, then," she finally said, "that my home needs assistance? That I haven't done enough?"

All of the power Bannickburn had felt himself gathering during the night seemed to have no effect on Jackie. "Of course not."

"Do you think abandoned warehouses are the least bit hospitable? Do you know what I had to do just so you could *sleep* comfortably in this place? I was on the run when I came here, remember? A little hitch with my old employer? So while I'm dodging the goons they sent after me, I still managed to bring in electricity, heat, water. I patched the walls, I fixed the ceilings—you have no *idea* all the stuff I did here. And you think I need you to buy me a chair to bring my home 'up a level'? My home is doing fine without your assistance."

Bannickburn knew this was a losing battle, and one he would not be able to fight well in his inebriated state. He surrendered. "I'm sorry. I meant nothing by it."

He watched Jackie's face—saw her considering whether she should still be mad at him, then deciding it was too late to bother. "All right," she said, then walked over to her bed. Bannickburn hoped, as he did every night, that she'd invite him over. As always, he was disappointed.

"I'm glad you had a good night," she said, stretching her legs and folding her arms across her chest. He thought she'd close her eyes and drift off for her customary three hours of sleep, but her eyes stayed open.

"You're being careful, right?" she said.

It was Bannickburn's turn to feel offended. "What kind of question is that? Am I a child?"

She sighed. "No, no, of course not. It's just . . . your friend. Shivers. I don't really trust him."

Bannickburn dismissed her with a wandering wave of his arm. "Don't take this personally, my dear, but you seem not to trust anyone. You've no reason to worry, though—James is a fine boy."

"Is he."

"Indeed."

She sat silently, chewing on her bottom lip. Then she spoke again.

"Do you know who he . . . Do you know what people call . . . Do you know everything about him?"

There was something she wasn't saying. Even in his drunken, increasingly tired state, Bannickburn could see that. Tomorrow he'd figure out what it was. Tonight he'd just reassure her.

"Of course I don't know *everything* about him. But he's been good to me, and that counts for a lot. Just like you've been good to me. There's plenty I don't know about you, too. But you're good to me."

She didn't like the comparison between James and her; Bannickburn could see it on her face. But she understood what he was saying. Whatever she was thinking of saying to him, she decided it could wait.

"Just . . . be careful. I know, I know, you're careful,

you know what you're doing, I know. So keep it up. When Shivers is around."

Bannickburn's lids drooped. He shifted in the chair, slumped down, shifted again. He was definitely going to get her some new furniture.

"I'll be careful," he said, his voice sounding distant inside his own head.

3

Bannickburn dreamed of fire. He dreamed of electricity. He dreamed of a storm moving over the highlands, of lightning flashing across the plains. The rain fell, watering him like a plant, and he grew. Not in size, though. He took the storm into him, and it filled him, and power rushed through his veins. The world was his.

Waking up in a warehouse, then, came as a disappointment.

Light trickled through the large room's three windows, filtered by the dark plastic that covered them. Bannickburn rubbed his eyes and looked groggily for Jackie. Naturally, she was next to her deck, jacked in. He'd have to make sure she got some sunlight today, if any of it managed to penetrate the clouds and grime that usually hovered over Avondale.

He tried to sit up straighter in his chair, but his back balked. He rubbed it, thinking maybe he should buy a bed. But the last thing he wanted to do was give Jackie an easy excuse to keep him out of her bed. He didn't like to be pitied, but if he needed to make her feel guilty about forcing him to sleep on a chair, that's what he'd do.

The more he shifted, the more aches and pains he found. Knees, wrists, and, most of all, head. He was old. He shouldn't be—middle-aged, sure, but not old. In his glory days he'd managed to keep a lot of the effects of age at bay, healing himself of any aches and pains without much thought. Now, though, a few decades of dangerous living had caught up to him, were taking their toll, and there was nothing he could do about it.

Well, nothing *here*. He'd met a few people, including his good friend James, who had showed him new ways to deal with pain and lethargy. He was careful—he'd seen the long-term effect of those substances and knew they weren't to be used lightly—but the chance to duplicate some of the effects he'd been able to perform in the Scotsprawl wasn't something he could easily resist.

Then, of course, there were the more permanent solutions. The replacement parts, the body enhancements. If he got enough of them, he'd almost be a mage again. But not really—and he would condemn himself to never regaining his old powers. Enhancing himself would mean admitting defeat, and he hadn't done that yet.

But right here, right now, he ached. Maybe he should get in touch with James. He'd asked Jackie if she had any contacts for these substances, and she'd steadfastly refused him. James, on the other hand, was always accommodating.

"Jackie," he said. She didn't glance at him. "Jackie!"

She heard him. He knew. He'd seen her hold a conversation in real life while her persona talked to someone else on the Matrix. Hell, he'd seen her have an RL conversation while hacking through some stubborn IC.

He grabbed a metal slug lying on the floor and flicked it between his thumb and forefinger. It spun through the air and hit Jackie in the shoulder. She didn't make a noise, but she flinched and rubbed the spot the disk had hit.

"Jackie!"

She glared at him and held one finger up in the air. He was on the verge of being offended when he saw it was her index finger. He considered looking for another slug, but thought better of it and plopped back down in his chair.

Exactly one minute later she turned to look at him, though she stayed jacked in. "What?"

"Good morning," Bannickburn said sweetly.

"Good morning. What?"

"I need to call James."

She rolled her eyes. "What are you, an infant? Then call him! The cell's on the table."

"I just thought that since you were already jacked in . . ."

"Call him yourself!" Her eyes glazed, nearly rolling back into her head. She was no longer focused on anything in front of her.

Bannickburn groaned loudly as he stood, but no sympathy was forthcoming. He ambled over to the cell phone and dialed James' number. In a moment, James, looking as alert and composed as he had the previous night, appeared on the small screen. His red hair was combed straight back and he showed no ill effects from the wagonload of alcohol he had consumed.

"Good morning, Robert."

"Hello, James. Thanks again for getting us all together at the casino last night. I had a fine time."

Shivers nodded, accepting Bannickburn's words as a simple statement of fact rather than any sort of compliment.

"And I hate to ask you for a favor so soon after an enjoyable night, but I need your assistance on a matter. That . . . gentleman you introduced me to last week? At the docks? I'd like to . . . renew my acquaintance with him."

Shivers' long face remained expressionless, his narrow mouth a small line. "I don't know who you're talking about."

"Of course you do. Large man, mostly metal on his right side, had a compartment in his chest holding a dozen vials?"

Shivers made a show of thinking. "No, I don't know anybody like that."

"Good God, man, it was just last week! How could

you . . . ?" Then Bannickburn understood what was going on.

"Sorry, James," he said. "Didn't mean to explode. It's early. I must be confused. I beg your pardon."

"No matter," Shivers said. "I'm truly sorry I don't remember. Look, why don't you come by later this afternoon? We can talk more in person."

Bannickburn felt like a complete fool, a pathetic amateur. How could he be dumb enough to try to set up a meeting with an illicit drug dealer over a cell phone? A determined decker, like the one sharing the room with him, could have hacked into the conversation without breaking a sweat. He had thanked James for the nice evening, then proceeded to put him at risk of an unpleasant run-in with any security forces that might be eavesdropping.

"I'd love to come by. Maybe I could even see you this morning," Bannickburn said hopefully.

"My schedule won't allow it. Drop by Carlyle's at three or so. We can have a late lunch."

Carlyle's wasn't far from the docks. Shivers had known exactly what Bannickburn was talking about the whole time.

"Fine. Thanks," Bannickburn said, and disconnected the call.

It was nine thirty now. It was five and a half hours until three, and he'd have to eat, and then go to the docks, then pull off the transaction. It could be seven hours before he had what he was looking for. Bloody hell.

"Take a fraggin' codeine."

Bannickburn hadn't even realized he'd closed his eyes until he opened them to look at Jackie. Each blink moved through his head like thunder. "Beg pardon, my dear?"

"Take a codeine. Stay away from Jimmy's friend."

"Do you even *know* Jimmy's friend?"

"I know the type," she snapped. "You'd be best off far, far away from him."

Bannickburn's skull rattled again. He winced. "I think I can decide what's best for me."

Jackie stared at him for a moment. Bannickburn considered saying how nice her eyes looked when she was angry, then thought better of it.

"If you come here with any trace of bliss on you," she finally said, "any at all, you can sleep in a dumpster. Or anyplace else. Anywhere but here."

"And when did you get to be such an upstanding citizen?" Bannickburn asked mockingly.

"Anywhere but here," she repeated.

Bannickburn knew she was serious. And he knew that if he used Bliss, there would be no way he'd be able to hide it from her.

Grumbling to himself, he grabbed his coat and walked out in search of codeine. Hopefully, he could at least ease the pain in his head enough so he could take a shower without the water feeling like a million needles poking his skull.

Sunrise had been maybe three hours ago. Any dust and grime that had settled overnight was wind-stirred into the air, a sea of black dots scattered in front of the clear blue sky. Not many people were out in Avondale at this time of the morning, and those who were didn't want to be. They slunk in dark corners, throwing resentful glares at anyone who dared to notice them.

What do I need James for? Bannickburn thought. *I'm surrounded by people who are likely dealers of illicit substances.* And the nearest law enforcement personnel were most likely miles away.

Sadly, though, he had no idea how to approach a potential dealer without an introduction. He had picked up several new skills in his time in New Seattle, but that wasn't one of them—and Jackie didn't seem inclined to teach him.

He sighed and continued down the road.

The Body Mall would carry what he wanted and might even have some bliss. But it was a ways away, and he'd

have to go through or around Glow City to get there.
Somewhere in Avondale there was someone selling what
he wanted. The trick, with Avondale's rapidly changing
retail—stores opened and closed every week, sometime
within the space of a single day—was finding the right
place.

The flea market south of Jackie's cellar had been shut
down a week ago, a victim of a battle between gangers
over the market's meager profits. Most of the retailers
hadn't found a new location yet—a good number of
them were still confined to their beds.

He'd heard of a tent city that had been hitting vacant
lots recently, keeping on the move so they could sell
goods lifted from other residents of the Barrens. As soon
as one of their victims caught up with them, that outlet
would shut down, too, but as far as Bannickburn knew,
it was still running.

The wind shifted and brought the usual smells of concrete dust and smoldering rubber, along with something
else. Bannickburn sniffed sharply. Popcorn.

They were getting bold, easier to find. They must have
been stealing from people in other neighborhoods lately.
Bannickburn walked faster.

The patched tents sat amid crumbled brick walls and
looked like a circus in a war zone. Merchants sat on
rickety stools but kept one foot on the ground, ready to
scatter at a moment's notice. A few of them had sparse
collections of wares on display, but most of the interesting and valuable goods were carefully packed away. That
way, the important merchandise could be on the backs
of the merchants when they fled.

Bannickburn looked for the red cross that most merchants with medical goods displayed near their tables.
Before he saw it, a collection of wood chips caught his
eye—especially the white-speckled black bark on one
long piece. He sidled closer.

He tried to appear disinterested, but as just about the
only customer on the lot, he couldn't deflect attention

to anyone else. The merchant next to the table, a dwarf woman with a rough burn scar covering the right side of her scalp, watched his every move.

"You've got a good eye, chummer," she said when she saw Bannickburn staring at the black wood. "Best piece of the collection."

"Can I touch it?"

"Go ahead."

He picked it up. The bark was still quite rough—it hadn't been handled much, which was good. If this was what he thought it might be, rougher bark meant more potential power locked inside. In the right hands, a piece of wood like this—unless it was fake—would suck in a spell like an elephant inhales water. Most of the time, creating a focus—an object that holds a spell for later use—takes considerable effort and more than a little personal cost. Enchanting something like midnight wood, though, is only slightly more difficult than striking a match. At least, that's how it used to be for Bannickburn.

Chances were, though, that if it was what it looked like, it wouldn't be sitting on a table in the middle of the Barrens. Unless the merchant was too dumb to know its true worth, which was always possible.

"I don't suppose you picked this up yourself," Bannickburn said.

"No sir, I don't leave these parts much. I've got one of those, how do you call 'em, networks? Supplier networks? Bringing me stuff."

"Must be a good network, to bring you pieces of this quality."

"Yes, yes, top quality."

"Not many networks can get this deep into Aztlan," Bannickburn said, running his fingers over the rough bark.

"No, of course not. But that's what I pay the good money for, isn't it? To bring valuable items to discerning people like you."

It was a fake. Bannickburn now had no doubts. If it

was real, the merchant would not have allowed him to give the bark the smallest rub, for fear of robbing the piece of some of its potency. And the Midnight Forest this wood supposedly came from was in Amazonia, not Aztlan. Any merchant skilled enough to get his hands on a real piece of midnight wood should know its country of origin. Bannickburn sighed in disappointment and moved on.

He'd almost forgotten his headache as he focused on the wood, but once he started moving again it returned, throbbing like an infant's heart. Thankfully, he spotted a red cross only two tables away.

He walked quickly even though he felt like crawling, then fell forward, catching himself on the table and using it for support. "Codeine," he croaked.

"Looks like you need more than that," said a slender man who was far too clean to have been in the Barrens long.

Bannickburn almost snapped at the man to just give him what he wanted, but then a note in the man's voice registered in his brain.

"What do you suggest?" Bannickburn asked casually.

The man raised a narrow eyebrow. "There are many options. So many options. It all depends on how much relief you want and how much you're willing to pay for it."

"Bliss," Bannickburn said. He was in no mood to joust. "I want bliss."

"Don't we all," the merchant said sardonically, but quickly returned to business when his joke made no impact. "I can get that for you," he said in low tones, though he probably could have shouted the words and no one in hearing distance would care. "Takes time, though. You come back, I'll have it for you. Fifty nuyen."

The price alone was almost enough to make Bannickburn walk away, but he took one more stab at it. "How much time? This afternoon? Later this morning?"

The dealer held up his hands. "Whoa, whoa, whoa.

No miracles. Tomorrow afternoon, maybe. Two days, definitely."

"Two *days*? I'm hungover *now*!"

The dealer smirked. "Then maybe you should buy some codeine."

Bannickburn handed over a few bills (there wasn't a credstick reader in sight), snatched the pills out of the dealer's hands, and stalked off.

"You know, if you're thinking of taking bliss for a little hangover, you might have a substance problem," the dealer called after him.

Bannickburn whirled and saw a revoltingly condescending expression on the dealer's face. Instantly he thought of a dozen perfectly lovely ways to wipe that look away. He particularly lingered on method seven—oh, that one would be quite rich indeed.

But he couldn't do any of them anymore, and he couldn't come up with any new methods until the hangover was cured. He had no choice but to turn back around and walk away like a kicked dog.

He clutched the pills in his hand and tried to think of last night. He wanted to bring back the swagger, the feeling of power. But it was entirely gone.

"There's an ork," Jackie said through clenched teeth.

Bannickburn opened his eye and was amazed to find that the light no longer hurt his brain. He blinked a few times. The pain didn't come back. That much was right.

Now he had to figure out what Jackie was talking about.

"An ork where?"

"An ork here. Outside. Looking for the way in. He knows someone lives here!"

"He hasn't found the way in yet, has he?"

"No." Red filled the hollows under her sharp cheekbones. "But he's too close. Go talk to him. He's on the west side of the building."

"Why me?"

"Because I'm not clumsy enough to let an ork get this

close. How do you think I stayed away from the fraggin'
assassins my lovely old boss threw at me? Because I'm
careful!"

"All right, all right. Back way?"

"Back way."

Bannickburn was sulking toward the back of the cellar
when a small pair of hands grabbed his shoulders and
turned him. Warm lips left an enduring impression on
his cheek.

"Be careful," Jackie said.

Bannickburn patted her hand. "What else would I
be?"

It was nice, he thought, to have a reminder of why he
was staying here. He continued toward the back of the
basement and opened a narrow door with several broken
slats. He smelled earth.

A short tunnel—concrete walls and ceiling over bare
ground—led to a staircase. He ascended six steps, then
pulled open a small stone door, no more than one meter
wide. He squirmed through and grabbed a piece of rebar
set into the stone wall and climbed up. Just below the
metal manhole cover, he crouched, listening. He couldn't
hear anyone moving in the alley just above him. Of
course, the ork could have moved since Jackie last saw
him, and might now be standing right where Bannickburn planned to come out, but he'd have to take that
chance.

He pushed the manhole cover up a quarter of a meter
and scanned the alley. Nothing. Moving quickly, he
shoved the cover entirely off, scrambled up, and replaced the cover. Hopefully it would look like he'd appeared out of thin air.

He brushed some dust off his brown kilt and
smoothed any obvious wrinkles. He didn't think it would
be necessary, but you never knew—sometimes even orks
cared about appearances.

He walked briskly out of the alley, turned left, and
spotted the ork immediately. The stranger was wearing
a suit. A nice suit. And staring right at him.

"Robert Lionel Bannickburn?" the ork said in a voice that combined a low growl with clipped enunciation.

Bannickburn was too confused by the ork's appearance to ponder whether it was a good idea to conceal his identity. "Yes?"

"Allan Tiberius Kross. I've been looking for you."

Having an ork looking for you was generally not a good thing, but Bannickburn was determined to regain his poise. "You've found me," he said nonchalantly.

"I believe you met an associate of mine last night? Quinn Bailey?"

"It's possible."

Kross smiled, an expression that, thanks to his lower fangs, didn't make him look any friendlier. "No need to be elusive with me, Mr. Bannickburn. I'm here to help you. More to the point, I'm here to tell you that Mr. Bailey would like to meet with you if you're available."

Bannickburn let a moment of silence pass so it wouldn't seem like he was responding too quickly. "That can probably be arranged. When did Mr. Bailey have in mind?" *Good God*, he thought, *I'm talking like the bloody ork*.

"Right now. I'm here to escort you."

Bannickburn's only plan for the afternoon was to recover from his hangover, and that seemed to have been accomplished. Oh, and he was supposed to meet with James, but the need for that seemed to have disappeared. He could cancel.

He wasn't particularly anxious to go off alone with an unfamiliar ork, but the day he let a lone ork intimidate him would be a sad one, indeed. And he wanted to talk to Bailey again.

"Lead the way," he said, and gave a quick wave to where he thought one of Jackie's cameras was, to let her know he wasn't being taken against his will. Then he was off.

4

Bannickburn had seen lots of kinds of nice in his time. There was subtle-nice, luxurious-nice, ostentatious-nice, and nice-considering-the-circumstances (which was the most common kind of nice in the Barrens). Bailey's office belonged to the category he called "academic-nice"—dark wood desk to match the pervasive bookshelves, volumes that looked pristine, either because new additions were constantly being made, or because none of them had ever been touched. There was even a globe (with tan oceans, not blue). Every chair in the room was leather and padded. Every person in the room—Bannickburn, Bailey, Kross, Shivers, and two unnamed, armed flunkies—squeaked when they sat down. As it turned out, Shivers had called to cancel their afternoon meeting before Bannickburn had the chance. Both had received the same summons.

"Good to see you, Robert," Bailey said. He looked even more dapper than he had the night before, a burgundy silk vest showing under his black suit. "I've gotta say I'm impressed that you can even walk today. The last time I saw that much alcohol disappear was when my friend Vida drove a beer truck off a cliff."

Bannickburn, leaning on one elbow, waved his hand casually in the air. "Was nothing," he said modestly. The size of the flunkies in the room made him a little nervous, but he was far too seasoned to let anything show.

"James here has been filling me in about your background, and while he was talking I had some thoughts. So I decided I'd invite you in, share the thoughts I had, see what they inspired in your mind, and we'd take it from there."

"Okay," Bannickburn said, since he couldn't think of a better reply. There were at least eight guns in the room protecting Bailey (Bannickburn counted two apiece on the flunkies, two on Kross, and one each on Bailey and Shivers), but the man himself sounded like nothing so much as a low-budget trideo director. What kind of business went on here?

"Now normally I wouldn't be in a position to go outside my organization for tasks like this, but, you know, in the shipping business, things don't always come in regular intervals—especially when you're dealing with goods from Asia. The train shenanigans alone out there give me hives. So sometimes things come in all at once, and my resources are stretched way too thin, and I have to look around and find someone who may know something about Siberian Blood Ice."

"Well," Bannickburn said. "Well, well."

"Wonderful," Bailey said. "I see you've heard of it."

"I told you," Shivers said. "This is what I told you."

"You know how valuable it is, I assume," Bailey said.

Bannickburn knew. Three years ago, a shaman in a small Siberian village lost control of his *ayami*, a powerful but jealous spirit that, in ideal circumstances, teaches a shaman all he or she needs to know. The shaman saw his *ayami* becoming too powerful, too controlling of him, and broke the bond between them. The *ayami*'s jealousy spiraled into insanity, and she brutally assaulted the shaman, tearing him into extremely small pieces. Then, for good measure, she killed every last person in his village. The magical energy expended in the spirit's vicious attack left traces that lingered to the present day.

The massacre was not discovered until several months

after it had occurred, by which time the blood of the villagers was firmly frozen into the snowy ground. The rest of the remains had been devoured by wolves.

The ice holding the frozen blood of the shaman had tremendous talismanic power, and sold for as much as three thousand nuyen per crystal. It made the midnight wood Bannickburn had been thinking about at the tent market seem like a plastic four-leaf clover.

The trick, though, was being able to tell the ice with the shaman's blood from the ice with the ordinary villagers' blood from some random piece of ice with a spot of chicken's blood, or possibly red paint, frozen in the middle. Another difficulty, of course, came from making sure the ice remained frozen—but most mages who knew its strength could usually find a way to keep it cold.

"It can bring in a nuyen or two," Bannickburn said.

"For damn sure," Bailey replied. "And it's close to us. It's real close, sitting in the hull of a ship right here in Tacoma, on the waterfront. So you can see we have a nice business opportunity sitting in front of us."

"I can see that, yes."

"But most opportunities like this don't come without a hitch." Bailey spread his arms. "Hey, let's face it, if making this kind of money was easy, everyone would be rich, right? So there are hitches. Hitch number one is the waterfront. It's . . . what is it, James?"

"It's a problem area," Shivers said.

Bailey slapped his hand on his desk. "Exactly! It's a problem area. We need to get our merchandise through there clean and unencumbered, without losing a good portion of our profit margin, if you understand what I'm saying."

It wasn't difficult to understand. "Problem area" meant "teeming with government security and organized crime muscle." "Clean and unencumbered" meant "keep anyone else, including Customs inspectors, from seeing the goods, because they might decide to take some for themselves." Or, if the officials were on the more honest side of the law, they might levy a large duty against such a rare imported item, thereby making Bailey lose "a good portion of our profit margin."

What it boiled down to was, Bailey wanted to smuggle some talismans through the docks. If Bannickburn really wanted to figure it out, he could probably guess what line of business Bailey was in, as a fairly narrow range of organizations got involved in such activities. If Jackie were there, she'd make him review that list immediately. On his own, though, he decided to hear Bailey out without burdening himself by thinking too much.

"This is all to say—what? You need a courier?"

"No, no, no. We have a courier. We need someone to carry the courier's coffee."

Bannickburn looked at Shivers, who was rolling his eyes. Kross was impassive. Bailey's oval face held a hint of a smile, but, as far as Bannickburn had seen, he always wore that expression.

"So . . ." Bannickburn started.

Bailey laughed. No one else in the room even smiled. "Relax, relax, I'm joking. Look, James told me you've hit some rough times, but who hasn't? I know a little bit about who you were—who you *are*—and I wouldn't humiliate you by offering pissant work. No, what I need is your particular set of skills, some knowledge of magic, which James assures me you have. We've got a lot of resources, my associates and I, but mages . . . well, we have a chronic shortfall in that area. Not that I need a *mage* per se for this, but I need someone who knows his stuff, because here's the thing—for every real piece of Blood Ice on the market, there are a thousand fakes. I need someone who can tell me exactly what's in this crate before my people go to the effort of moving it. Simple enough?"

So far, yes, it had been simple enough. Any hesitation Bannickburn had about the job vanished when Bailey got down to terms. The sum he was offering for a simple identification job indicated that Bailey thought he could set a new record price with this shipment of Blood Ice.

Bannickburn felt a small trace of guilt about misleading Bailey. More than once, Bailey had referred to Bannickburn's "abilities," and the elf knew he was talking about more than just a simple knowledge of talismans. But Bannickburn didn't bother correcting him. He had told James some of the story of Valinscarl and the Stinklands, but not the whole thing. It was quite possible that James, and therefore Bailey, thought Bannickburn had kept some of his powers. And Bannickburn was guilty of letting them believe that, since there was no way he was going to tell them how far he had fallen. The tactic seemed to work—he hadn't said anything, and he'd gotten the job. Dishonesty pays, he'd learned several times, even if it leaves a small bitter taste in the mouth.

Now he was on his way to the docks, with Kross along to show him the way and even provide a little conversation. In most of his experience, Bannickburn had found that spending any time with an ork meant enduring a lot of silence, but Kross was polished, courteous, and surprisingly refined.

"The '45 is much better than the '44. Subtler," Kross said.

"I'd heard the '45 varied greatly by region."

"What year doesn't? However, for particular areas— Belgium comes to mind—the '45 is the equal of any year in the past half century."

"And you don't deep-fry them?"

Kross widened his eyes in horror. "Never! Destroys the nuances of the flavor! Just bludgeons it. No, locusts are best stir-fried, lightly, in olive oil. Truly a delicacy."

"So I've heard, so I've heard," Bannickburn said, lying with a straight face. "Perhaps I'll have the chance to try them someday."

"I'd recommend the Big Rhino. Touristy sometimes, but top-notch when it comes to insects."

"I'll keep it in mind."

His nose was full of the smell of salt and seaweed. In his short time in Seattle, Bannickburn had already discovered what a joy the docks were to walk in. Security from every AAA and a number of the smaller corps patrolled the area, but they spent as much time keeping an eye on each other as they did on any outsiders. They walked along the corp-controlled docks, while Lone Star and other private security forces patrolled the government docks with a swagger completely out of proportion to their actual influence. Sailors loitered on nearly every corner, leaving empty bottles as a testament to their presence. When the security troopers weren't watching each other, they were keeping an eye out for any drunken sailors who thought it might be funny to throw a bottle at something. The sailors found that sort of thing amusing fairly frequently.

In the middle of all this walked a number of people who looked guilty, and an equal number of people striving to look innocent. Bannickburn imagined that, at some past point in time, the people who looked guilty were probably innocent of everything (except poor genetic inheritance), while the people who looked innocent were undoubtedly guilty of something. But then the criminals had figured this pattern out and started deliberately looking guilty, which, ironically enough, deflected attention away from them.

But the security patrols caught on to that act soon enough, causing the guilty parties to try to look innocent again. These days, Bannickburn figured, the docks held a healthy mix of guilty people who looked guilty, guilty people who looked innocent, innocent people who looked guilty, and innocent people who looked innocent. One could spend a long, entertaining afternoon trying to decide who was what.

The spring sun, not the most common sight in Seattle, gave a certain luster to the decades of grime coating the warehouses. Rusted cranes creaked as broad pallets of cargo swung back and forth. Some of the cargo was

worthless—boxes and boxes of sand shipped by mer-
chants working some arcane financial scam far beyond
Bannickburn's understanding. Much of the cargo was
mundane, while a small portion of it was highly illegal.
One single crate, on a ship called the *Juniper*, held what
Bannickburn and Kross were looking for.

Kross had grown silent and had fastened the top two
buttons of his charcoal suit jacket, which Bannickburn
supposed meant he was ready for business. Bannickburn
stroked his sideburns to make sure they were
presentable.

The *Juniper* lay ahead, a relatively small freighter that
looked like it was built for speed. Black mold and barna-
cles clung to the chipped white paint on the narrow
prow.

Two groups stood on the dock. One wore Lone Star
uniforms and looked serious and patient, ready to wait
as long as they needed to until someone nearby commit-
ted a crime. The second group, positioned closer to the
ship and dressed in clothes whose chief purpose was to
provide fabric on which they could wipe their hands,
appeared equally determined to do nothing until the first
group dispersed.

Bannickburn started working on ways to talk his way
past either group, but both of them parted for Kross
before he could say a word. The workers looked relieved, while security looked indifferent. One Lone Star
officer even offered a hesitant nod to the ork. It wasn't
returned.

"So far, so good," Bannickburn said as they boarded
the *Juniper*.

"Not really," Kross grunted. "I'd prefer that no one
was here. But *que sera, sera*. At least some of them are
our people."

Bannickburn felt certain Kross wasn't referring to the
Lone Stars.

Two armed guards stood on the foredeck, in gray uniforms with Russian military insignia prominent on their
shoulders. That meant Kross and Bannickburn had just

entered Yamatetsu territory. Bannickburn wondered if
the megacorp was cooperating in this venture somehow,
or if the guards were being used as unwitting dupes. *Oh
well,* he thought. *Not my concern—at least, not yet.*

Kross walked firmly toward the guards. "Ensign
Teskiev, please. Allan Kross to see him."

The guards made a point of standing motionless for a
moment, silently appraising the two visitors. Then one
of them walked through a metal doorway, while the
other raised his Steyr assault rifle and leveled it at Kross,
obviously deciding he represented the more significant
threat. Bannickburn bristled.

A few moments later the guard returned with an unshaven, tank top–wearing man in tow. The sailor chewed
on an apple.

"Mr. Kross," the sailor said, spitting out small chunks.
"I'm glad you could come by, but I'm afraid there has
been a problem. Some people"—he made a vague gesture toward the people clustered on the dock—"have
convinced themselves that some of our cargo might be
illegal, and have planted themselves on the dock to keep
an eye on us. I'm terribly sorry."

Kross frowned. "I can't say I'm happy about this, of
course."

"Of course. I understand your disappointment. Perhaps if we spoke in the officers' mess for a time, we
could discuss the matter in further detail and greater
comfort."

"Gracious of you. Please, lead the way."

Bannickburn waited patiently for the sailor's little
floor show to finish. While he understood the value of
creating deniability as well as the next runner, he wished
the sailor could just bark an order to the guards to let
the strangers through and forget they ever saw them.
But such authority wasn't always easy to find.

Ensign Teskiev nodded at the security guards, who
stepped aside but made a point of arranging their faces
in the most intimidating possible expressions. The one

with the Steyr kept it raised. Bannickburn grinned widely at both of them as he passed.

A short walk led to the officers' mess, which was nothing more than two card tables surrounded by eight metal folding chairs. The unpadded feet scraped loudly on the corrugated floor as the three men pulled the chairs back and sat down.

"I don't see any goods in this room," Kross said. Apparently, Bannickburn thought, the ork's graciousness and manners did not extend to small talk.

"Patience, my friend. Patience."

Bannickburn thought of a few conversation starters as the moments ticked by—"So, Siberia still cold?" or, "How many pieces will your superiors carve you into if word of this little operation gets out?"—but he decided not to use any of them.

Soon, the door to the room opened, and a short woman in a ridiculously white uniform, complete with a flat cap, carried in a covered tray. Small wisps of mist spilled out from under the cover.

"Enjoy," she said as she placed the tray on the table in front of them, then turned smartly and walked out the door.

Teskiev removed the cover from the tray. The mist, as it turned out, was not steam from hot food but rather chilled air spilling out. A thin layer of frost covered the tray as soon as it was exposed to the open air. In the middle sat four diamonds of ice, each with a spot of red in the center.

"We must leave the items on the tray as much as possible," Teskiev said. "To maintain their core temperature. I'm sure you understand."

"Of course," Kross said. "I assume these are not all the crystals on board?"

"No, just a sample. A random sample, naturally."

"Fine." Kross glanced at Bannickburn. "It's your turn now."

Back in the Scotsprawl, when he had his powers, the

whole operation would have taken a few seconds, and
Bannickburn wouldn't have needed to touch the items.
Now, he had to be slower, more methodical. But something with the amount of power Blood Ice was supposed
to hold still should be relatively easy to spot.

"I was told equipment would be supplied," Bannickburn said.

"Yes, yes. Don't worry, our kitchen staff is more than
just one person."

Sure enough, in a few moments a half dozen more
white-suited people entered and unloaded five carts'
worth of equipment. Soon, a limited but functional
magic shop existed in the officers' mess.

Teskiev stood. "You have three and a half hours until
the room must be cleared for dinner. I wish you luck."

"Three and a half . . ." Bannickburn sputtered. "These
things take time, you know."

"Then I will not distract you any more with my presence." Teskiev walked briskly away, followed by the six
kitchen staffers.

"All right. Start doing whatever it is you do. Is there
anything I can do to help?" Kross asked.

Bannickburn looked over all the equipment—the
knobs, the dials, the magnets, the electrodes—and decided he didn't want anyone else in the world touching
it.

"I'll take care of it," he said. Kross nodded, folded
his arms, and stood near the door to the mess in a sort
of watchful coma.

The next two hours were bliss. Bannickburn was in
his element, and he was being paid to be there. He knew
exactly what to look for, how to measure it, and he could
stop every few moments to peer through the frosted ice
and glimpse the single red spatter inside each crystal.
He thought of the things he could do with a talisman of
this power, and didn't bother putting his thoughts into
the past tense.

At the two-hour mark, he knew. In his gut, he knew.
But thoroughness compelled him to complete the testing,

because even though he *knew*, he couldn't *feel* it. His mind told him what it was, but to his touch, it was nothing more than cold water. And he had to get this right. The number of guns he'd seen in Bailey's office convinced him of at least that much. One more hour of work would serve as confirmation.

After that hour passed, Bannickburn turned to Kross. "They're genuine," he said. "All of them." He wanted to pick them up, squeeze them in his hand, let the water and blood mix on his skin, certain that he couldn't hold power of that magnitude without feeling *something*. But, since Kross would probably rip his arm off the second he wrapped his hand around the crystals, he refrained.

Kross nodded, needing no time to recover from his near slumber. "Good," he said. "I'll call Teskiev."

Bannickburn expected him to use an intercom, or at least stick his head out the door, but Kross had a simpler idea. He slapped the wall near the door four times, and the echo of the banging metal shook Bannickburn's teeth. He figured either Teskiev would come quickly, or the vibrations of the blow would shatter the ship and sink them into the bay.

Luckily, Teskiev came first. "Were your results satisfactory?"

"Quite," Kross said. "We'll take the whole shipment."

Belowdecks, two metal briefcases sat on top of one crate next to a second, open crate. Guards—at least a dozen of them—lined the walls of the large hold. Every last one of them had the brim of his cap pulled low, shadowing his eyes. They all looked incapable of any expression except grim determination.

"Do you have the mold for these guys on board, or is it kept back in Russia?" Bannickburn asked. He received no response.

"Would you like to inspect the briefcases?" Teskiev asked, and Kross nodded once.

Bannickburn left the job to him, as he knew little about what the briefcases were supposed to do and how they were supposed to do it. Kross, though, seemed as familiar with them as Bannickburn had been with the analytical equipment in the mess, and the job was done quickly.

"They seem excellent. Thank you." He reached into a hidden, buttoned pocket of his vest and pulled out three credsticks, tossing them one at a time to Teskiev. "For the ice. And for the briefcases," he said. "Both coded to your captain. And this one is coded to you. As a token of our gratitude."

Teskiev bowed his head slightly, but remained expressionless. Kross, though, wasn't looking for gratitude. He turned to the crates.

"Come here," he said, and Bannickburn, assuming he was the one being addressed, stepped forward.

Kross reached into the open crate and pulled out a square box, no more than a quarter of a meter on each side.

"Caviar," he said. "Excellent stuff, really. We need to pull it out."

"Perhaps you would like a case? As a token of our esteem?" Teskiev said.

"That's very generous of you," Kross said. "Thank you." But he was careful, Bannickburn noted, to keep his face as neutral as Teskiev's. Kross put one box to the side, then stacked the others by the crate. Bannickburn joined him in pulling them out.

Once the boxes were out, Bannickburn and Kross removed a few large armfuls of packing material. It was cold, chilled by the refrigerated walls of the crate.

The bottom of the crate was a crude fake. It looked like the bottom of a crate, but any casual inspection would show that the false bottom was a good decimeter or two higher than it should be. However, it had done the job.

Kross and Bannickburn reached in together. They had to feel around to find a grip, but eventually Bannickburn felt four spots of spongy wood that looked exactly like the rest of the bottom. By squeezing it down, he could get a grip. Kross was waiting for him.

They pulled it up. Air whooshed into the bottom of the crate, swirling the mist below the false bottom. A metal case sat below, filling almost the entire base. It had two handles, one on each side of the case's top. Again, Bannickburn and Kross pulled it out. Bannickburn's back gave a twinge, but he wasn't about to let anyone in the room see the slightest trace of pain on his face.

They set it next to the caviar, undid four clasps, and opened it. More whooshing air, more swirling mist.

Kross waved the fog away. Below it were several small metal vials, lined up tightly, like extra-large bullets in an ammunition belt. Bannickburn counted maybe sixty of them. Sixty! True, there was an awful lot of blood in the human body, but sixty pieces of Blood Ice in a single place was a remarkable sight. Nearly two hundred thousand nuyen worth, if Bailey played his cards right. It would either be a nice little payday, or a really helpful haul for any mages Bailey might be working with.

Still, it didn't seem to justify the effort. A fifth of a million was nice, but paying Kross, Bannickburn, and whatever Yamatetsu people Bailey had to pay off wouldn't be cheap. But if Bailey could live with a narrow profit margin, then Bannickburn had no reason to be concerned.

They arranged the metal vials in the briefcases. Either the vials or the briefcases were magnetized—the vials stuck firmly to the inside walls once placed. Once all sixty were placed, Kross sealed the briefcases and pressed a button on the side of each one. Air blew out of the briefcases, dropping the internal pressure and temperature, preserving the ice.

"Let's go," Kross said. "Ensign Teskiev, please convey my compliments to your superiors."

"Of course. The corporals will see you out."

Two of the identical guards stepped forward, and Bannickburn and Kross followed them to the foredeck.

Then it started. Quickened heartbeat, dry mouth, clammy hands. On the surface, nothing changed. Inside, Bannickburn was all adrenaline. He hoped he'd get to punch someone.

"So what's the plan from here?" Bannickburn asked. "Nightrunners waiting for us on the other side of the boat? Secret passage from the prow to the docks?"

"We walk out the same way we came in," Kross replied. "Hold these."

Bannickburn took the box of caviar Teskiev had given Kross along with the two cases of Blood Ice. He wasn't sure why he needed to carry everything, but apparently Kross thought he'd need his hands free in the near future.

Bannickburn didn't know what to think of Kross' exit plan. Waltzing the goods right out the front door seemed risky, but it also increased the odds that he'd get to punch someone. "Okay," he said.

They walked down the pier. Disappointingly, the Lone Star guards were gone—either bribed away or called to a scene where something was actually happening. They had been replaced, though, by five people whose appearance screamed "hired muscle," right down to the spiked brass knuckles being lovingly caressed by a man each of whose hairy hands seemed only slightly smaller than Bannickburn's chest. The dockworkers that had been there before were still waiting, eyeing the newcomers cautiously, while making certain not to appear intimidated.

The sailors of the *Juniper* parted to let Bannickburn and Kross through. The five hired goons tightened together in a line, leaving no room to get around them on the pier. The two people on either end of their line each stood with half of one foot hovering over water.

The man in the middle, the one with the brass knuckles, held out a single thick arm, palm up. He looked like a grizzly bear in a suit.

"Stop," he said, somewhat unnecessarily. "Jig's up."

His voice was a low rumble that Bannickburn more felt in his spine than heard.

Kross seemed affronted at such an ancient cliché being used in his presence. "I rather think it isn't," he said.

"We want those cases," the bear-man said.

Kross snorted. "Funny. So do I. And I have them."

"We're doing you a favor," the big man said. "You and your people wouldn't know what to do with the stuff. We do. Give it here."

Bannickburn leaned closer to Kross. "Who is this guy?" he whispered.

"No one you need to worry about," Kross said, loud enough for everyone standing around to hear. "Just a speed bump."

The big man wiggled his fist in front of Kross and Bannickburn, so that the spikes on his knuckles glistened in the sun. For the first time, Bannickburn saw that the weapon was actually a permanent part of the big man's hand.

"Might be more trouble than that," the big man rumbled.

"I'm sure you're very tough," Kross said, his voice oozing condescension. "But your timing's bad."

"Oh, really?"

"Really. You see, I understand some of the ship's guards are getting ready for target practice. And I also understand they're rather poor shots. Stray bullets everywhere, if you understand what I'm saying."

The bear-man glanced quickly at the foredeck, where ten guards had appeared. None of their weapons were pointed at him or his friends, but it was quite clear that the weapons *could* be pointed at them without much effort.

Kross glanced at them, too. "You could probably kill us both. You might even get a hand on one of the cases. But then you'd be completely shredded by their deck guns, and they'd just take the case back on board. Hardly worth it, don't you think?"

The hairy man looked warily at the guns. "Fine," he finally said. "But they can't keep you covered for long. Once you're out of their range, those cases are gonna be ours."

"If you say so."

Bannickburn was poised and ready. He knew they couldn't just saunter away with the bear-man and his friends in tow. If they were going to get away from the five of them, it was going to happen right here. He just had to wait for it.

The five assorted goons lined up on the dock didn't have enough space to turn around easily. The two on either end waited while the middle three awkwardly stepped back to let Kross and Bannickburn through. It was all Kross wanted.

He raised his right arm over his head. A burst of fire clattered from the Russian guards, coming nowhere near the goons, but close enough to startle them. Kross charged, Bannickburn right behind him, with the dockworkers bringing up the rear. Bannickburn didn't know who the workers were, but they were clearly on his side.

Kross had one goon off the dock and into the drink immediately, but two others grabbed him. Bannickburn headed for the middle of the group, swinging Kross' box of caviar. He hit something firm but rubbery, and the box shot back.

He had caught the bear-man in his midsection. The hulking man looked at Bannickburn with beady eyes burning under his thick brown eyebrows. He wasn't happy.

The dockworkers—minus one, who had fallen into the bay—were grappling with a goon to the left, who had enough hidden blades to keep them wary. Kross was still struggling with his two assailants. That meant Bannickburn had the bear-sized man all to himself.

He suddenly realized he wasn't ready for this. He'd prepared for some talismongering, not for hand-to-hand combat against someone twice his size. He had no weapons, potions, foci, or anything else useful with him, and

his opponent could easily rip him in two with his bare
hands. Still, he'd get to hit someone.

The bear was reaching for a gun at his waist. That
was bad. Bannickburn's left arm, holding the caviar, was
moving away from the bear. He hoped the Blood Ice
was packed well.

He raised the steel case, twisted hard, moved it forward as fast as he could. It caught the bear solidly on
the forearm.

The bear shoved Bannickburn's arm away, rotating
the elf's torso. Bannickburn didn't fight the momentum
he took from the blow, but instead raised the box of
caviar as the left side of his body pivoted around. The
box slammed into the bear's face.

Both men staggered backward. Bannickburn's wrist
had jammed, and his arm fell loosely to his side. The
bear blinked in pain, and there might have been a few
drops of blood falling into his thick beard, but Bannickburn couldn't be sure.

"Dammit, elf! Careful with the caviar!" Kross yelled.
His cultured tones had vanished, and his voice was a
mean growl.

"It's the only weapon I've got!" he yelled back.

"Then use your fraggin' *legs*!" Kross yelled. He
shrugged off the one goon still clinging to him and bar-
reled toward the still-unbalanced bear, wrapping him up
around his midsection. He hit, and a combined mass of
over 225 kilograms slammed into the pier. A plank
cracked loudly.

Bannickburn moved, running past the bear. This
didn't seem like a great plan, but it was better than
hand-to-hand combat.

He was one step past the bear when a hand grabbed
his shoulder and spun him around. One of the goons
Kross had been fighting had caught up to the elf.

Bannickburn reacted. The caviar fell to the pier. His
fist clenched and slammed into the goon's chin. His
knuckles exploded in pain as the goon's head jerked
back. The goon wasn't knocked out, and he wasn't going

down, bu͏͏ ͏e didn't have a hand on Bannickburn. It was enough.

Bannickburn ran. He was startled by heavy footsteps behind him, but when he turned he saw it was Kross.

"You nearly left my caviar. Stupid fraggin' elf." Bannickburn noticed Kross was still talking in his growl.

"Just . . . stupid . . . had to . . . bloody hell." Bannickburn's breaths came in gasps too short to let him put together any kind of sentence. He decided he'd better just run.

Footsteps like an earthquake let him know the bear was on his feet and after them. Bannickburn longed deeply in his soul for the power of invisibility. He'd have to go shopping for some foci when he had the time. And a lot more money.

"Right. *Right!*" Kross yelled. Bannickburn turned right.

"Second door, left!" Again, Bannickburn obeyed. He was inside a dim warehouse. He couldn't see much, but a beam of sunlight piercing a filthy window showed him the only thing he really needed to see. Light fell through the dust-clogged air and illuminated salvation.

"Is that—?" Bannickburn started.

"Sidecar!" Kross barked.

It was a Harley. A beautiful black-and-chrome hog. No fancy paint, nothing to its design that wasn't muscle. Its engine was already rumbling. Bannickburn was in love.

He jumped in the sidecar just as the box of caviar fell into his lap.

"Hold on to it this time! No using it as a weapon!" Kross ordered, then passed along his briefcase. Bannickburn had an awkward fit with the two cases and the box, but it beat running.

Heavy footsteps came after them. The floor of the whole building shook, sending shivering waves of dust into the air.

But the bear was too late. Kross put the hog into gear, squeezed the throttle, and the engine pushed them immediately out of reach. Bullets flew to their right, to their left, and between them, but drew no blood.

Calls had already been put out. Other security would be looking for them. But they were in the warehouse district, and they were mobile. It was too chaotic there to pen in a single motorcycle. They might have to circle around a few times, but they'd make it out.

Bannickburn spent most of his time on the ride nursing his knuckles, watching them swell around the abrasions from the goon's face.

Kross took a brief moment to look at Bannickburn's hand as he drove.

"You're supposed to punch with your hand, not your knuckles!" Kross yelled over the noise of the hog. "Didn't anyone ever teach you that?"

No, Bannickburn said, but only to himself. *Haven't had to fight with my hands much.*

5

If any birds more musical than pigeons had a reason to live in Avondale, Bannickburn was convinced they'd be singing. The sun shone, Jackie was smiling at him, and he had excess cash—excess cash!—in his pocket. Life was as close to good as it had been since Valinscarl had left him crumpled in the mud of the Stinklands.

He frowned as he sat on his battered chair. He remembered the way the sky had looked—purple and orange, like a burning vineyard. Valinscarl had stayed to gloat as long as he dared, until Bannickburn's friends arrived to scoop him off the dirt. Valinscarl's right arm hung limply at his side, his face was burned, his scalp blackened and hairless. He was entirely spent, or he would've cast the spell to finish Bannickburn off. But he was still standing, and someday, soon, when he had healed, Valinscarl would cast magic again.

The fragger knew. As he stood over Bannickburn and laughed through his scalded throat, Valinscarl knew that Bannickburn was finished as a mage. And the toxic mage enjoyed the moment more than Bannickburn had ever seen anyone enjoy anything.

But Bannickburn had rebuilt. He had a life. He had money. He had, to some small degree, respect. Sure, no one feared him. But it was only a matter of time.

He sipped at his tea. Earl Grey, the real stuff. He'd bought an entire case after the Blood Ice run, and he hadn't managed to drink his way through it yet. A few times, he'd even wandered off to find real milk, not powdered, to pour into it.

"I'm as good at burying information as I am at finding it," Jackie said, talking to someone on the telecom. "There's a real art to it, you know. It doesn't take much effort to hide something where no one can find it, but the true skill is hiding it where only a few people—the right people—can get to it."

She fell silent as the other party spoke into her ear. Bannickburn loved hearing only one side of her conversations, so he could guess at the other.

"I'll spell it out for you, then," she said. "I've got the information. It *will* get out. The only question is how. Either you live up to the agreement as I described it— as *I* described it, not the curious version you claim to remember—or the information goes to a place where you won't find it, but anyone you *don't* want to find it, will. It's as simple as that."

Another pause.

"I'll send you the routing instructions. I'm glad we understand each other." She terminated the connection.

Bannickburn smiled in admiration. She was barely over a meter and a half tall, weighed under forty-five kilos, had a face (to Bannickburn's mind, anyway) like a granite angel, and the soul of a shark. On the Matrix, she was a samurai.

"Scare them enough?" he asked.

"Think so," she said with a demure smile. "If I did, I'll buy you dinner tonight."

"Wonderful." Things just kept getting better. A couple of months ago, before he'd met James, he and Jackie were scrounging for food, once even holding up a delivery boy in what was a leading contender for the most pathetic moment of Bannickburn's life. Now, thanks to the Blood Ice run and a continuing series of odd jobs

Bailey kept throwing him, Bannickburn could buy his own dinner—but he didn't have to, because Jackie was finally getting paid.

He could almost feel the rhythm of the world welling up from the ground. In the old days, in the Scotsprawl, he could always feel the currents of power flowing beneath his feet, pulling him. He knew when the flow had been interrupted, could feel disasters from hundreds of miles away the moment they occurred. He was not just standing on top of the world—he was an integral part of it.

After Bannickburn's battle with Valinscarl, when his abilities had been seared out of him, he went numb. He had literally stumbled around each time he tried to walk, his feet feeling like they never really touched the ground. He hadn't just had a leg or arm amputated; the whole world had been cut away.

That had been just over two years ago. Now, for the first time, he could feel it coming back. Not like it had been; nothing that happened more than a block or two away registered with him. But he was in touch with the way this city moved now—he'd thrown himself into its current, let it take him along, and he was prospering. Sure, he wasn't wealthy yet—if all of his prospects and plans went away today, he only had enough funds to get by for a month or two—but he was in the current. If he let it, it would keep carrying him.

In fact, he really must be getting more attuned to the city's rhythm—he could even hear it now, a light, rapid tapping, like the amplified heartbeat of a hummingbird.

Then he looked at Jackie. Her leg was bouncing up and down like she had a spring welded to her heel. That was the source of the noise. Her eyes darted back and forth, looking at him, looking away, looking at him.

"Something on your mind?"

Her eyes focused. "What? Mine? No, not really. Why?"

"Your leg."

She looked down at it curiously. It kept bouncing. She squinted at it, apparently willing it to stop. It didn't.

She gave up on it. "Since you ask, I should tell you

I've found something interesting," she said. "I've been doing a fair amount of negotiation lately, buying and selling a few items I've come across, and I've met some people who know your friend James."

"Mmm-hmmm."

"Did you know he has a nickname?"

Bannickburn shrugged. "Most people do. I didn't know a particular one for him."

"Well, it's really not a nickname. . . . What they call him is 'Jimmy the Shiv.'"

Bannickburn smiled after a brief moment. "I suppose that's somewhat clever. James Shivers, Jimmy the Shiv. Maybe a little obvious, but it gives him an aura of toughness."

Jackie's leg stopped bouncing. Her eyes were focused on his. "This is not just something to give him an aura. This is something he's earned."

"We've all been in rough spots, haven't we? So he used a shiv. Good for him. Shows he can improvise."

"You're not getting what I'm saying."

"That's because you're not really saying anything, dear girl."

Jackie took a deep breath, either to gather her thoughts or prevent herself from cursing him out. "It's a mob nickname. It's something that made guys call him."

Bannickburn blinked, considered what she said, then blinked again. "He's Mafia?"

"I think so."

"Think so?"

"He walks like a mobster, talks like a mobster, smells like a mobster . . ."

"Smells? What does a mobster smell like?"

"I don't know, gun oil and blood. Look, it's just an expression, okay? I haven't tied him to any group yet, but only because I haven't tried. Give me an hour or two, I'll have your proof."

"Don't bother," Bannickburn said airily. "It doesn't matter. So what if he's a made man? Do you trust anyone in this city who is *not* a criminal?"

"No, but . . ."

"Then what's the difference? He's a criminal, like everyone else, he's just more . . . *organized* about it."

"I think you're being a little cavalier about this. Don't underestimate what they can do."

Bannickburn stood up, walked toward her, and patted her on the head in a gesture that was both affectionate and patronizing, and tended to drive her crazy. "I've met combat mages from Ares on the open field. I've been ambushed by toxic spirits in the Stinklands. And just a few weeks ago I punched a man the size of a bear in the face. I can handle it."

Jackie was not convinced, Bannickburn could tell, but he was gratified to see that she was going to pretend otherwise for a time. "Okay," she said. "Just watch yourself."

6

Bailey desperately wanted a scotch. Failing that, a strong cup of coffee might be useful. But he didn't dare drink either one. He was walking a fine balance at the moment, and adding caffeine or alcohol might push him off one of the many cliffs on which he was teetering. He had to stay in control, so he had to drink water, unsatisfying as it was.

"The casino," he said to Shivers, who sat in a leather chair running his finger around the rim of a tumbler of bourbon. "The casino wants to control their floor. That's okay. I like to control my floor, too. That's what the rug is for. But they're playing a dangerous game here. If we stay away, so do our accountants. A ban on us won't hold."

"There's no ban," Shivers said.

"True. True. Just a request. And not even a request for us to completely stay away, is it?"

"No, it's not."

"Just a request that we limit our numbers so as not to draw the attention of the authorities. Do I have that right?"

"You have it exactly right."

"Okay, then, here's what we do. I'm going tonight. You're going. Boone is going. Anyone else who's not otherwise occupied is going. We're dropping a fair pile of nuyen on their heads. And then we're telling them that if we hear any complaints, our accountants will make our considerable losses of that evening disappear from their coffers, and that'll only be the start. And if they decide to complain, our accountants go public with what they know."

"Losses?" Shivers said. "Does that mean you'll be playing?"

"No, of course not. The rest of you will, though."

"Are you ordering us to lose?"

"No, just observing a sad fact. Most of you have the card-playing skills of lungfish."

Shivers finger traced a few more laps around his glass. "Why a lungfish?" he finally asked.

"Dunno. Just popped to mind. So—what else is going wrong today?"

"Cabel woke up long enough to say a few words."

Inside, Bailey jumped to alertness, startled. Outside, he slouched a little deeper in his chair. "What did she say?"

"Complained a little about the pain. Then said something about the Finnigans."

"And what was that?"

"Nonsense. Something about them and the Tir."

"Something in particular?"

"No."

Good and bad, Bailey thought. Cabel hadn't said enough to alert Shivers or anyone else who heard about anything, but she also hadn't said anything that told him anything useful about what had happened to her. It was confirmation of a sort, though. The wheels Bailey had heard about were, in fact, turning. But even if Cabel knew what was happening, she wouldn't be giving any details for a few days at least. If she survived that long.

He needed more information, and soon. He had an uncomfortable feeling that Sottocapo Martel had been displeased with him lately.

"Oh, there's one more piece of news," Shivers said,

with an offhandedness that guaranteed this was going to be bad news.

"What?"

"There's another visitor out in the hall."

"And you knew this when you came in," Bailey said flatly.

"Yes, I did."

"And you didn't tell me."

"No, I didn't."

"Because you were trying to irritate both me and whoever's waiting."

"Right."

Bailey grinned and nodded. "Nice work," he said. "You're an annoying prick, but you'll be the type of lad who helps me die with a smile on my face. Bring whoever it is in."

Shivers put his thumb and forefinger in his mouth and let out a whistle that Bailey half expected to shatter his glass. The door opened, and an ork in a herringbone suit walked in. He looked grumpy, even more so than a normal ork.

Bailey stood. "Kross," he said.

"Quinn," Kross responded in his polite growl, and they shook hands.

"Herringbone?" Bailey asked.

"I make it work."

"Okay. What can I do for you?"

"Nothing. I'm here to help you."

Alarm bells—several of them, insistent and loud—went off in Bailey's head. "Help? You've already done that. And I even thanked you."

"I'm to do it on a more regular basis. With anything you need. Sottocapo Martel is anxious that the many initiatives you're working continue progressing, and I'm here to help them keep moving."

Wonderful, Bailey thought. *I've got my own personal spy.* He had just the assignment for Kross.

"I'm glad to have your help, and your timing couldn't

be better. I've been having trouble with some of my suppliers in Aztlan, and I think it's probably time for someone to physically go down there and straighten things out. You seem like the perfect man for the job."

"I'd be happy to do it," Kross said.

That was too easy, Bailey thought. "Okay. Great. I'll get you started immediately."

"And what else would you like me to do?"

"Else?" Bailey asked. "You'll be in Aztlan. That should be enough for you."

Kross laughed, much too long and too loud to be genuine. "No, no, no, I'm not going to Aztlan. I said I'd take care of it—but delegation is the key to good leadership, isn't it? No, I imagine I can take care of just about anything you give me while staying right here in town."

"Great," Bailey said, not even trying to sound sincere. "That should work out fine."

The trick, he told himself, would be keeping Kross away from Cabel, or anyone who might talk about Cabel. Kross was welcome to learn a lot of things about Bailey's way of doing business, but information about Cabel's mission wouldn't get out until Bailey was good and ready.

He'd get Kross out of his hair for the afternoon, then make a few calls and see what more he could learn about Cabel's mission. Then he'd take it to Martel himself. In this one thing, at least, he'd stay in front of the pack.

The wallpaper was dark green with a satin sheen, the wall sconces were brass and emitted a soft light, the customers were discreet, and the steaks were as thick as two hands placed on top of each other. Real beef, not a trace of soy in it, worth its weight in gold (which was reflected by the prices on the menu). Sottocapo Alexei Martel could be found at the Brigham Steakhouse every evening.

Bailey ran his hands down his lapels. Appearance mattered. The mob had long ago learned that rampant criminality went down a lot smoother when neatly groomed

and dressed in tailored suits. The first thing Martel
would do to judge Bailey's work was give him a once-
over. A loose hair would be almost as damning as a
thousand missing nuyen, so Bailey had spent half an
hour getting his wavy black locks into place. Judging by
the grins several women (and a few men) gave him on
his way to the restaurant, he'd done himself up right.

"Mr. Bailey," the maitre d' said. A thin man with a
thinner mustache, he was the first line of defense in the
Brigham's war against noise. He spoke in a leathery
voice just above a whisper. He looked harmless, but was
backed by a quite lethal security system hidden in the
foyer's nooks and crannies. No one got into the Brigham
who wasn't supposed to be there.

"Mr. d' " Bailey said, one of about a thousand jokes
that amused him more than anyone else.

The maitre d' gave no acknowledgement that humor
of any sort had been attempted. "Please follow me," he
said. "Your party is here, waiting for you."

Of course he's already here, Bailey thought. Martel,
one of the few full-time carnivores left in the world,
would break out in hives if he was more than 100 meters
away from meat for two hours.

He sauntered through the tables as the maitre d'
walked primly forward. The tables were generously
spaced, and the patrons hunched over them, bringing
their heads together over flickering candles. The conversation in the room rustled like a dozen snakes on sand.
Bailey couldn't make out a word anyone at any of the
tables was saying, which was exactly as everyone
intended.

Martel sat in a corner booth, mainly because a regular
chair would never hold him. He was built like a buffalo,
and jokes about his weight were common among those
under his command (as long as he wasn't in the room,
of course). Some people called him fat, but Bailey had
never seen a hint of anything besides metal and muscle
in the man's body. He stood smoothly as Bailey approached, carrying his size with grace.

"Mr. Bailey," he said in a voice like a long bow stroke on the thickest string of a cello. "Please sit down."

Bailey sat down without extending a hand toward Martel. The sottocapo didn't seem to appreciate human contact, and if he ever got his right cyberarm on anyone else's hands, it was usually for the purpose of mangling, not greeting.

"Good evening, Sottocapo Martel," Bailey said cheerfully. "From which portion of the cow's body will you be dining tonight?"

As was the custom when he spoke to Bailey, Martel simply ignored any remarks he found inconsequential. Knowing this, Bailey usually tried to make as many frivolous comments as he could.

"I understand you've welcomed the new assistant I dispatched to you," Martel said.

"The ork? Yes, yes indeed, Sottocapo, and I want to thank you for your generosity in sending him my way. Big dumb muscle is easy to come by in this city, but big *smart* muscle is wonderful. And the fact that he's such a fashion plate only makes him more delightful."

Martel placed a triangle of red beef in his mouth and chewed slowly. Bailey pretended to enjoy the sight.

Martel swallowed. "Mr. Kross is a very valuable commodity," he said. "I did not dispatch him to you lightly."

The trick of talking to Sottocapo Martel, Bailey had discovered long ago, was learning how much information Martel packed into his words. In contrast to Bailey, who had mastered the art of speaking for hours without really saying anything, Martel said as few words as possible, expecting the listener to pick up on every nuance and inflection. Thus, the two brief sentences Martel had just uttered said a lot more than they appeared to. Bailey translated them as: *I'm paying Kross a lot of money, and there are plenty of things I could have him do, but of all of those I chose to send him to you. Don't waste the family's money—put him to use on some important assignments. Besides, one reason I sent him to you is to spy on your operation, and how can I do that if you assign him grunt work?*

The last sentence of the translation was tricky, as Martel did not necessarily want his subordinate to know that Kross was a spy. But Bailey had known it instantly, which meant he knew the real reason Martel wanted the ork put to good use, so he included that motive in the translation.

"Certainly, Sottocapo Martel. He'll only be washing the windows in *my* office—I won't let him so much as touch a pane in any other room."

Martel was chewing again. Bailey took advantage of the opportunity to flag down a waiter and order some food of his own, if only so he'd have something to do while Martel was processing his bites.

"Thank you for joining me tonight," Martel said when his mouth was clear. "You have many important duties. I know they press on your time."

Bailey translated again: *I've given you lots of assignments that I think are pretty important. You should be working on them now, but you're meeting with me, so the best use of your time at the moment is to tell me how your progress is going.*

"Yes, Sottocapo, and I'm honored, of course, that you would entrust me with these jobs. Most of them are progressing well. I expect Pietro Vacini's secret cannoli recipe to be in my hands within a day; our chefs should be attempting to duplicate his creations by dinner tomorrow."

Again, Martel showed no signs that he'd heard Bailey speak. Bailey grinned and proceeded to real business. "I think the Gates problem will be under control shortly. I've got a two-part strategy that involves annoying the hell out of them, followed by impressing them. I think it'll work."

"You will be employing your strongest skills," Martel said with a small nod.

Bailey raised an eyebrow. *It's possible*, he thought,

that Martel just made a joke at my expense. Martel's face remained expressionless, but Bailey thought he detected a hint of self-satisfaction in the large man. *At this pace,* he told himself, *we'll be bantering like old friends in a mere quarter century or so.*

"There are a few steps I need to take to get the Gates situation all squared away, but I'm not at all worried. As long as I can draw on some of our flexible resources." Which meant money to hire outside help.

"Of course."

"Now, I *am* worried about what's going on in the Tir. The 'others' "—Martel never liked anyone to say the Finnigan family name in his presence—"are, I believe, very close to getting their hands on the item. Time's running short, shorter than I thought, but it's something I can deal with. I've been moving plans ahead to compensate, and we should be able to derail them without effort."

"They already have it."

Bailey's mouth opened, but, oddly, no words came out. It was never good, he thought, for your superior to know more about the progress of your project than you did.

"Are you . . . I have a—a source. Someone I'm trying to talk to. She hasn't said anything about that."

"Your courier doesn't know."

That sentence was only four words, but it carried a wagonload of bad news for Bailey. Martel already knew about Cabel's mission. Not only did he know about it, he knew more than Bailey did about what Cabel had learned and what she hadn't. And to top it all off, Martel had his own source that gave him better information than Bailey had on what was supposed to be Bailey's most important project.

That was all quite bad. But Bailey would be damned if he'd let Martel see him without his composure for another second.

"Then we're moving ahead," he said brightly. "They may have it, but they don't have a way out yet." Bailey was guessing at this last bit of information, but he needed to sound like he still knew what was going on. "I'll have people down there before they can do anything useful with it."

"Analysis would not take long."

"I know, I know, they wouldn't need a lot of time, but they're going to have to stay on the move as long as they're down there. They may have better relations with the Tir than we do right now, but all that means is that they won't be shot on sight. Now that they have it, the Tir's going to be on their tails until they get out, and getting out of Portland while holding it is going to be about as tough as getting out of this place without dropping a couple hundred nuyen. We still have some time. My people will be there before it's too late."

"You've chosen them?" There was a note in Martel's voice that might have sounded impressed. Or it could just have been the calming effect of the steak.

"Yes. The leader's all lined up," Bailey said. It was a terrible lie, but it had all just come to him. Who should do it. How. What the incentive would be. And how to get Kross out of his hair. It would work. He'd need a little help, but it would work. "It'll be taken care of."

Martel said nothing, which Bailey took to be a sign of trust, though it could just as easily be an indication of disgust. Bailey spent the rest of the night telling stories about gambling in casinos, winning the hearts of lovely young women, and drinking prodigious amounts of alcohol, while Martel slowly chewed his steak, and then ordered another and another.

7

Bannickburn opened doors. He slid her chair back from the table with the grace of a ballet dancer. He spoke to the waiters in French. He smiled. He listened. He laughed. And as the evening wore on, he was amazed to discover that the act he had put on so many times before to impress scores of young ladies was no longer an act. He didn't listen to Jackie to show off how attentive and sensitive he was. He just listened.

He'd always worried this would happen. The greatest peril of age, he'd always thought, was a reversal of your natural tendencies. Those who spend their youth innocent find themselves growing more and more cynical as the years pass, ending in a bitter and jaded condition that Bannickburn had always believed was wholly appropriate. Those who caught on to the rhythms of life early, on the other hand, and who grew caustic in their youth in an attempt to keep pace with the savagery of the world, often came to an unfortunate juncture in middle age when they grow more naïve, more trusting, more open to the good things of life.

Bannickburn had watched in horror when that happened to one of his mentors, thinking that the desire to rhapsodize on the beauty of a flower was a fate worse than death. Now he felt it happening to him—odd feelings working through his normal armor. The worst of it

was, the change was not entirely unpleasant. His whole
nature should be rebelling against it, but it wasn't.

Maybe he should just put a gun to his head while
there was still time.

". . . with so little IC around it, well, God, that's just
a joke, isn't it? You might as well just leave it on your
reception desk! You might as well put it on a fraggin'
billboard in the middle of downtown. You're just *beg-
ging* me to take it when you leave it so open.

"But the real problem," Jackie continued, "was they
didn't know its worth. They thought of it just as pure
data. They never thought about how to use it against
anyone. They just thought it was . . . *science.* How pathetic is that? It just wouldn't be *right* to leave information that valuable in the hands of those people."

Bannickburn decided he didn't need to blow his brains
out after all. How could he *not* find a creature as beautiful, crafty, and jaded as this one appealing? It wasn't his
age's fault that she was perfect.

"And it's the funds from this data that's paying for
our meal tonight?" he asked.

Jackie snorted. "Hardly. The actual funds have barely
started to trickle in. This dinner just comes from using
the information to put the right leverage on the right
points."

"Blackmail?"

"It's an unpleasant word, but I guess"—she shrugged—
"it applies."

Simply delightful, Bannickburn thought. *I'm eating
truffles and she hasn't even begun to pull down the real
money yet.*

"How long do you expect this particular revenue
stream to last?"

"I'm not sure. I'm still learning how to play these
things out." She tossed and re-tossed her salad without
actually bringing a lettuce leaf to her mouth. "The first
few times I had something like this, I was a little blunt,
a little direct, I guess. Mistakes of youth."

Bannickburn hid a smile. She didn't like to speak of

her age, but Bannickburn was fairly certain she hadn't yet hit twenty.

"I got some nice sums up front," she continued, "but that was it. I've seen, though, how other people tease it out for a while. The initial money is much smaller, but if you milk your pigeons long enough . . ."

"Milk your pigeons?"

"Yeah, yeah, mixed metaphor, sorry. Anyway, if you string them along for long enough, you can keep a decent cash flow coming to you. You don't get the rush of the immediate big payoff, but the total money in the end comes out to more that way. I think I could stretch it out for a year at least."

"And you have other similar . . . projects that you're working on?"

"You'd better believe it."

"So how many do you think you need to have before it's enough? Before you, you know, move out of the Barrens, find a nicer place, settle into a more regular lifestyle?"

She gave him a look that made him feel the exact difference in their ages. "Enough?"

"Enough nuyen. Enough power."

She dropped her fork, sat back in her chair, and lightly rubbed her right temple, apparently thinking of something she hadn't bothered to contemplate before. "Enough? Drek, I don't know, Robert. I've never thought about it that way. The money is useful as a way of keeping score, I guess, and for getting a nice meal but . . . what would I do, buy a SIN? Open a regular bank account?" She shook her head. "I don't see that happening anytime soon. I mean, is that how you thought of things back in Scotsprawl? Did you think of just working until you had enough?"

He hadn't. Of course he hadn't. But he had been young then. With the amount of power he had, he felt young right into his forties. He never even thought of the word "enough." There was no such thing—only "more."

But the day he'd lost it all, he'd aged about two decades. Survival wasn't a given anymore—it was an open question. Ridiculous minutiae, like where his next meal would come from, dominated way too many of his waking hours. Since he'd come to Seattle, he'd thought long and hard about what would be enough—what would give him safety and security. But Jackie, so blessedly far removed from any effects of age, and still growing into her considerable powers (though hers were of a completely different nature than his had been) thought now like he once had. Which was wonderful, but Bannickburn couldn't be sure how well he'd be able to put up with a young version of himself these days.

Of course, this young version of himself came with a wonderful smile, angelic and devilish at the same time. That helped.

"No," he finally said, answering the question that hung awkwardly in the air. "No, I never thought that way. And you shouldn't, either."

She returned her fork to her salad. "I think you need to have more fun in what you're doing. Yeah, we gotta run to survive, but you have to enjoy the rush, too, right? If it's all about putting bread on the table, you're just another wage slave, and who wants that?"

He thought of the way he'd felt leaping onto Kross' motorcycle and getting away from the goons at the dock. That *had* been fun.

"You're right," he said. "You're right. And I have been enjoying it all more lately."

"It's because of Shivers, isn't it?"

"And his boss. Bailey."

"Right. Quinn's his first name, isn't it?"

Bannickburn nodded, and he could almost see the information being filed into Jackie's brain for later use.

"The work they're giving me has been good. Fun sometimes."

"Okay," she said. "I'm still not sold on these guys, but if the work's good, okay. Just keep your guard up."

Bannickburn grinned widely, and his brogue thickened

as he spoke. "Keep my guard up? Lass, you don't get
to where I've been without knowing *that*. I've thrown
too many knockout punches myself not to have learned
how to avoid them. Good God above, you'd think you
were speaking to an infant."

She laughed. "All right, all right. You're the almighty
Robert Lionel Bannickburn, I know. You can handle
yourself."

"And you'd be well not to forget it!" he said, but his
tone remained light.

"I couldn't if I tried. Especially as long as I have to
look at those horrendous sideburns."

He thumped the table in mock anger. "Now you've
done it, lass! Two things you never insult in a Scotsman
are his clan and his 'burns! I've no choice now but to
force-feed you haggis!"

"Evening, Robert. Is this young lady giving you trouble?" said a friendly voice. Jackie looked up, and while
her face didn't exactly fall, it also didn't remain open
and cordial. Bannickburn pivoted right and saw Quinn
Bailey standing behind him.

"Quinn! Fancy meeting you here!"

"Yes, I love a good coincidence. I guess it's inevitable,
since we share the same tastes." He threw Jackie a leer
that would have been offensive if it wasn't so over the
top. "In many things."

Bannickburn chuckled. Jackie remained impassive.

Half a century of life had taught Bannickburn how to
handle the situation from here. He might not have the
drive and power of youth, but he'd be damned if he
hadn't learned at least some social grace.

"I'd love to invite you to join us, Quinn, but I'm sure
you understand that some evenings are not to be interrupted." He smiled at Jackie, and she grinned back. It
was genuine.

"Of course, of course. Just giving you my good wishes
for the evening. Perhaps, though, if you have some time
tomorrow morning we could talk? You're going to like
what I've got to tell you—you're going to like it a lot."

"Certainly," Bannickburn said. They exchanged a time and a place, Bailey said a smooth good-bye, and Bannickburn returned his full attention to Jackie.

"What, in your experience," he asked, "is the difference between setting up a bribe and setting up blackmail?"

She was off and talking again, allowing Bannickburn to marvel at her all over again, and wonder how long it would take for her to rise so far that she left him behind.

The date ended the way Bannickburn believed all dates should, and he reflected on the end of the evening in careful detail as he reclined in bed, savoring each moment on that particular piece of furniture. He wished Jackie were still there with him, to provide visual reinforcement of his recent memories, but she'd gotten up to jack in to the Matrix. Bannickburn wasn't sure if it was a meeting or datachasing or both, but it had her whole attention.

He drifted into and out of sleep, but every time he opened his eyes, everything in front of him looked the same. The black chair with the narrow "S" back, the soft blue lights blinking on Jackie's wide array of electronic devices, the dim lights from the wall sconces—everything was the same, and Jackie sat in the middle of it in the exact same position.

Then he opened his eyes and she wasn't in her chair anymore. He couldn't see her anywhere, but half of the basement apartment was pitch black. If he got up, he'd probably find her there, but he didn't feel like getting up.

Then she walked out of the darkness, light catching her long white T-shirt in a way that woke Bannickburn up a little more. She looked serious, though, which likely meant conversation instead of anything else. Her eyes bounced this way and that, and her shoulders twitched involuntarily. She wanted to talk, but she was still coming down from being online. Where she probably wished she still was.

"Are you awake?" she asked.

"If you want me to be," he said, with all the gallantry he could muster.

"You know who Bailey is, don't you?"

The question took him by surprise. He hadn't thought about Bailey since the man had left their table. "What do you mean?"

"You know what I mean."

He pushed himself up into a semiupright position. "No, I'm too drowsy. Give me a moment, though, and maybe I'll come up with it."

That was a lie. He knew exactly what she meant. And she was right. Ever since the run with Kross, he'd had a pretty clear idea of who Bailey was, and what kind of position he occupied. After all, there weren't a whole lot of people who used ork muscle to run talismans off the Tacoma docks. But Bannickburn kept telling himself that if he never actually admitted what Bailey was, then that meant he wasn't becoming involved with the type of person he knew Bailey to be.

"Holy flaming drek, Robert, you know he's Mafia. You *know* it. Part of the Bigio family, to be precise. A caporegime, just as brutal as any of them, only he's got manners and a veneer of civility. But that's all it is, just a thin surface. And that's who's giving you marching orders."

"No one's giving me orders," Bannickburn said. He was feeling much more alert now.

"No one besides him is giving you work, either. You're getting sucked into the family, and that's not a safe place to be."

"This is what you've been doing all night? Finding out Bailey's background and preparing this speech? Wouldn't it have been more fun to stay in bed?"

She snorted. "Finding out about Bailey took about ten minutes. I did it while I was shopping at Hacker House, which was one of about fifteen things I did on the Matrix tonight, thank you very much. Even you could have found it out if you'd wanted to."

Bannickburn decided that, in the light of the rest of

the night, he'd not take offense at that remark. But the confidence of her words raised his hackles a little—on the Matrix, she oozed power, while he was just as weak online as he was everywhere else. He knew how she must feel when jacked in, and he envied her for it.

"All right, then," he said. "Yes. Bailey's Mafia, and, as it turns out, the Mafia pays well. Are you telling me you've never worked with organized crime before?"

"No. I mean, yes, I've worked with organized crime."

"And are they more powerful than the corps? More ruthless than the corps?"

"Sometimes."

"And sometimes not. So I'm not sure exactly what it is you want me to be worried about."

Jackie paced back and forth a few times, and Bannickburn let a few glimpses of her legs distract him. But then she was ready to speak.

"You should know this already. You're almost thirty years older than me and you haven't exactly been spending your time in a cave. But you want to pretend you don't, so I'll tell you. Any Johnson is dangerous, any Johnson might double-cross you and try to kill you—we know this. But at the end of the day, even if the corps—or the government—don't want to *be* respectable, they want to *seem* respectable. So they'll put in the token effort. But the Mafia doesn't care about being respectable. That's the last thing in the world they want. They want to look intimidating, tough—*evil*. So while the corps are occasionally forced to do good or decent things that they don't want to do to keep up an image, the Mafia never is. It's just the opposite—when the Mafia wants to be ruthless sons of bitches, they have nothing holding them back, and even when they *don't* want to be ruthless sons of bitches, they sometimes have to be, because they have an image to keep up. No one we deal with really has a conscience—but mobsters never even have to *pretend* they have one."

"Okay. So. They're bad guys. Maybe I like them, but they're bad guys. I'll be careful."

"It's too late for that," Jackie said, her voice rising with concern and anger. "You're in. They've got some of their hooks into you. You may not know it, but they do. You can't be careful anymore. You can only get away. It's the leaky faucet that becomes a flood."

"What?"

"Drop by drop. They wear you down. They're patient, and they know how to get their way. It's just a trickle, so you don't notice what they're doing until you're completely swamped. Completely overwhelmed."

Bannickburn didn't notice any leaks. He'd done some work, that was all, and he could walk away any time. As far as he was concerned, that meant he was being careful enough, and could proceed as he'd planned. But he needed a way to end the conversation amicably.

"Okay," he said. "Okay. Let me just meet with Quinn tomorrow. I'll tell him I'm booked, that I can't take anything new for a while. I'll take a few steps back. Okay?"

She stopped her pacing and looked at him squarely. Her gaze could detect bulldrek as effectively as any of Bannickburn's old spells. He wasn't sure how well he held up to her analysis, but finally she decided to act like she believed him, regardless of whether she actually did or not.

"Okay," she said, and returned to bed, allowing Bannickburn to pretend the whole conversation hadn't happened and that the night—well, the morning, now—was still proceeding perfectly.

8

Bailey had friends who considered themselves experts on various parts of a woman's body. He knew a leg guy, a breast guy, a neck guy, even a small-of-the-back guy. He had listened at great length to their monologues on their favorite subjects, and had to admit that each of them made excellent points. But none of them knew eyes like he knew eyes, and that was their critical mistake. The better you are at reading eyes, the better chance you have at studying whatever other elements you would like to examine.

He'd had about ten seconds to assess the look in the eyes of Bannickburn's lady friend the other night, and he hadn't seen anything good. Mistrust, hostility, and an active, predatory intelligence. That wasn't a good combination. He had a pretty good guess what she'd been telling Bannickburn since Bailey had left the two of them to their dinner, and he'd spent most of his morning working up a counter plan. Part of it involved getting to Splat before Bannickburn.

The restaurant likely wouldn't last more than a few months—it was too crowded, too profitable to survive so close to Redmond. Soon, it would be hit by the inevitable series of break-ins, robberies, and vandalism, leading to either closure or buyout by the Bigios or Finnigans, who were adept at using the promise of protection to expand their empires. Once they bought it, the mob might keep it open but would most likely shut it down, eliminating competition and making sure profits kept flowing to their regular joints. And Redmond would get back to the business of being barren.

For this brief moment, though, it was warm, lively, and served fantastic omelets. Plaid wallpaper covered most of the dents and divots in the walls, and the lights only blinked occasionally with the poor flow of electricity. The windows were clean, the plates were slightly less clean. The clientele, for the most part, had woken up only an hour or two before, so they were too low-key to throw the dishes at each other, which allowed the dishes to survive long enough to gain stains.

When Bannickburn arrived, he looked impressively alert. Bailey knew he'd probably had a late night—but then again, that was the norm for people in Redmond, which was why Splat served breakfast all day.

Bailey saw him across the crowded room and waved him over. Bannickburn sauntered to the table, and Bailey could immediately see that the elf's girlfriend had gotten to him. But Bailey was ready.

"Morning, Robert."

"Morning, Quinn. For a few more minutes, at least."

Quinn smiled, then launched into his prepared speech before Bannickburn could open his menu.

"There's something I've got to tell you before I tell you anything else. Robert, you've been working for the Bigio family lately. That's right, the mob. I'm a mobster. Boogety boogety boogety." Bailey wiggled his fingers in mock menace. "I'm sure you've heard how frightening we are, and it's all true. We're bad, bad people. If they had fried baby on the menu, you can be sure that's what I'd be ordering."

Bannickburn kept his face blank, and Bailey plunged on.

"We're not nice people. I won't pretend we are. I've killed people, and some of them probably didn't deserve it, but that was what needed to be done at the time, and if it makes you feel better about me, then I'll assure you my poor heart bled a little just before I put a bullet in their sad brains. I'm not going to try to convince you that, sure, we're the Mafia, but we're not that bad—we're actually nice! Because we're not."

"This is a hell of a pep talk so far," Bannickburn said. "Should we order our food before you further explain what a bastard you are?"

"Ah, if you've learned anything in your life, I'm sure you've learned about that vast spectrum between nice people and bastards. I'm somewhere in there, and you are, too, and I'm fairly certain we're not that far apart." Bailey motioned for a waiter, who started to ignore him, did a double take when he saw who was waving at him, then walked over.

"I've always loved that speech," Bannickburn said. "The one at the end of every action trideo, where the bad guy takes a minute to tell the good guy how much alike they are."

"Me, too. I guess you should be saying, 'Then I'll see you in hell,' any minute now."

Bannickburn leaned forward, his gray eyes carrying a hint of a burning ember. "Why the speech, Quinn?"

Bailey replied smoothly, "Because I should put all my cards on the table before I ask you to do what I want you to do. This is what you have to know if you're going to do the job, and I thought it would be best if I laid it out right off the bat."

The two men gave the now-patient waiter their orders, and he scuttled off to make sure they were kept happy.

Bannickburn took a few moments to respond, and Bailey spent the time running a few of his more extreme methods of persuasion through his mind, choosing an option to employ in case Bannickburn resisted. It turned out to be unnecessary, though—he had used the right bait.

"What's special about this job?" the elf asked.

"It's a favor to a man we value highly—a guy named Victor Kreb."

"Never heard of him."

"Good. You shouldn't have. He's an accountant, and accountants work best when they're totally invisible."

"One of your guys?"

"He's done a number of favors for us, saving us a considerable amount of money and a great deal of legal and corporate hassle. He's someone we wish to keep as a friend."

"Right. And now there's a problem?"

Bailey grinned wanly. "There's a problem. He has a daughter, Angeline, who has been spending a significant amount of time with Murson Kader."

"Kader?" Bannickburn whistled. "Great holy dragon dung, even I know that name."

"Yes. When you disembowel so many people in such a public fashion, your reputation tends to spread quickly. Now, as an old romantic, I was hoping the relationship between Angeline and Kader would lead to a fairy-tale ending, but that's not the road you generally follow when you're dating a psychopath."

"I would imagine."

"The relationship recently . . . ended. Badly. Messily."

Bannickburn's eyebrows raised. Bailey thought he might be looking genuinely concerned, but it wasn't an expression he saw very often, so he couldn't be sure.

"Is she okay?" Bannickburn asked. "Is . . . are her insides still . . . inside?"

"She's alive, and we hope someday she'll be okay, though she'll have plenty of scars—physical and mental—to carry around the rest of her life."

Bannickburn shook his head sorrowfully. *Drek*, Bailey thought, *he's going to be even more of a pushover than I thought.* Bailey continued talking so that he could strike while the iron was hot.

"Naturally," Bailey said, "Mr. Kreb wants revenge, and his first thought was to turn to us. He didn't mince words—either we help him, or he's done with us. Since his abilities are not the kind that are easily replaced, we're not anxious to see him take his talents elsewhere.

But you don't take out a guy like Murson Kader lightly—someone that high up in the Finnigan family isn't going to fall without a loud, disruptive crash."

Bannickburn was too shrewd. He saw where this was going and started to backpedal. "If *you're* not going to go after Kader, with all the tools at your disposal, I'm not sure what you think *I* could do about the situation." His mouth twitched, attempting to open but staying closed, and Bailey intuitively understood why. His brain was telling him to say, *This job is too big for me,* but his pride wouldn't let the words come out. Bailey picked up the pace of the conversation to lay a little more bait in front of Bannickburn before the elf had time to back out.

"I wish we could be involved. I, personally, would love to deliver some of the repayment Kader has coming. But as you know, the situation between my family and that other family is a bit tense, and if anyone with Bigio connections gets caught assaulting someone of Kader's standing, we'll all have trouble. Large, unpleasant, city-wide trouble.

"Now the good news is that Mr. Kreb is not entirely carried away in anger, and still has a rational mind in his head," Bailey continued, stepping on Bannickburn's words as the elf tried to break back into the conversation. "He knows we can't kill Kader, and that even hiring someone else to kill him is too risky. He is willing to settle for embarrassment and humiliation."

Bannickburn had been sitting more and more stiffly in his chair as Bailey's story proceeded, until it seemed he'd be forced to stand. But Bailey's last line, combined with the timely arrival of breakfast, loosened him up. His body slowly eased back into place. He bit into some fatty bacon, soggy in the English style, and chewed on it thoughtfully.

"Embarrassment and humiliation," he said, and his exhaled breath was smoky. "To avenge a girl's honor." He chewed some more. "That doesn't sound like a ruthless-son-of-a-bitch-type job."

Bailey spread his hands. "Ah, but there's the beauty of it. We're ruthless sons of bitches to everyone in the world but our own. Our own, we protect like . . . well, hell, like family, of course."

It was, perhaps, the largest and most ludicrous lie Bailey had ever uttered. The Mafia took care of their own the same way a family of newborn pigeons did, kicking and scrambling and pushing whoever looked weak out of the nest to die on the street. But the trids had done a wonderful job of promulgating the myth of Mafia family loyalty, and Bailey was not about to squander all their hard work.

Bannickburn was still thinking, and Bailey opted to remain silent. He didn't have to draw Bannickburn a picture—the implication should have been clear. *Do this, and you, like Kreb, earn our friendship. Do this, and we'll take care of you.*

Bailey hoped he wouldn't have to spell that out for Bannickburn, because that might push him into a series of ever-larger lies. But he thought he'd coated the hook in enough inviting, meaty bait to get Bannickburn to chomp down.

"That's the outline of *what* you want," Bannickburn finally said. "But you haven't said anything about the *how*. Have you thought of that any, or are you leaving that to the poor lad you intend to rope into this task?"

Bailey smiled and, in his head, pictured himself reeling in a fine catch. "Oh, I've thought about it," he said. "I've thought about it plenty."

9

The guy in the leather coat looked pretty tough. His wrists were as thick as Bannickburn's neck, his shades were black as tar, and his tusks were white, sharpened, and gleaming. The fact that he had an ork even taller than himself pinned to the ground while he rained blows on his opponent's head only added to the favorable impression.

This was the kind of guy Bannickburn needed, but he couldn't approach him here. He needed background on him, he needed to know if he could trust him, and he needed the stench of ork sweat to dissipate somewhat before he could think about getting any closer to the guy.

But the fact that he could even consider ways to draft this particular specimen was exciting. He hadn't given orders to anyone since that terrible day in the Stinklands—at least, he hadn't given orders that anyone had paid attention to. Now, though, he had money, and a mission that should be fun. He should have his pick of runners for his team.

All he had to do was figure out how to contact them.

The easiest thing he could have done was the one thing he truly wanted to avoid—relying on Jackie. He was quite certain she could present a long list of good candidates after a few minutes on the Matrix (or maybe just off the top of her head), but this was *his* mission, and he wanted to take care of things himself. Plus, he wasn't sure how Jackie would react to the idea that he was getting in deeper with the Bigios.

He also had been forbidden from asking Bailey and Shivers for any names, since a central goal of the run was keeping the Bigios at arm's length from the whole thing.

So he was on his own. He knew how this was supposed to go—he had to use his network. Unfortunately, he didn't really have a network in this city, but he was nothing if not adaptable.

He had about a half-dozen conversations with casual acquaintances in the Barrens. Each of them went pretty much like this: he'd walk up to them smoothly and non-threateningly, make a few remarks about the weather, then get to the heart of the matter.

"Hey, remember that guy (or lady) you mentioned to me a while back? The one you said was looking for work?"

The contact, in each case, looked dubious and uncertain. "Which one was that?"

"The one who hit the streak of bad luck? You said they're pretty good at what they do?"

A moment more of confusion before clarity rippled across the contact's face. "Oh, oh, right, you mean . . ." and they'd say the name of a friend.

"Right! Right! That's the one! How's he (she) doing?"

"About the same. It's tough, you know? Not enough business to go around."

"Yeah, I know. Believe me, I know. Living off the crumbs from the guys at the top, right?"

The contact would then follow with some form of defense of their friend, saying that the person in question was very skilled at what they did, and the fact that they had hit the skids recently was due to the unfortunate quirks of a hostile universe rather than to any lack of skill on their part.

"Really?" Bannickburn would say. "It sounds like there's a story there. What happened?"

And the background would come out. By the time the contact was done speaking, Bannickburn would have a decent estimation of the target's skills, reliability, and history. Out of the six contacts he spoke to, he got the names of two people he wanted to interview.

One of them, he found out after a little effort, was lying at the bottom Lake Washington, presumably held down at least in part by the weight of several lead bullets scattered throughout her body. The other, a skittish, rat-faced man called Steeltoe, seemed to be gradually warming up to the run, until Bannickburn uttered two fatal words.

"Murson Kader."

"Murson *Kader*? What the hell kind of drek is this? *Kader*? And you're offering"—Steeltoe looked at a number Bannickburn had written down—"*that?* You go after someone like Kader, it's a good idea to disappear for a while, right? Relocate, get somewhere he can't find you? That's what I'd do. And you can't do much work when you're trying to stay out of sight. Job'd have to pay for that downtime, give me enough to survive for a while. You're not there yet. Pay is nowhere *near* there. You get more money, you can come talk to me about Murson Kader."

Bannickburn tried the direct approach. "Look, I don't mean to be blunt here, but however much it is, it's more than you've made in a while. Maybe this isn't the best time to be picky."

The man snorted, an unpleasantly wet sound. "It's always the right time. You want me to do something that could make me end up dead, you better pay me enough to let me live it up while I'm still alive. You're not offering enough, so for the time being I think I'll stay alive and poor instead of dead and slightly less poor."

So, by the end of the day, after working over what passed for his network in this godforsaken city, Bannick-burn had made absolutely no progress. Steeltoe's reac-

tion to Kader's name briefly made him reconsider doing
the job at all, but then he decided that Steeltoe was
scared not because Kader was so tough, but because
Steeltoe was so far down the food chain. It was like a
cockroach looking up at a cat—the cat's only scary when
you're something that easily fits in its mouth.

The key, he thought, was to find some people who
were normally a few more rungs up the ladder. If they'd
been a little closer to the top, Kader wouldn't look so
bad. To get these people, though, Bannickburn would
probably need to put a little more money out there and
reduce his take, a decision that caused physical pain in
Bannickburn's abdomen. The fact that it was for a noble
cause (as long as he thought of the mission as avenging
a young lady's honor, not keeping a mob accountant
happy) marginally reduced the burning.

Even with his cut reduced, though, he still wasn't sure
he could pay for the kind of help he needed. What he
needed, he was realizing, were some suckers just like
himself—people who, for one reason or another, were
willing to do this job for a little less money than they
normally would receive. Maybe they'd be attracted to
the cause, maybe they were desperate for some quick
cash, or maybe they used to be at the top of their game
but, through misfortune, had fallen.

Bannickburn hoped to avoid recruiting anyone from
that last group—one per team was enough.

This was a much more difficult mission than the one
he'd conceived this morning. In the Scotsprawl, in the
last few years, he had gotten a little sloppy. He'd gathered teams of just about anyone willing to take his cash,
without bothering to take any of the normal precautions
that would ensure he was getting decent help. The recruiting part of his life had started to bore him, as it
seemed like an endless parade of losers and suck-ups.
He'd assembled teams when he needed them, with all
possible speed, sometimes just making a few telecom
calls and pretty much hiring whoever answered.

The slapdash approach had naturally led to some poor

teams, but it never really mattered. If the people he hired did their job, that came as a pleasant surprise. If they didn't, then he just expended a little extra energy to cover their asses—and energy used to be something he had in excess.

Until the Stinklands. He'd been left utterly alone, his former friends lured away by Valinscarl's promises of money and power, and his team of hired guns asleep at the switch, unaware that their boss had stumbled into the most powerful magic ambush he'd ever seen.

He would pay for that mistake for the rest of his life, and he wasn't keen to repeat it. This time, he'd have a quality team. If he'd learned anything today, it was that he couldn't put together such a team on his own—at least not soon enough to please Bailey. He needed help to get this done—assuming he could convince the help he had in mind to be friendly.

His first thought was to buy flowers for her, but he rejected that. Too base, too common. He needed something from the heart, something that wasn't a rote gesture of apology, but instead a true show of respect and affection. He'd scour the markets all night if he needed to, so that he could find the right thing.

10

"**F**lowers?"

"Mere blooms, of course. Radiant, beautiful in their fashion, but their glory is fleeting when compared to yours. An inadequate gift, to be sure, but when faced with a beauty such as yours, what offering would truly suffice?"

Jackie balanced her spine on the black "S" of her chair, leaning back and propping her legs on a table. "Charming. How much more buttering up do you need to do before you get to whatever point you need to get to?"

Bannickburn curled the left side of his mouth, fully prepared for her to see right through him. "It's a big favor I'm preparing to ask. I'd estimated that a full ten minutes of groundwork would be necessary before I even broached the subject."

"'Groundwork?' How romantic. Are you asking a favor or laying some concrete?"

"I beg your pardon. Such a common phrase should not be used in association with an uncommon lady. But mere words tend to fail me in the ethereal glow of your presence."

Jackie snorted. "Right. Well, much as I'd like to watch you tie your tongue in knots for ten more minutes, I have a busy night ahead of me. Let's just pretend you already flattered me for ten minutes, and you can go ahead and say what you really want to say."

Bannickburn strode forward, a long step that was more like a glide, and slid the vase of flowers on the table near Jackie's feet so that, in her line of vision, they'd appear right next to his face. He'd picked pale colors—whites, yellows, and blues—specifically so they'd complement his appearance. "I need a favor," he said.

"So you said."

"I'd like you to help me with something."

"And now you're just redefining terms. Come on. I'm a busy woman. Get to it."

"It's nothing, really. I just picked up some work, and it's something I can't do on my own. I need a team."

"You just picked up some work? From Bailey, I'm guessing."

"Yeah," Bannickburn said, then braced himself for the inevitable lecture about dealing with the Mafia.

"Okay," Jackie said. "We've got you and me, so that's two. What else do you need?"

Bannickburn scratched his eye. Then he loosely dragged his fingers through his thick, windblown black hair. Then he realized his mouth was hanging open.

"You? Two? What do you . . . ? You heard me say 'yeah' when you asked about Bailey, right?"

"Yes, I did. Look, you're a big boy, Robert. You made your choice. I'm sure you took any advice I gave you into consideration, and I assume you have a reason to keep working with Bailey. I like you, I can help on almost any kind of run you can think of, and being on your team will allow me to keep an eye on your butt. So I'm in."

"Humph," Bannickburn said, still trying to overcome his surprise. "All right. Just don't let my arse distract you from the task at hand."

"Yes, sir. So what else do you need?"

"Muscle, transportation, and a face."

"What kind of face?"

"Innocent, naïve. Someone who can pull a hustle."

"Okay." She paused, took a deep breath, then spoke again. "We need a mage."

Bannickburn nearly leaped out of his chair. "No, we don't!"

"Robert . . ."

"I've got that aspect covered."

"No, you don't."

"Yes, I do. Who could we find as good as me?"

"Robert, don't make me say it."

"Say what?"

"Robert . . ." Her voice was a plea.

He knew what she didn't want to say. Since he didn't want to hear her say just how many mages were currently more powerful than he was, he gave in. "All right, all right, I might need some magical help. But just a supplier, you understand? Just some stuff I can use. Not anyone for the run itself."

She sighed. "All right, Robert. All right. What's the pay?"

"Little over a grand apiece."

"Eh. It's a pay cut, but as long as the job's quick . . ."

"Should be."

"Okay." Jackie furrowed her brow and stared either at a black spot on the floor or at nothing at all—Bannickburn couldn't be sure where her eyes focused. "We'll want some good people willing to work for cheap. That narrows the field a little."

"You read my mind."

She kept staring at nothing for a few more seconds, then suddenly pulled her head and looked at Bannickburn again.

"I've got it," she said. "Cayman."

"We're going to the Caymans? Sounds lovely. Perhaps, though, it should wait until the job's done."

"Ha ha. Hold on, I'll set up the meeting."

She jacked in without offering any further explanation, which was par for the course.

*   *   *

There was a time, Bannickburn believed, when wealthy people asked to meet you in places containing wealth, and poor people asked to meet you in places wracked by poverty. Then people took it into their heads to conceal their personal riches (or lack thereof), and rich people started slumming in rat holes while poor people would blow a month's worth of earnings just to lunch with you in a trendy restaurant.

Then, of course, people started catching wise to this pattern, so it changed again, and everyone went back to their customary haunts. Then they changed again. And again. Now, when you met someone, you couldn't tell a fraggin' thing about them based on the surroundings. Bannickburn found that a distressing development.

They were in a library in Bellevue—one that had a number of battered decks and scratched trideo screens for public use, and a few actual books. Bannickburn had followed Jackie into a glass-enclosed meeting room, where a large man in an olive green jacket sat waiting. It was a pretty good room, Bannickburn had to admit. Probably rent-free, providing privacy for conversation but keeping everyone visible in case the meeting went sour. The problem, of course, was that someone in the library could have Finnigan connections, and would remember seeing these faces together in a meeting. That was why Kross, who had been loaned to Bannickburn by Bailey, sat in a van a few blocks away, watching images transmitted from a camera lodged just above Jackie's left ear. She was careful to make frequent long, slow pans across the room. If Kross saw trouble, they'd be on the move quickly. Bannickburn had made sure, though, that Jackie wasn't wired for sound. If Kross wanted to know what they were saying, he'd have to read lips, and Bannickburn wasn't planning on moving his mouth much as he spoke.

The metal chairs, pads on the legs worn away long ago, scraped across the linoleum floor. The big man, who Bannickburn assumed was Cayman, winced.

"I hate that sound," he said. "Someday I'll remember that before I book this room." He nodded at Jackie. "How're things, angel?"

"Good, thanks," she said, taking a seat, without so much as offering a hand to Cayman. Bannickburn followed suit. "You?"

"About the same, which is a fraggin' shame since things were supposed to be way better by now. How's the troll?"

Bannickburn happened to be looking at Jackie the moment the question was asked, and he was glad he was; otherwise he would have missed the most remarkable expression that briefly flared on her face, then disappeared. Her eyebrows pushed together and fell into a "V", her lips pulled back far enough to bare her fangs (if she had possessed any), her nostrils flared. Then she was her normal, calm self again. No one could have failed to catch the warning that look conveyed.

"Ah. Right," Cayman said. "Never mind, then. What can I do for you?"

"I'd like you to meet my friend Bannickburn. He's got a proposal for you."

Cayman shifted his glance to Bannickburn, and his face hardened. All the changes were subtle—his thick jaw became slightly firmer, his gray eyebrows lowered, his chin ducked down a little. The affable man who had greeted Jackie when they walked in now looked like a mugger about to demand that Bannickburn hand over all his cash.

"Hello," he said, and the word dropped out of his mouth like a cinder block.

"Pleasure to meet you," Bannickburn said in his friendliest voice. He'd seen a million hostile glares in his lifetime, and saw no reason to start letting them affect him now. "I hear you're competent."

That didn't make the glare friendlier. "Okay."

"I'd like to offer you a relatively small amount of money to piss off a powerful and irritable member of the Finnigan family."

Cayman looked back at Jackie, but his expression remained hard. "I'm here because I trust you, Jackie, even though I can't remember why. But we're two minutes in here, and your man's squandering your capital pretty quick."

"Relax," Jackie said. "We've got two words for you that will change your whole perspective. Robert, hit him with the two words."

Bannickburn obliged. "Murson Kader."

It didn't seem possible, but Cayman managed to look even angrier. He stood up. He muttered a few things that might not even have been words. He took three steps to his right, executed a quick turn that showed he probably had military service somewhere in his past, then walked back to his chair, but stayed on his feet. He stood quietly for a few more beats, then abruptly slammed his palm on the room's brown plastic table. Bannickburn expected the blow to snap the table in two, and it made enough noise that people outside the room jumped, then looked angrily at Cayman. A librarian sternly raised his index finger to his lips.

"Dammit," Cayman said. "Dammit dammit dammit."

Bannickburn let the name sink into Cayman's brain for another few moments.

"It was supposed to be on my terms," Cayman finally said, after crossing the small room a few more times. "I was going to go after him when I was ready."

"That day didn't seem to be getting any closer," Jackie said gently, but Bannickburn saw the words still stung Cayman.

"I was going to do it," he said stubbornly. "It's tough to find the time, though, you know?"

"I know," Jackie said. "For you and Hamlet both." Bannickburn grinned while Cayman scowled.

"All right. I'm interested," Cayman said. "But you've gotta tell me a little something about your boy here."

He was being baited, Bannickburn knew. He decided this wasn't the time to rise to it. He deferred again to Jackie.

"You're not just interested," she said. "You're in. We're getting Kader, and you're helping." She outlined the mission to Cayman while he continued to scowl.

"You're only *embarrassing* Kader," Cayman complained once the briefing was done. "I'd rather have him dead."

"Of course you would. But this is what you have in front of you right now. You know you want to do it, but you don't want to appear too eager by agreeing to it immediately. That's fine, you can delay for a while if it makes you feel better. But you're in."

Cayman's scowl deepened, then vanished. Suddenly, he was smiling.

"Ah, girl, you're a treasure. You're younger than most of my clothes and weigh less than my right arm, but you still think you can bully just about anyone 'cause you know so much. An absolute treasure."

While Cayman was becoming more relaxed, a new worry struck Bannickburn. "Hold on. Before we get any agreement on the table here, I need to be sure you're not going to go freelance on us. If you decide it would be fun to kill Kader in the middle of the run, you'll bring down the entire Finnigan family on us. You want to be in, you've got to stick to the plan."

Cayman, to Bannickburn's surprise, didn't scowl. Instead, he nodded briefly, as if acknowledging that the point had to be made.

"I'm a professional," he said.

That wasn't good enough for Bannickburn—those were just three words anyone could say. But this was why he had Jackie's help.

"His record back up his words?" he asked her. It was a crude power play—annoying Cayman by talking about him as if he wasn't there—but it would do what it had to, showing Cayman the dynamics of the team he was joining.

"Yeah," Jackie said. "From everything I've heard, Cayman's got a list of grudges several kilometers long, but he's never let that interfere with a mission."

"Does he ever settle a grudge on his own time?"

"Of course."

"Good." Bannickburn turned back to Cayman, who had endured the exchange impassively "Okay, let me put my cards on the table. I'm doing this thing quickly and on the fly, so I'm not offering any guarantees. You're in the job until I say you're out. My choice."

"You want to do it that way, I'll need some money up front. To convince me to play along."

"I'll pay you at the start of each day. If I decide to part ways with you, you get to keep that day's money. You make it to the end, you get a five-hundred-nuyen bonus. Fair?"

Cayman snorted. "I make it to the end, I get the bonus of seeing Kader looking like an ass. That's way more incentive than your money. But yeah, it's fair."

"Okay." Bannickburn took out a black credstick. "You're hired. Today's task is finding the rest of the team."

"What else to you need?"

"Rigger, especially one who can handle small drones, and a face."

"And a mage," Jackie added. "For some supplies, mostly."

Bannickburn glowered. "Yeah. What she said."

But Cayman was stuck on an earlier word Bannickburn had said. "Face?" he asked, looking oddly apprehensive. "What kind of a face?"

"Naïve, trusting. Kind of guy who'd look like a good mark."

The familiar scowl returned to Cayman's face. "Damn," he said.

Once, near the docks of Tacoma, Bannickburn had seen a fight break out between five scruffy individuals. He'd been accompanying an old friend of his, a hulking man named Claymore, on some unspecified errand. The five people stood around a large wooden crate, more than fifty cubic meters in size, and battled. One guy took a knife to the throat and lay on the docks, gurgling, for a long time before he fell silent. Another fell into the water and thrashed clumsily around until one of her opponents figured out that she was now an easy target and shot her. The other three were still fighting when Claymore said it was time to leave.

"Wonder what was in the crate," Bannickburn had said.

Claymore had snorted. "Crate was empty. In a lot of parts of the Barrens, that would make a pretty good house. That's why they were fighting over it."

Bannickburn was in one of those places right now, not too far from Paradise Lake, standing in front of a crate very similar to the one that had been the object of the battle, and he found himself missing Claymore. If he'd lived, he could've taught Bannickburn almost as much about the city as Jackie.

Cayman walked up to the front of the crate and knocked on the crooked door that had been clumsily carved into it.

"Prime!" he bellowed. "Prime! Get out here!"

The door swung open, but no one was standing on the other side. Cayman's pounding had unlatched it.

"Drek, Prime, nice security!" Cayman yelled. "Anyone who wants could walk in here and shoot you without a thought!"

A man, a good twenty or so years younger than Bannickburn, stumbled into the doorway, blinking rapidly in the bright sunlight. He wore a green bathrobe that had probably once been quite nice but was now worn and tattered. The man tied it shut, attempting an air of wounded dignity.

"Nobody wants to shoot me," he mumbled.

"That's your problem," Cayman said. "If you were any good at your job, people would be lining up to take shots at you."

"Okay," the man said, easily shrugging off Cayman's insult. "Thanks for dropping by to remind me I'm incompetent. Anything else I can do for you?"

"Yeah. Get dressed. Your robe stinks. Then the elf here would like to talk to you."

"Okay," the man said again, then wearily pulled his door shut and went inside.

Cayman turned to Bannickburn. "That's X-Prime," he said. "He's a complete moron, but he's got the face you want."

"A complete moron?" Bannickburn said. "Don't know that that'll help us."

Cayman looked around, then motioned Bannickburn closer. "Okay, look, between you and me, he's not a complete moron. He's got a few years of running under his belt, and there are some things he does pretty well. But I can't let him know I think that. You understand?"

"No," Bannickburn said.

"I've known him since he was completely green, fresh from being a corp drone. He really was next to worthless then, and that's the relationship we have. I know everything, he knows nothing. That's our dynamic, and I'm not changing it."

This all made very little sense to Bannickburn, but he didn't feel like interfering. "Okay."

They stood silently for another minute or two, until X-Prime pushed the door open again. His eyes were focused, his brown hair was combed, and he wore a black T-shirt over rust-colored pants. Now that the runner's face was a little more composed, Bannickburn could understand why Cayman had brought him here—X-Prime looked like he'd just wandered in from the potato fields. Wide eyes, light freckles across the nose, and a small mouth that always looked on the verge of quivering made Bannickburn stifle an urge to con him right on the spot.

"What is it?" X-Prime said, in a voice much harder and wearier than his face.

"You're on the job again. The elf's hiring you. I'll tell you more about it on the way."

"On the way where?"

"To find Spindle."

"She's in, too?"

"I hope so, yeah."

X-Prime looked at the horizon, then glanced at his watch, then back at the horizon. Then he shrugged. "Okay."

He closed the door to his crate and threw a padlock over the latch. Cayman raised an eyebrow at the lock.

"You know all that lock will do is hold the door nicely in place while someone kicks it in."

X-Prime shrugged. "It's a visual deterrent."

Cayman rolled his eyes. "Fine. Let's go." He walked away, with Bannickburn and X-Prime lagging behind.

The situation was making Bannickburn wary. X-Prime seemed like a dog that had been kicked too much but followed his master anyway, and the pathetic lock on his crate didn't make him look like the wealthiest or smartest resident of the Barrens. Based on his first impression, Bannickburn wasn't sure how the hick had survived a week in Redmond.

But he had. By Cayman's account, he'd actually survived a few years. Clearly, there was more to him than the first impression.

He let Cayman draw a little further ahead, then spoke low to X-Prime. He didn't know how much time he'd have, so he was blunt.

"Look. You're here at the moment because Cayman recommended you, but I'm not hiring just anyone he leads me to. Neither of you has given me much reason to trust your abilities." Most runners would have taken instant offense at this remark, but X-Prime's hangdog expression remained unchanged. "And if I'm going to actually hire you, I need a reason."

X-Prime's face still didn't change—except for the eyes. Something danced back there, some sign of life and intelligence.

"Break into my house," he said.

"What?"

"Break into my house. You saw the lock. You saw

the walls. Piece of cake, right? Go break into it. Then we can talk more."

Bannickburn pondered for a minute. Then he made a call.

"Hello. Have you missed me in the past hour? No? Pity. Look, I know I said I'd leave you alone for the afternoon, but it turns out I lied. I need you to do me a favor. I need you to break into a crate."

"What would you use for this?"

"Renraku Arachnoid."

"Why?"

"Climbs walls better than other drones."

"Climbs walls? Doesn't that make it more visible?"

"Depends on which walls you climb. Lotta times, casinos have good corners or stupid decorative pillars, where you can hide without exposing the drone. Nice to have that option. Plus, they look neat, and they're only a few centimeters long."

"And you have one? Or could get your hands on one?"

The slender elf stood at the opposite end of a rickety card table from him and said nothing. She bounced on one heel, and the table legs creaked. Her name was Spindle, and she'd appeared quite agitated the moment Cayman introduced her to Bannickburn, a mass of nervous energy and facial tics. The more Bannickburn asked her about the potential job, though, the calmer she became—the tics settled down, her narrow, triangular face smoothed. She was still bouncing a lot, though. And at the moment, she looked irritated, taking offense at Bannickburn's effrontery in assuming she might not be able to get the machine she wanted to use.

"Okay, sorry," Bannickburn said. "I'll assume you can get your hands on it. How do you get into a place like Gates?"

"Sewers. Another good reason to use the Arachnoid— waterproof and maneuvers well in pipes."

"The͓   ͓ep the casino floor regularly."

"I can always throw on more electronic counter measures than they'd be expecting. But the easiest thing to
do is not be seen—the way I understand the job, you
don't need me watching all the time. The less I transmit,
the worse chance they have of noticing my drone."

She knew her game. And her heel wasn't even tapping
anymore. He felt more confident about her than he did
about X-Prime and even Cayman. The two of them had
spent most of his interview with Spindle making fun of
each other in a corner of the room.

"Okay. I think we're on track here. You want in,
you're in."

A tic made a brief reappearance on Spindle's drawn
face, forcing her right eye closed. She controlled it as
quickly as she could.

"I'm in," she said. "It's not . . . it's not good for me
to go too long between jobs."

"How long has it been since the last one?" Bannickburn asked.

Spindle looked at the floor a moment before looking
back up. "Two days," she admitted. "The edginess is
coming in quicker and quicker. Gotta keep on the job."

"I understand," he said, and smiled. He *liked* this one.
Maybe he should just keep her and dump the other two.

On his hip, his phone vibrated. "Excuse me," he said,
and walked into a corner and answered it.

"It's Jackie," Jackie said. "What are you trying to do,
kill me?"

"No, of course— How? I mean, what do you think
I'm doing that might kill you?"

"This crate! This fraggin' *crate*! The padlock's a fraggin' *mine* that'll detonate on vibration if I hit the fraggin'
walls too hard! And he's got some sort of electrical fence
built into the walls! And that's just what I found for
starters. There's no *way* I'm trying this by myself."

"No. No, of course not. Don't worry about it. You
did enough. Go home."

"Yeah. Thanks. Did you mine my place while I was gone, too, or can I expect that to be normal?"

"It'll be normal. Bye."

He snapped the phone shut and turned to X-Prime. "Great holy hell, man," he said. "What do you have inside that crate?"

X-Prime just smiled, and Cayman looked at him oddly, like a proud parent. Maybe these two would do after all, Bannickburn thought.

He'd walked for two hundred meters before he remembered that he'd forgot to ask Jackie about a mage who could be a supplier for this mission. Oh well, he thought. It could wait.

11

Always take a moment. That was Bannickburn's rule. The lead-up to a run was usually hectic and stressful, what with the attempts at concealment and the looming possibility of death, but it was also some of the most fun you could ever have in your life. Usually you had a decent bankroll to buy some new toys, and you had the intoxicating feeling of power, of being the only person in the world (well, one of only a few) who knew what you were up to. Soon, at least a few other people would know about your work, and most of them would be quite sorry. For now, though, the knowledge and the delicious anticipation were all your own.

So Bannickburn always made sure to enjoy at least a single moment in the day before a run, to stop and just soak it all in.

The moment he found in this day came when he was looking at himself in a mirror. The past two hours had been extremely clumsy and inefficient, using wigs and spirit gum to accomplish what he'd once been able to do in a few short seconds of spellcasting. But in the end, the effect was what he needed. His sideburns had vanished (without, of course, being shaved off), his hair was light brown, his face rounder and softer. He didn't recognize his image in the mirror as himself, which was exactly the way things should be. So he looked in the mirror and he relished the sight.

It wasn't perfect, though. A few shadows he'd applied looked a little off, a few hairs didn't look natural, and the bulged skin near his ears still made him appear like he was suffering from some bizarre disease. But he was making progress, and he was enjoying it. He hoped the rest of the team was having as much fun as he was.

Jackie, naturally, was on the Matrix, flowing through the network like a single cell in the universal bloodstream—that is, if blood flowed at the speed of thought. She was free of physical constraints and was all sensation—sight and sound, but mostly power. It passed through her like light through a prism, still flowing rapidly, but changed by her touch. She loved that feeling like nothing else in the world.

She always took the first moments after she jacked in for sheer pleasure before getting down to business. After one more deep breath—using lungs that seemed far, far away from where she currently was—she focused on the job at hand. First stop, Gates Casino. Not the flashy casino replica that most Matrix clients saw, but their back offices.

The icon for the online offices was quite literal, a bland, flat office building behind the sprawling neon palace of the casino. The IC back here would probably be pretty good, but not nearly as tough as it would be if she were trying to get near any of the casino's many pots of money.

The first obstacle was glaringly obvious. The ground in front of the main door that would give her access to the Gates offices was black and shiny—a tar pit that the Gates people hadn't bothered to alter from its out-of-the-box appearance. If she were trying to sneak into the node, the tar pit might cause her a problem. Using a deception utility or other similar means would probably trigger it, and black hands would reach out of the tar and try to throw her offline. But she'd planned for this in advance, and had a fine set of stolen passwords to use. The tar pit blinked out of sight when she submitted the right word, and she was in.

Too easy. The real fun in breaking into a system was in wrestling it to the ground and making it do your bidding. Using a password felt too . . . *legitimate.* But she was on a tight time schedule, and the job would work best if the Gates people had no indication that trouble was afoot. Pummeling a system was fun, but it tended to leave traces. For now, secrecy was the way to go.

Once she had access to the node, she blinked into the main room of the office building. No alarms sounded, no guard dog icons came charging, and no other form of IC was launched at her. She wouldn't have to mangle the guy who'd sold her the passwords.

The room was mostly empty. It was big, with high ceilings and distant walls. The floor looked like gray granite, and a few granite columns broke up the huge space. There was no furniture, no décor, no doors. Apart from the columns, there was nothing extraneous here. It was a simple room with the simple purpose of funneling staff into the node.

A few icons zipped by now and then, mostly the drab gray of corporate terminal users. Jackie had picked the time for her break-in carefully, going in at seven p.m., after normal business hours but before the action in the casino really started hopping for the evening. She saw a few icons that looked like janitors, and assumed they were utilities instead of people. She watched them carefully as they blinked by—many of them were probably doing routine maintenance on the casino's Matrix, but she'd run into more than one system that liked to disguise some particularly nasty brands of ripper IC as janitors. Ripper IC—programs that tried to rip your icon apart, kick you offline, and damage your deck while they were at it—was no fun. Thoroughly uncivil, so it was best to stay away from the stuff if you could.

There was nothing in the central room to guide the visitor about where to go, as visitors weren't welcome here. She could spend a long time blinking here and there in the node, looking for the right room, but that seemed wasteful. She could try asking one of the other residents of the node where to go, but few of them seemed like actual humans, and none of them would likely stop to help her. And asking for directions in a building like this was a good way to set off alarms.

She was on her own—well, she and her dog.

"Here, Rover," she muttered. A small Scottish terrier appeared in front of her, jumping up and down, its mouth moving like it was yapping. No sound came out, though—she'd fixed that part of the utility the first time she'd used it. It was loosely rendered—its fur looked more like plastic than hair, and it was a purple color generally not found on dogs—but it was still adorable.

She scooped up the dog and spoke quietly into its ear. "Customer record. Murson Kader." Then she dropped the dog into a large cloth bag that went well with her icon's flowing white dress. She let the utility stick its black nose out of the bag. It was unnecessary, since the utility wouldn't actually smell anything, but she liked the way it looked. And she'd long ago realized the importance of image and appearance in the Matrix.

Rover made a suggestion, and she followed it. The entry room blinked out of existence, and a smaller foyer blinked in. It was even more bare than the original entry room, a space that resembled the inside of a steel safe. She saw nothing that looked like a file, but spotted a hallway off to her left.

It made sense. The Gates bosses didn't want just anyone looking at their files, so jumping right into their file area would be prohibited. She'd have to clear another test before she got what she wanted. No problem. She had passwords for that.

She watched the hallway for two minutes and saw the same people come in and out of the various doors multiple times, many of them tracing circuitous, repetitious routes in even that small amount of time. Slave programs, she guessed. Slave programs that were being kept

fairly busy. At this time of day, keeping the customer
records up-to-date would be one of the few activities
that would have them hopping. Rover, actively squirm-
ing in her bag, had led her to the right place.

Time for him to go. "Home, Rover," she said, then
called her next utility. "Here, Asta." She had another
terrier in her hands, identical to the first one, but red
instead of purple.

She pointed Asta down the hallway. "IC, Asta," she
said. The dog reacted like a basset hound in a terrier
body. She dropped him to the ground and he prowled
forward, legs bent, nose sniffing every inch of carpet.

There was something in the hallway. She knew it
immediately—Asta was only this careful when he
scented IC in the area. If there was nothing, he usually
knew it in seconds.

The fact that there was IC in the hallway didn't
change anything, since Jackie didn't have a wide range
of available strategies. But it was good to know what
obstacles might be waiting, on the off chance that things
went wrong.

Asta had a bead on something. The dog stood patiently, one leg cocked, nose pointed proudly forward.
Jackie absolutely loved the ridiculous way the small dog
mimicked a pointer's stance, which was why she had
programmed it that way.

She picked up the terrier and instantly knew the information it had gathered. There was probe IC to make
sure nothing untoward happened in this part of the
node, and a pretty good ripper that would jump in if
anything went wrong. *Good to know,* she thought, *that
the casino truly values its patrons' privacy.*

If all went well, she wouldn't see a trace of the ripper.
She zoomed down the hallway, hoping her passwords
would keep up their sterling work to this point.

The floor made a subtle transition from charcoal gray
to thundercloud gray as she entered the hallway, and
then she was in. No alarms. No problem.

Except she wasn't alone. A samurai, fully armed and

dressed in crimson, stood in the entrance to the hallway. He looked beautiful, right down to the gleam on his sword blades and the ridges on his helmet. Some programmer had really cared about this one.

Unfortunately, the attention to detail hadn't extended to the IC's voice. When the samurai opened his mouth, he spoke in a polite, bland Midwestern-UCAS voice.

"Hello," the samurai said, looking at nothing in particular but certainly speaking to Jackie. "I'm afraid you've made an improper turn. Please exit this corridor and return to areas of the building for which you have proper access."

Jackie imagined the entire conversation that awaited her—she wouldn't go anywhere, and the samurai would become increasingly less polite, and she might try to talk her way out of it, but of course there was no way to fool a stupid piece of IC, so they'd fight. The whole conversation seemed boring and unnecessary. Time to switch utilities.

She sent Asta away and called on another of her fleet of dogs—Daisy, a yellow dog who appeared in Jackie's arms with an Ares Crusader in her mouth. Jackie grabbed the gun, dropped to one knee, and unloaded half a clip at the samurai.

The samurai whirled the two katana blades he carried and blocked every bullet. *That's the downside of the Matrix*, Jackie thought. *Every little piece of code thinks it's a superhero*.

The samurai lunged, the steel of his blades slashing out impossibly far, and she rolled, firing wildly, since she didn't have to worry about hitting innocent bystanders. *And there's the upside of the Matrix*, she thought.

She pushed herself up with her hands, flying backward as the second blade whizzed in front of her face. She had a clear target now and unloaded a few more rounds right at the samurai's face. Again his sword easily knocked them away.

Then he came forward, a blurred mass of spinning steel. She staggered back, arms flailing, barely able to hold her gun, not able to fire it. The swords came closer and closer. Twice, she flinched as the cold metal brushed over her skin. Glancing blows only, though. For now. If those blades made any more solid contact, her icon would suffer, and she'd probably be jacked out post-haste. She couldn't have that.

As she gradually yielded ground to the samurai, she saw a few of the blank gray icons pass right by the fight, paying her no mind. Her fight with the samurai was far outside the bounds of their programmed behavior, so to them it didn't exist.

Jackie was running out of room. She could just blink out of the corridor at any time, of course, and evade the IC that way, but that wouldn't get the job done. The IC would still be waiting for her when she came back, maybe with some backup security protocols as reinforcements. She had to get this done now. She felt a little sad about what she knew came next, but she had one more weapon on her, and she chose to use it.

"Daisy!" she yelled as she stumbled backward. "Sic!"

The terrier leaped up gracefully, yapping silently, flying toward the samurai's face. The samurai registered no surprise as he swiftly raised his blades and cut the dog into several small pieces. The distraction had lasted for the briefest moment, but it was enough. Jackie had already fired.

The samurai couldn't cut the dog and block all of Jackie's rounds. Two of them snuck through. One grazed the samurai's temple, furrowing the flesh, but drawing no blood (a common practice, Jackie knew—most IC programmers thought that a display of blood only served to encourage attackers). The second caught him in the neck, near where his jugular would have been if he had one. He went down.

Jackie zoomed toward him, and even though she had a bare five steps to cover, she was almost too late. The samurai, knowing he was finished, had dropped one sword and raised the other to his belly, ready for seppuku. *No*, Jackie thought. *Not yet.*

She kicked the second sword out of his hands, then uploaded a simple medic utility. She didn't need the samurai saved—she just needed him alive a little longer.

The medic, at her request, carried with it a few pieces of rope, representing her best suppression utility. She used these to bind the samurai. The knots weren't great—the samurai would probably break free soon—but if her calculations were right, he'd get his bonds off at about the same time the neck wound finished him. At that point, of course, his death would raise holy hell across the entire Gates Matrix—but by then, Jackie should be long gone.

She was sorry about the loss of Daisy—it would take a good few hours of programming to rebuild that particular utility—but the dog had done the job. She called Rover back, and had the purple dog point her to the right spot.

The dog directed her to a room that, appropriately enough, looked like a file room. Tall gray cabinets lined each wall. Rover pointed Jackie to the right drawer, and she pulled it open.

True to the room's design motif, the drawer held numerous icons that looked exactly like tan file folders. They were even alphabetized. She found one with Kader's name on it and pulled it out.

She didn't open it, instead calling Asta back to help her. The red dog gave the folder a good sniff, and Jackie had the findings immediately—scramble IC. The data was encrypted, and if the IC caught Jackie breaking in, it would be thoroughly trashed. A good password would get her past the IC, but the samurai in the hallway had been pretty solid proof that her passwords weren't working in this part of the system.

But there was a dog for every occasion. The one she needed was a blue one named Petey, and soon the dog was in her hands.

She pointed him at the folder, then did a very undoglike thing with him. She pushed him forward until his nose touched the folder, then kept pushing. His head disappeared into the folder, and his tail wagged furiously. Jackie kept pushing until the dog's entire head was submerged, then she stopped.

Pure code flowed through her, garbled letters and numbers that only a few people really understood. She couldn't describe how she perceived the code—she didn't see it, she didn't hear it, she didn't even really feel it. It just *was*.

The only limit on Jackie now was the speed of her own mind, which, when she was in the Matrix, hardly felt like a limit at all. She didn't read the code, she didn't write any new instructions, she just pushed here and pulled there—intuitively, almost the way an infant reaches for light, except it was all inside her head. The dog got her into the folder and offered a few helpful hints, but for the most part, this was Jackie's work. Work she had done a thousand times before, and loved every time.

She didn't really know which of the million tiny maneuvers she performed made the difference, but in one microsecond, the folder was closed, then it was open. There was a brief tunnel into the data about Kader, narrow and temporary, but it didn't need to last long. She pulled all the data in the file out and copied it to two places—her deck at home and the private data haven that the few people who knew about it considered to be the most valuable collection of data in Seattle. The tunnel then closed, but the data was hers.

She pulled Petey out of the folder, the shock of losing the code feeling like a brief cardiac arrest. She casually flipped the folder over her shoulder. It flew through the air and neatly dropped into the appropriate drawer, which slid shut. Then Jackie was gone.

She made a quick stop at the foyer and went out the main entrance of the node. She didn't want the system to get worried about her staying inside for an inordinately long time. The lobby was quiet as she left. The dying samurai hadn't manage to raise the alarm yet.

She jacked out and sagged limply in her chair, as reality, with its heavy gravity and snail's pace, reasserted its claim on her.

Cayman had offered to slap X-Prime several times. All for the good of the mission, of course.

"It'll make your expression just right," Cayman insisted. "The right mix of vacuity and wounded pride."

"Not to mention several ugly bruises," X-Prime retorted.

"Please. You know I could hit you all day without leaving a mark. Come on, just a few blows."

"No. I think I can look stupid enough without your help."

Cayman couldn't argue with that, and he'd sent X-Prime off, while he sat at one of the Gates Casino's many bars and watched his progress.

X-Prime wandered slowly through the crowd, stopping at various tables and widening his eyes in authentic-seeming amazement at the large sums of money being wagered, the bright colors, and the spinning wheels. Prime wasn't playing anything yet, though. For that, he'd need some money.

While X-Prime kept laying the groundwork for his part of the mission, Cayman turned his attention to the rest of the bar, looking for the right tourist. Finding a tourist in the Gates Casino was about as difficult as spotting a felon at San Quentin, but finding the *right* tourist was another matter. He needed someone impressionable and confident, who'd listen to what he had to say and act on it.

He found one. A woman in a simple black dress, leaning on the bar, swatting away cheap pickup lines like flies. She could almost have been a native, except most natives would have long grown weary of the parade of flirting tourists and moved on to another bar to do their regular drinking.

He didn't try to look charming as he walked toward her—she'd sense that right away. He just ambled over, though he made an effort to raise his chin a little, making sure the light from above didn't cast dark shadows from his brow across the rest of his face. He didn't smile, but he didn't scowl.

Still, she looked at him warily as he approached.

"Hi," he said. "If I tell you that the last thing in the world I want to do is buy you a drink, could I sit on this stool?"

She didn't quite smile, but his bluntness amused her enough to lower her defenses a touch. "Go ahead."

"Thanks," he said. "It's nothing personal. I just gave all my money to the blackjack dealer, is all."

"Then why are you staying at the bar?"

"I'm thirsty. Sometimes watching other people drink helps ease the pain."

Now she laughed. "God. You're quite pathetic, aren't you?"

He gave her a half grin back. "Yeah. Thanks for noticing."

"Look, the last thing in the world I want to do is buy you *two* drinks. But you seem like you could use at least one. What'll you have?"

"That's very kind of you. Gin and tonic, thanks." The safest drink order in the world, Cayman thought. Makes you appear civilized but not snobby, thirsty for alcohol but not desperate to get drunk. Tougher than a daiquiri, less aggressive than bourbon. The perfect, nonthreatening order.

The drink soon sat next to Cayman. He took an appreciative sip. "Thank you," he said after swallowing. "This is actually much better than just watching."

"I would hope so."

He sat silently for a moment, putting all his effort into looking casual and relaxed. The next part of the conversation would be tricky.

"What I'm going to say next is going to sound awfully cheesy, but bear with me for a minute. Do you come here often?"

The woman in the black dress rolled her eyes. "Oh, come on."

"I know, I know. But that's not how I mean it. I'll

just put it right out on the table—I come here a lot. But I think I'm going to stay away for a week or two."

"Why's that?" Suspicion still dominated the woman's voice, but she was still talking.

"You see that guy? Bigio family. So's that guy. The woman over there. The dwarf. The guy in the black hat. All Mafia." They weren't, but Cayman said it with conviction.

The woman seemed to buy it. "It's the city," she said. "What're you gonna do?"

"I know, I know, but I thought the standards were higher here. I mean, I don't like the Mafia looking over my shoulder when I've got a big stack of chips in front of me. That makes me tighten up, and if I play tight, I lose more."

The woman was still watching the people Cayman had pointed out. "There do seem to be a lot of them here."

"Yeah. I was thinking of talking to someone about it, but who? What are they going to do about it?"

"You could talk to security," the woman said. "Have them beef up their presence. If it's making you not want to play here, I'm sure they'll listen."

"Really? Naw, I'm just one person. They're a bunch of mobsters. The guards won't care about one complaint."

"Then I'll come with you," she said. "I don't want them in here, either."

The two of them stood and crossed the casino, looking for a guard to talk to. On the way, Cayman lifted a few chips from the woman and passed them to X-Prime, so he could start the gaming part of his evening.

Cayman thanked the woman profusely once they registered their complaint, then surprised her by leaving her alone for the rest of the evening.

By the time he was done, Gates Casino security had received a dozen complaints about the quality of people on the casino floor. In response, the security chief decided to put some additional guards on the floor over the next week or two. Extra eyes should make sure everything proceeded smoothly.

* * *

At 12:35 A.M., Bannickburn walked right in front of Cayman. He paused briefly, making sure the big man had a good chance to see his face. Cayman saw him but didn't recognize him, and Bannickburn moved on.

He smiled, sweating a little beneath the layers of his disguise. *Perfect*, he thought.

He lingered in the casino longer than he should have. He wasn't really having fun—the costume only grew hotter, and he didn't have any extra money to wager at present. But standing around the casino sweating was still more fun than what he had to do next. He'd put it off as long as he could, but there could be no more waiting. As soon as he left the casino, he was going to drag himself to a meeting with a mage named Twitch. He was going to ask this lowly street mage to help him, the mighty Robert Lionel Bannickburn, with magic.

The utter humiliation of it had gnawed on him all day. He'd reviewed the plan for the run over and over, seeing if he could cut magic out of it entirely. He almost had it—he was a hair's breadth away from being able to cancel this stupid meeting altogether. But there were a few stupid things—minor things, emergency measures really—that he couldn't handle, that he had no answers for besides magic. He would have to swallow his pride— a big, bitter pill that he was pretty sure his throat was nowhere near wide enough to handle.

12

The bottle sang sweetly. It was a wordless melody, lilt-
ing and seductive, reinforced by the rich red-brown
color of the cognac. Bailey had placed it on a higher
shelf, hoping that would silence it, but the move had no
noticeable effect. He'd just have to keep ignoring it until
the time came when he could give in to its siren call.

Maybe it would help if he left his office. Couldn't hurt.
He walked out his door, down the silent, dim hall and
out into the quiet Tacoma night. Too quiet—he could
still hear the cognac's attempted seduction.

He had only a short walk in front of him. Several
people, over the course of his life, told him that the
amount of walking he did was unnecessary. There was
this thing called the Matrix, they told him, that would
allow him to visit just about anyone, anywhere, instanta-
neously. He could work with a decker in New York, in
Germany, in the Philippines, if he wanted. There was
no reason to stick with a decker who was just down
the street.

But Bailey valued face-to-face contact. You couldn't
read an icon like you could a person, which was why all
the serious gamblers in the world avoided Matrix-based
casinos. There was no sense in playing with pigeons who
could hide their tells.

He had a handful of deckers he employed in various

capacities, but for crucial tasks, he turned to Slidestream, who was conveniently stationed two blocks away from Bailey's office.

Slidestream's building was built to discourage attention, whether from passers-by admiring the architecture or surveillance teams trying to find out what was happening inside. The curtains were drawn across all the windows, and Bailey knew that lead panels sat behind each window. More lead was embedded in every yellow brick wall. The building was a plain rectangle, the roof was brown, the doors were steel, and everything about its appearance was bland.

The front door glided open as Bailey approached. Bailey was being monitored and, he was happy to note when no alarms went off, recognized. He passed through the door, and it slammed shut behind him. Around him, various security systems allowed him to pass. The corridors looked like a neglected high school—chipped off-white linoleum, chicken-wire windows in the doors, harsh fluorescent light spilling everywhere. No one but Bailey was out—none of the tenants here shared his view of the importance of physical travel.

Slidestream's office was on the first floor, at the back of the building, close to the rear emergency exit. Like the front door, the yellow plastic door to the office opened automatically as Bailey walked up.

Slidestream was, naturally, jacked in. He claimed to do his best work on his back, so he lay on an enormous bed that dominated the office. There really wasn't anyplace for visitors to sit—Slidestream wasn't in the habit of having anyone else in his office.

"You don't have to be here," Slidestream said, his eyes barely able to focus on Bailey. "I have nothing to show you."

"Does that mean there's no progress, or you're just not going to show me what progress you have, in fact, made?"

Slidestream's disdain came off him in waves. He was small, no more than 1.3 meters, of stout but not heavy build, and clean-shaven, mainly to prevent people from mistaking him for a dwarf. His most notable skill, besides his decking, was his ability to radiate intense contempt and scorn that far outdistanced his size.

"I would show you if I could, but it's impossible. First off, you don't have a datajack implant, so my machines are not available to you. Second, even if you could see what I was working on, I wouldn't have anything to show you now. The routine's designed to give me access to the Gates surveillance systems for a pretty brief period—tomorrow evening. If I go in too soon, just to give you a sample look, there's an increased chance they'll detect the intrusion, and by tomorrow the entire access structure will have changed. I'd blow the whole thing just to give you a quick look in. And I'm not doing that."

"Okay," Bailey said. "Then we'll have to work it this way. I'm going to ask you a question, and you're going to answer it honestly. Before you answer, though, I should tell you that I highly value honesty and integrity in the people I deal with, and that I treat people right if they treat me right. If that's not enough incentive, I should tell you about this neat chip I have that fits right into a cranial jack and delivers enough amps to make an elephant go up in smoke. You have no *idea* what it does to your prefrontal lobe."

He paused to let Slidestream decide if the threat was serious or not, then threw out one more piece of information.

"And it smells terrible. Like bacon soaked in tar and burned on a charcoal grill. So I'd like to avoid using that if I could."

Slidestream nodded, looking a little shaky. The description of the odor usually did the job.

"Okay. Lucky for you, the question is simple: will I get a good view of the Gates Casino tomorrow night in my office?"

"Yes." His head might have trembled a little, but his voice was firm.

"Good. Good. That's all I needed to know. You have yourself a good evening." He strolled away without any further niceties, since he found that people who'd just been threatened with possible brain burn usually weren't interested in polite chitchat.

The cool night air was refreshing, but less so than getting the answer he wanted. So far, so good. He needed his own eyes on this run. He trusted Bannick-burn to a point, but there was nothing like watching things unfold for yourself.

Back at Bailey's office, an impatient James Shivers paced back and forth in front of the locked door. His black leather trench coat made his red hair—spiky today—look that much lighter. He glared at Bailey as soon as he walked in.

"You told me to meet you here at nine," Shivers said.

"And here I am."

"At nine twenty."

"Why, James. I had no idea you were such a stickler for promptness."

"It's nighttime. The last place I should be is in some slaggin' office."

"All right, all right. I won't keep you long. Did you see our friend Robert today?"

"Yeah. He was in the makeup chair for a while and was pretty bored, so I kept him company. He felt like talking."

"You mean about his plans for tomorrow?"

"No, about Glasgow's football team," Shivers said. "Of *course* about tomorrow. He gave me most of the details."

"Then come inside, spill your guts, and you'll be free to go."

Shivers, still impatient, walked through the doorway on Bailey's heels. He threw the door closed behind him.

Ten minutes later, the door opened again, and Shivers stalked out, no happier than when he arrived. Bailey, by contrast, sat in his leather armchair, hands behind his head, feet on his desk. Things were lining up just fine.

Then he remembered one thing he'd forgotten to say. "Jimmy!"

Shivers whirled quickly and stalked back, his face twisted, ready to yell at Bailey if he made a stupid joke.

Bailey, though, just had a simple order. "Stay away from Gates tomorrow. No matter how much Bannick-burn wants you to watch his handiwork. Stay away."

"Yeah, yeah. Okay if I go there tonight, Dad?"

Bailey would have appreciated it if Shivers would at least feign respect on occasion, but since Bailey wasn't big on fake shows himself, he supposed it was only fair to let Shivers get away with expressing himself honestly.

"Yeah. I want plenty of us there tonight. Go bleed some tourists of their hard-earned dough."

Shivers left without another word.

The office was quiet again, except for the high, clear song of the cognac. He now had tomorrow squared away. He had no pressing need to think clearly. He could give in.

13

"It's not just the bad pay and the life-threatening situations I love about a run," Jackie said. "It's the *glamour.*"

She sat in a worn lawn chair whose seat would probably have given out if she weighed five kilograms more. A trideo display in front of her showed the image of a sewer in all its murky glory. The tiny attic room she sat in was dark, and small mammals and large insects skittered through the darkest corners. They were only a few hundred meters from the Gates Casino, but they might as well have been in a different world.

"Maybe we can get the ork to eat a few of the roaches," Spindle said. "Clean the place up a little."

The ork, Kross, sat silently behind them and did not bother to dignify Spindle's remark with a reply. His arms crossed and his right leg folded over his left, he wore his impatience poorly. Spending a whole run merely as an observer was clearly not his style.

Jackie watched the trideo as Spindle moved her drone forward. There wasn't much time—the drone needed to be in place by the time X-Prime started playing, to get as much useful footage as possible. Sadly, they wouldn't be able to just leave the drone's surveillance on the whole time and watch the entire show unfold—the risk of detection was too large. They'd have to make do with small snippets: a minute here, a minute there, using any clues Cayman managed to pass along about when they should start filming and when they needed to have the whole project done.

Light, cut into long narrow strips by a grating, dropped into the sewer ahead of the drone.

"That's it," Spindle said. "We'll sneak through there and get this show on the road."

Jackie leaned back and watched some sort of beetle crawl near her toes. Her part wouldn't come for a while. All she could do was wait and watch as Spindle gathered the data she'd need.

The guy at table eight had more tics than patch of tall grass in the woods. He had more tells than an old gypsy woman with a crystal ball. Anyway you sliced it, he was easy money. And as soon as he ran out of chips, he signaled one of the wandering cashiers and bought a new stack. The gamblers would've been lining up to get a shot at him, but that would tip off too many people to what was going on. Instead, those who didn't have a seat lingered a table or two away, or made irregular circuits around the casino, checking for an opening every few minutes, or, if they were smart, paying the dealer to save a chair for them when a spot at the table was empty.

That was how Murson Kader got his seat. Not that he personally paid off the dealer. He always had a few associates tour the poker tables an hour or so before he arrived, checking for the best table and making sure their boss would be able to play there. They had found the pigeon at table eight without too much difficulty, and secured a space for their boss. Eight minutes after he walked in the Gates Casino doors, Kader was seated two chairs away from the young man with the slick brown hair and the large but dwindling pile of chips.

Kader's head was half flesh, half grinning metal skull. The odd thing was, the two halves didn't really look much different. His flesh was pulled tight over broad, firm bones, and his one real eye bulged in its socket. His permanent grin carried no hint of humor.

His fingers, long and bony, were built for a game like gin, where he would need to hold numerous cards. Texas Two-Step, which only required the spidery extremities to grasp two cards at a time, seemed like a waste of his abilities.

Kader dressed like an undertaker, which was wholly appropriate, right down to the black, brimmed hat covering his bald, gleaming metal-and-flesh scalp. When he played poker, he always took exactly five seconds, no more, no less, to decide whether to call, raise, or fold. Compared to the mark at table eight—or even compared to a *good* player—he was a poker-playing robot, an efficient, chip-raking machine.

The mark did not seem too pleased to see Kader. He probably would have been happiest to sit at a table with just the dealer and himself—but even then he would have found a way to lose.

Kader wasn't much for niceties at the table. He didn't introduce himself to anyone or direct remarks to his fellow players. In the course of conversation, it came out that the mark's name was Alex, but that meant nothing to Kader. The mark only mattered for his chips, not his name.

The other players at the table seemed preoccupied by figuring out just what Alex's strategy was. He played a few bad hands, possibly trying to bluff, but his betting was so timid that he never forced any other players away. Inevitably, it turned out they had better hands, and Alex lost.

Sometimes, when he folded, Alex would turn his cards over as he threw them in, which no real gambler ever did. Once, the other players caught him folding a pair of jacks. Another time, he threw out the ace and queen of clubs. This caused no small degree of agony among the other gamblers, as they couldn't help but think of all they could have done with those wasted cards. Still, by not playing them, Alex was continuing to wave good bye to considerable sums of money, which helped lessen the other players' pain.

In the end, the other gamblers adopted Kader's strategy—they didn't think about why Alex was doing what he was doing. They just accepted it—assumed that no matter what he did, he'd lose money—and they shifted their focus to the other, more skilled players.

Kader caused them a lot of trouble. His demeanor and movements were all predictable, but he kept changing his betting patterns, so no one could get an easy read on them. Only some unlucky draws and a few ill-advised doubling bets placed when he traded in his two hold cards after the fifth shared card was dealt kept him from completely dominating the table. The other gamblers tried to work together to slow him, but poker is not a team sport, and they mostly succeeded at passing chips between themselves rather than realizing any gains.

Then, right around the time the others expected Alex to signal the cashier for more chips, one of them glanced at his stack. The first surprise was that he still had one— the other players had all assumed he'd be down to a dozen or fewer chips at this point, but he had a healthy collection. That led to the second surprise—it was possible that in the last hour or so his stack had actually grown bigger.

No one at the table had a clear memory of how that might have happened. Had Alex been the only one to bet on a few hands, sneaking his way into some small but useful pots? Had he bought more chips while they weren't paying attention? Neither lapse in attention seemed likely to anyone at the table, but the physical evidence of the chips showed that *something* had happened.

The chips didn't calm Alex down any. The whole table watched as he glanced at his cards, waiting for the cheek muscle beneath his left eye to twitch upward, the sign that he was holding something good. The higher the twitch, the better the hand.

On one particular hand, his face stayed still, but he threw in fifteen hundred nuyen anyway. None of the other faces around the table changed, but everyone felt like raising a skeptical eyebrow. The bet was clearly a bluff.

Four of the seven other players folded, grudgingly, wishing they could be the one to expose Alex's ploy. Three others, Kader included, stayed in. A few raises were placed, and Alex called them all. Finally they were ready for the flop.

It came out queen of spades, eight of clubs, six of hearts. Alex and Kader stayed in, the other two went out. Kader saw his chance. He had a stack of chips twice as big as Alex's. All he had to do was put in a bet that would equal Alex's remaining chips. If he had a brain in his head, Alex would fold, taking a significant loss but staying in the game. If he was insane, or really liked losing, he'd match Kader's bet, reveal his bluff, and be out of the game—or forced to buy more chips.

Kader made a bet more than big enough to sink Alex if he matched it. Everyone waited for the inevitable fold. It didn't come. Alex called Kader's bet, going all in.

An involuntary sigh left the lips of most of the players. This was it. Kader was taking all the mark's money, leaving none for them. Too bad.

Kader turned over ace-queen, both clubs. A strong hand, even if Alex hadn't been bluffing.

Alex turned over the other two queens.

Kader remained expressionless, but the other players couldn't help but gasp and blink a few times. Clearly, Alex had suppressed the tic—at least this once.

The final two cards did nothing to the hand—a four and an eight that gave Alex a full house he didn't need. He took the substantial collection of chips into his now-large stack.

It was time to get serious. Whether he had finally learned something or whether he'd been playing them all along, Alex's money would now be a little more difficult to take. The other players decided they couldn't play lazy anymore.

The battle became more even. Most pots went out uncontested, with only one player willing to place a bet. The few times more than one bet went down, the betting was light. No one took much damage, no one gained much ground. They were feeling each other out all over again.

The new evaluation of Alex tagged him as just a poor poker player, rather than a spectacularly bad one. His tells and tics had decreased, but he still didn't have much of a feel for when to play, when to fold, and how to draw other players into a bet. Once they stopped relying on his face to tell them what he had, and focused solely on his betting patterns, the other players started siphoning away Alex's chips again.

Then luck kicked in. On one hand, Alex held ten-six, while one of the other players went in with jack-jack. Alex was on the verge of a big loss when the final card, a seven, filled Alex's inside straight and he took the pot. On another hand, his suited nine and ten beat an ace and jack when the final card gave him a club flush.

Every hand wasn't like that, but too many were. The players kept going up against Alex, knowing that, in the long run, skill beats out luck most every time. And Alex kept getting the cards and winning pots.

The last straw came in a head-to-head against Kader. His face still blankly dour, Kader drew Alex into a pot with a relatively small eight-hundred-nuyen bet. Alex stayed in. After the three-card flop (nine-six-two), the two players made a few more jabs at each other, raising and re-raising, but never large amounts. The pot grew slowly, but it grew.

The fourth shared card, the jack of diamonds, gave the advantage to any player holding another jack. Kader and Alex seemed neither fazed nor encouraged, and another tepid betting exchange ensued.

The fifth card was a queen. Finally, the two players

decided to go for the jugular. The bets hit twenty-five hundred nuyen, and went up from there. Neither was ready to go for a knockout blow, but both were hoping to do some real damage. Finally, Kader put his last chips into the pot. Thanks to his run of luck, Alex had about half his stack remaining in front of him.

Kader got ready to turn over his cards, but a quick wave from Alex stopped him. Alex had one more option left to him—double his bet and replace his hold cards with two new ones. He took it.

All his chips were in, and he was depending on the luck of the draw to put him over the top. It was a ridiculous move, but that kind of thing had been working for Alex recently.

He flipped over the two cards he was throwing away as he discarded them, an unusual move. Ace-king. Fine cards to bet with, but, given the shared cards, probably not a winner. Every other gambler at the table agreed, without saying anything, that he should have folded after the fall of the fifth shared card.

Alex received two new cards. Kader showed what he had—queen-jack. Two pair, both of them high. A quality hand.

Alex flipped over his draw. First a ten. Then an eight. Kader made an instinctive reach for the pot, until he realized—8-9-10-jack-queen. A straight. A winner.

Kader and Alex stood at the same time. Alex was not foolish enough to reach a conciliatory hand to Kader, who was already stalking off. He gazed at his considerable stack of chips for a few moments, then apparently decided he'd ridden his luck long enough. He raked in his chips so he could cash them in.

By the time he'd assembled all of them, Kader was nowhere in sight.

Bannickburn wasn't sure what the best part of X-Prime's performance had been—the fact that he'd cleaned Kader out, like he was supposed to, or the fact that he'd won so much from the other players in the meantime. Since all of X-Prime's original stake came from Cayman's pickpocketing exploits, the final winnings were pure profit. It would make a nice bonus for the team.

First, of course, they had to finish the mission. Kader was mad, but he wasn't humiliated. Not by a long shot.

True to the propensities revealed by the file Jackie had stolen (a file that provided crucial information for X-Prime as he worked to win Kader's money), the mafioso had retired to the bar to reduce the pain of his losses. When he won, Kader drank wine; when he lost, he drank whiskey. By all accounts, Kader could hold his liquor quite well, so Bannickburn could take his time before approaching him. Which was good—walking up too soon would look suspicious.

Kader was in the Gates Casino's twentieth century–themed bar, with the taillights of finned automobiles sticking out of the wall and hard plastic furniture everywhere. Bannickburn was nearby, in the Old West Saloon, which had a few cowboy hats on the wall and little else that looked like anything from a saloon. Bannickburn also understood that this bar served sarsaparilla, but he'd never bothered to find out for sure. Regardless, with the evening he had in front of him, he chose to stick with water.

He waited for Kader's anger to coalesce into icy hatred—he figured it would take fifteen to twenty minutes—then wandered over. He walked slowly but directly, knowing where he wanted to go, but being in no particular hurry to get there.

Kader saw him approaching, and gave him a look like he was eyeballing Bannickburn to determine his coffin size. The person Kader saw looked nothing like Bannickburn—his sideburns were covered and transformed into heavy cheeks and jowls, his hair was sandy brown, his nose broad and misshapen, his brow almost Neanderthal. He looked like hired muscle who'd taken a few too many punches.

Kader didn't welcome him, but he didn't stop his approach. Bannickburn knew there would be no use for small talk, so he got right to the point.

"Tough loss," he said.

"Who the hell are you?" Kader hissed.

"Your new best friend. Got a minute?"

"No."

"You want your money back?"

Kader turned to look at Bannickburn directly, looking to the elf like a mannequin in a cheap haunted house slowly rotating toward him.

"I don't know what you intend to sell me. I don't care. Take your scam elsewhere. I'm done giving away money for the night." He returned his attention to his whiskey, assuming Bannickburn would follow his orders.

"You were cheated," Bannickburn said. "I've got the proof. Just thought you'd be interested."

"I have no doubt I was cheated. But I have no confidence in you, whoever you are."

"You can call me Miller. All you need to know is I'm a sympathizer."

"With what?"

"With people in your line of work."

Kader didn't respond, didn't nod, didn't acknowledge Bannickburn at all. Bannickburn wasn't making much headway. Kader still was paying far too much attention to his glass, and he showed no interest in the conversation. But he was still sitting there. He hadn't forced Bannickburn away yet, and that had to be worth something. Bannickburn soldiered on.

"I don't know everything that's going on with you, but I know this much—you can't let people take advantage of you. You were cheated. The guy's walked away from your table, he's spending your money on some prime rib and aged scotch. I assume you can't let that kind of thing go on. I can help you end it."

"You have proof of the cheating?"

"Yup."

"Then why not take it to casino security?"

"You trust them?"

"More than I trust you," Kader said.

"You shouldn't. Because they're the ones screwing you."

Kader tried not to show any interest at Bannickburn's words, but he failed. His jaw clenched, his eyes tightened. He was getting angrier, and that meant he was getting interested. The hook was going in.

"That's right," Bannickburn said. "You know how Gates feels about the Mafia."

"What's that got to do with me?" Kader said, almost reflexively.

"Oh, nothing. Nothing at all. But maybe, somehow, someone on Gates' security staff got it into their head that you're Mafia. And they don't want Mafia in their place, so they're making sure you lose. If that means sending in a dupe to look stupid and then cheat you out of your money, then that's what they'll do. Or should I say, that's what they did."

Kader took two deep, raspy breaths before speaking again. "That's a significant accusation."

"Damn straight it is," Bannickburn said. "Damn straight. It's the kind of accusation that means nothing without some rock-solid proof."

"And?"

"And that's exactly the kind I've got."

14

It was a tricky doctoring job. Straight trideo manipulation, Jackie could do. Give her enough time, and the job would be seamless. She'd even been getting better—the time she needed to do an acceptable job had gotten shorter and shorter, but it was still longer than the amount of time she had tonight. That meant there were going to be seams. Luckily, for this job, that was okay.

Which was part of the trick. The manipulation had to be good enough to fool an amateur viewer who would nevertheless be giving the footage a careful look, while fake enough that a professional would be able to dismiss it fairly quickly.

She hoped Kader was feeling talkative, or that Bannickburn would at least run his mouth long enough to give her a few extra seconds. Every little bit of time helped.

Spindle sat next to her in the small attic a few hundred meters from the casino, keeping track of her surveillance drone. The video feed was off for the time being, and Spindle was trying to move it out blind. It was slow work.

Jackie's mind raced as she altered angles, combined shots, and tried to make the altered trideo footage look vaguely like reality so that Kader would be convinced that something that had never happened really had. Soon Cayman would be here for the relay, and she'd have to hand off whatever she'd managed to do. After that, she had one more little task—another test of her Gates passwords—and then she could relax. Jack into the Matrix and have a little fun, instead of this cut-and-paste drudge work.

She didn't bother to see what Kross was doing. She assumed he was still sitting behind Spindle, face grumpy, arms folded and driving creases into the elbows of his silk suit, still angry about having nothing to do. Spindle's tight green tank top at least gave him something to look at, but that didn't seem to be enough to cheer him.

Keeping Kross happy, though, was not one of Jackie's concerns. She was content to ignore him.

She heard heavy footsteps walking up the stairs toward their attic. Kross, playing security guard, jumped to an alert position, but Spindle and Jackie didn't bother to turn to the door. Jackie knew it was Cayman approaching, and she knew that meant she had to be done.

It had been exactly like fishing for marlin, an activity Bannickburn hated. He'd prefer to just sail out in a boat, zap the water with a healthy dose of electricity, and see what came to the surface, but a few people had once convinced him to spend an excruciating afternoon watching them attempt to reel in a single fish. They'd pull it in a little, then give it some play, then pull it in a little more, and on and on and on. And when it finally was over, they had a big wet fish that needed to go through an exceedingly disgusting process before it was ready to be consumed.

The evening's labor had been almost as difficult, with Kader shying away every time Bannickburn thought he had him interested. But he'd finally done it, and his reward should be a lot better than a dead fish.

Cayman had walked by ten minutes ago—stumbled by, really, putting on a fine drunk act. When he bumped into Bannickburn, he passed a small disk to him. That disk now sat in a portable trideo player that Bannickburn was about to show Kader.

"Just watch," he said, and flipped open the player's screen. "Example number one. From the end, the hand where he cleaned you out. Take a look at his draw."

The trideo image started with an overhead view of Alex at the table, clumsily shuffling his chips as he contemplated his next move. It was the last round of betting, just before he threw in all his chips to get two new cards. He threw in a raise, and it was Kader's turn to think. Bannickburn paused the image briefly, making sure he had it zoomed in on the dealer's hands and the card shoe, then restarted the playback. Offscreen, Alex made his do-or-die bet. The dealer reached for the shoe and pulled out two cards.

And palmed them.

The move was incredibly fast. Bannickburn had to slow the replay down to one-quarter speed before Kader caught a hint that something was amiss. At one-eighth speed, the mobster started to see what had happened. At one-sixteenth, he was sure.

The two cards from the shoe disappeared somewhere—maybe up her sleeve, maybe disintegrated by a quick spell—and were replaced by two cards deftly hidden in her large hands. Those were the cards Alex received. Those were the ones that gave him his final victory over Kader.

Kader clenched his jaw, but said nothing until the replay crawled to its conclusion.

"Show it again," he said.

Bannickburn obliged. It was an incredibly quick move, two cards flying in one sleeve and two new ones out the other. The dealer's arms partially covered the move, making it difficult for the camera to get a clear view, and even harder for the other players to see anything. But this close in, and in slow motion, was indisputable proof. She had cheated, and Alex had benefited.

Kader watched it five times, his face showing nothing. Then he stood and took a quick stride forward.

"Bad idea," Bannickburn said.

Kader strained forward like a rottweiler on a leash. "It's the only idea. There's no choice in the matter."

"It's what they want."

"They wanted my money. They got it. Now I'm going to take a little back."

"You kill him on the floor, you play right into their hands. They kick you out, you never come back."

Kader was staring toward the last place he had seen Alex, his eyes nearly pulling themselves out of his skull, but he didn't move. Bannickburn had hooked him again.

"I'm not just letting him take my money," Kader said. "I'm not just letting him walk away."

"No, of course not. But go through the official channels. Report him to security. Let them take care of him."

"They won't take care of anything. You say they helped set me up. They'll just let him go."

"Not if you expose him publicly. A lot of people noticed this guy, a lot of people saw what happened. You expose him in public, the casino will have to do something about it. They can't just bury it, not with the evidence we have. They'll have to do something. And if you do it in public, you get a little payback against them—telling people the casino let a cheat run wild inside. NewsNet will probably pick it up. They'll *have* to do something to this Alex fragger, because the damn newshounds will keep after them until they do."

Kader's eyes slowly eased back into their sockets. He was listening.

"Killing Alex would be fun, sure," Bannickburn said. "But exposing him and Gates together—that might be even better, huh?"

"Okay," Kader said. "Okay. But you're going to help me make it very, very public."

Bannickburn had no problem with that.

*   *   *

Bannickburn was in mid-rant, fake jowls shaking with every angry word.

"I don't want some pansy floor guard, and I don't want some candy-ass head of the *floor*. I want the head of security for the whole damn place. And I want him *here*, not in some fraggin' office where he can try to sweep everything under the rug. He's going to answer and he's going to answer *now*."

Kader said nothing. He just loomed behind Bannickburn to give greater weight to everything Bannickburn said.

Bannickburn was in full-throated roar, and he knew from long experience that he could continue like this for hours on end if necessary. The chief would have to come out sometime.

And he did, finally, summoned more by the murmuring crowd around Bannickburn than by anything Bannickburn had said. Three times before the chief got there, guards had made a move to pick up Bannickburn and physically remove him from the casino. All three times, menacing glares from Kader, as well as from other casino players who seemed to sympathize with Bannickburn, stopped them in their tracks.

The guards had done at least one useful thing, though—they'd found Alex and brought him over. He stood, nervous and resentful, between a pair of them. He tried to shrink into a puddle when the security chief arrived. Tall and thin, she was built like a whip. Her sharp features betrayed no worry about the increasing tumult in the casino.

"Good evening, sir. I'm Liselle Byatt, head of security, and I'd like to help you, but the first thing I'm going to have to do is ask you to lower your voice so we can talk."

Bannickburn complied with a glare. "There's not much talking to do," he said. "You just need to take a look at some trideo footage."

Byatt smiled. "Sounds easy enough. What would you like me to see?"

Her smile vanished once the footage started playing. Her face hardened, like hot metal under cold water. She threw an angry look at Alex.

"Don't let him go *anywhere*," she said. The guards flanking Alex obediently grabbed his arms.

But then Byatt, looked again and something in her expression changed. She didn't look any less angry, but now she didn't seem sure where her anger should be directed. She looked at all the players involved in the drama in front of her, and decided not to speak to any of them.

"Keep all of them right here," she told one of the guards.

"Are you sure?" the guard replied, glancing at the gathering crowd. "Maybe it'd be better if you finished somewhere . . . private."

"No. At the moment, I don't trust any of these people to move a muscle in my casino. They started it here, they can wait here until I figure out how it's going to finish. Keep them here. And don't let them fiddle with any sort of device. Have all of them keep their hands where you can see them."

"Yes, sir," the guard replied, and Byatt stalked off.

Kader took a smooth step, gliding toward Bannickburn like a specter.

"Where is she going?"

"I don't know."

"She should've taken action already. Right here. Right now."

"I agree."

"I don't like this."

"Neither do I. But here we are."

Kader moved his face closer to Bannickburn's ear.

"You're closer to me than he is," he hissed. "I could kill you first, then worry about him."

Bannickburn turned, his prosthetic nose nearly bumping Kader's real one. Neither man moved his head back. "You're right," Bannickburn said. "But if you do that, the guards would kill you before you got him. And isn't he the one you really want?"

Kader considered this. "I'm not here alone," he finally said.

Bannickburn knew this all too well. Kader's flunkies
had been trailing close behind, ready to free their boss
from the grip of casino security at the drop of a hat.
Kader knew he needed to put up with the security tem-
porarily, so he'd waved them back. They remained close
by, though, and their considerable bulk made them easy
to spot in the crowd.

Bannickburn decided to not say anything. He just
cracked a corner of his mouth in a smile and let Kader
guess what the grin meant.

Then Byatt returned with a nervous-looking dwarf in
tow. The dwarf clutched the small trideo player in her
hands, and her blond braids swept across it as she
scanned back and forth across the gathered crowd. Her
round face puckered.

Bannickburn could almost see the steam coming out
of Byatt's ears. She'd seen what she was supposed to,
he guessed. Now things were going to get really fun.

"Georgia," Byatt said, apparently addressing the
dwarf. "Tell them."

Georgia muttered something. She might have said,
" 'Tis fade," which would make no sense, but Bannickburn couldn't be sure because the dwarf was so quiet,
while the muttering of the surrounding crowd only got
louder.

"Louder, Georgia," Byatt said.

"It's fake," Georgia said. "The trid footage. Doctored.
Our dealer never did that."

"What the *hell* . . . ?" someone yelled, but it was one
of the goons, not Kader himself. Kader kept silent, with
murder in his eyes, trying to decide where to direct his
killing gaze.

"I don't know what kind of game you people are playing, and I don't want to know. I just want the three of
you out. Take Mr. Primus, Mr. Miller, and Mr. Kader—"

Then another voice joined the conversation. "Kader?
Is that Murson Kader?" It was a man in a tuxedo with

the official Gates Casino green-and-gold cummerbund. Another high-ranking official. With, thanks to Jackie, perfect timing.

"Yes," Byatt said. "The tall corpselike guy over there."

The tuxedoed man turned to Kader. "Mr. Kader, I'm Tyrone Lawton of the Vault Department. I need you to step aside with me to discuss a . . . matter."

"Kader's not going anywhere," Byatt said, "except out. My people were about to show him to the door."

Lawton fidgeted and wiped his brow with a gleaming white handkerchief. "I'm afraid I need him to stay, so this matter can be addressed."

"What are you talking about, Lawton? What's going on?"

Lawton looked at Kader, taking note of the muscular goons behind him, then looked at Byatt. His eyeballs nearly twitched out of his skull. He leaned close to Byatt and whispered something in her ear.

Unfortunately for Kader, Byatt did not feel like being nearly as discreet as Lawton. "Counterfeit!" she yelled. "What in hell are you talking about?"

"Just that," Lawton said meekly, "there's no real value in the credsticks. They're attached to accounts, and the accounts are trying to claim they have money, but they don't, really. It's tricks and nonsense—no real money."

"How much?"

"Mr. Kader has bought twenty thousand nuyen in chips with these credsticks tonight."

Byatt placed her hands on her hips and glared at Kader. "Fake videos and counterfeit credsticks. We've had a busy night tonight, haven't we?"

And Kader finally snapped. His mouth twisted, and a guttural growl wormed through his chest. His brow creased, reddened, and grew moist with sweat. His hands lunged for Bannickburn's neck, so he could break it with one violent twist.

But Bannickburn wasn't there. He was running, barreling toward Byatt, watching her draw her automatic, hoping he had enough time.

Behind him, Kader's goons echoed his growl, only louder, and moved forward. A slot machine got in their way, and they pushed it over. Glass broke, coins rattled. Some patrons dove out of the way, while others scrambled to see if any money had fallen out.

The first shots were fired. Not by Byatt—she was still raising her gun, looking for the sweet spot between Bannickburn's eyes—but by someone behind Bannickburn. The elf ducked his head and hoped the armored fabric sewn into his costume would do the rest of the work.

Byatt took a step back, apparently bracing herself for a blow from Bannickburn, but he veered and bulled into Georgia instead. She was less than one and a half meters tall, but she was plenty solid and she didn't go down easily. Bannickburn had momentum on his side, though, and they both tumbled to the floor, rolling and rolling.

Byatt didn't take a shot—she didn't want to hurt Georgia, just as Bannickburn had expected.

Georgia didn't make a noise after Bannickburn hit her, probably because she was hyperventilating in panic. Bannickburn felt a twinge of guilt, but then he was at the end of a row of slot machines, and he had to worry about making his escape. He managed to gasp a quick "sorry" to Georgia as he dashed between the patrons, most of whom looked for a hiding place, while a few managed to at least glance at him between pulls on their machines.

Now he moved. The next part of the plan had to happen quickly.

He stayed as close as he could to other patrons, partly to prevent security from getting a clear shot at him, partly to prevent any monitoring mages from getting a good look at his aura. He zigzagged a little between the rows of machines when he needed to, but for the most part he traveled in a straight line. He knew where he wanted to be.

Sweat trickled between his real cheek and his fake

one. It suddenly felt like he wasn't getting enough air through his disguise. He kept sprinting, and every breath stabbed his side with pain.

He had a solid ten-meter lead on the nearest guards, which would only buy him a second or two. He had to make that enough.

He ran into a crowded restroom and dropped the bomb he'd pulled out of his pocket. A loud flash made everyone inside jump, then the smoke made them panic. Luckily, it spread quickly and thickly, and most of them couldn't find the door. That was good—Bannickburn needed them present for a little while longer, and their natural confusion would only aid what he was about to do.

He entered the third stall and pressed himself into the back corner. He was now standing in one of the only spots in the casino not visible to security cameras. Any mages working security would still be able to see his aura, but it would be lumped in with everyone else in the small room, difficult to make out individually. And things were about to get hairier for anyone trying to keep track of the mysterious Mr. Miller.

Bannickburn lit up a small cigarette and inhaled sharply. After a mere three tokes, he'd burned through the whole thing. His lungs smoldered painfully with smoke, but he needed to take it all in quickly. He felt the smoke work its way into every crevice of his lungs, then seep outward through the rest of his body. His chest, his arms, then his legs felt light, insubstantial, ready to drift on the slightest current of air. The intensity of the situation dissipated, and Bannickburn felt a certain distance from the chaos around him.

His hands, feeling like clouds riding a breeze, peeled off a layer of latex and ripped off his shirt while reversing his jacket. His second mask was showing now, this one much tighter, giving him a long, lean face. His hair was now blond, and he wore a white blazer with an aqua shirt. Hopefully, this second disguise would be completely unnecessary.

The Little Smoke he'd inhaled made him feel dizzy, and he stumbled awkwardly out of the restroom stall. No one glanced at him. Now the other men around him seemed strangely unable to find the door. They bumped into the walls and each other, and a few unlucky souls sat down in urinals. A few of them found the way out.

The confusion power of the Little Smoke was clearly working well. From the way he felt, and the fact that no one registered his presence, the concealment seemed pretty effective, too.

A few guards walked into the restroom, but as soon as they came in they started acting just as disoriented as everyone else. Bannickburn moved patiently, drifting between people, until he finally came near the door. It opened, and he blew out.

He looked for another crowd in which to lose himself. He hoped the security mages were becoming as confused as the people in the bathroom, but he didn't want to take any chances.

The most promising spot looked like the front entrance. Casino security had locked down the entire building, and a considerable number of patrons were milling around the doors, waiting for the all clear so they could get the hell out.

Bannickburn joined them, amused at how people became clumsier and more disoriented as he drew near. He slid into the middle of a throng and stayed there, hoping for safety in numbers.

The front doors opened, and the crowd shoved forward eagerly. The guards pushed them away and cleared a little space for a couple of DocWagon medics with a gurney. The medics didn't seem to be in a hurry—the patient was either going to be fine or was already dead.

The medics actually knew far more about what was going on in the casino than anyone besides Bannickburn. Beneath the medical scrubs were Cayman and Spindle, hurrying to pick up their comrade.

The gurney disappeared between the rows of slot machines. Bannickburn waited, and after a few minutes the medics reappeared. A sheet-covered body lay on the gurney. The medics were still taking their time.

Bannickburn scanned the rest of the casino, but he couldn't see Kader or his goons. He didn't think they'd slipped out—with any luck, casino security had taken them to a nice, secure place.

The gurney came closer. A bloodstain had appeared near the right shoulder of the body, under the sheet. Bannickburn hoped it was fake, a show-business touch thrown in by Cayman, but there was a real chance that X-Prime, who was under the sheet, had been hurt.

By now, the casino personnel should be convinced that X-Prime—Alex—was dead. One of X-Prime's duties, while waiting for Bannickburn to prod Kader into action, was to ingest some Cold Slab, an interesting little experimental drug they'd gotten from the same people who supplied the fake DocWagon outfits. The drug had dropped X-Prime's pulse to nearly nothing and made his breathing so slow and shallow as to be undetectable. Any decent medical equipment would show he was still alive, but the casino hadn't bothered with that. He looked dead, the meat-wagon docs who came by said he was dead, and that was good enough for them.

Spindle and Cayman carried X-Prime out, leaving Bannickburn to make his escape. He decided there was no time like the present. He dashed through the crowd, feeling like steam in a wind tunnel, and slipped through the main casino door just as it closed behind Cayman. No one in the casino noticed or cared.

15

Naturally, he checked NewsNet first. It wasn't the top
story of the day, but it was there, read by an earnest
young man who lowered his voice to show that he
thought it was a serious item.

"Chaos at the Gates Casino last night, as a reputed
mobster and a mysterious con man accused the casino
of shifty dealing. The mobster, Murson Kader, an alleged
associate of the Finnigan crime family, lost over twenty
thousand nuyen at the casino, only to accuse a dealer of
cheating on behalf of another player. Though Kader and
his associate, a man only identified at this point as 'Mr.
Miller,' claimed to have trideo proof of the cheating,
that proof turned out to be doctored. When his evidence
was questioned, Kader flew into a rage, inciting a brawl
that spread across the casino and claimed one life. The
deceased, a SINless man known only as Alex, is believed
to be the man who won most of Kader's twenty thousand nuyen at the poker table.

"Lone Star Security Services, in conjunction with
Gates Casino management, is working to develop an appropriate response to the situation, including determin-
ing what charges to file against Kader. The case is
complicated by the fact that the credsticks Kader used
to gamble at the casino were counterfeit. Mr. Miller re-

mains at large, and Lone Star has provided the following mock-up of his appearance."

An image that looked vaguely like Bannickburn's disguise from the previous night appeared on the screen. Bannickburn squinted at it, then smiled. His brain seemed surrounded by a gauzy cloud, and he had trouble summoning the motivation to do more than switch between the nets. Detoxifying (he preferred that term to the more colloquial "coming down") was never easy.

He switched to INN. He had to wait to see the coverage he wanted, but when it came, it was most gratifying.

"We've just heard from Liselle Byatt, security chief of Gates Casino, announcing a lifetime ban on Murson Kader from all Gates Casino properties, both in reality and on the Matrix. Byatt also hinted that this is only the beginning of the punishment the casino will seek, though Mr. Kader's extensive contacts may limit the casino's actions against him."

Beautiful, Bannickburn thought. *All quite beautiful.* Report after report alleged—which, to the public, was as good as a statement of fact—that Kader was a liar playing with counterfeit money. And now he was banned from Gates for life.

This was enough, but Bannickburn wanted more. "What's the Matrix buzz?"

Jackie blinked several times, trying to focus her eyes, but she was too involved in the Matrix. Her expression stayed slightly dazed. "These people are savvy. Most of them know Kader wouldn't show up with counterfeit credsticks. They figure he was duped, not crooked." Then she smiled. "But they don't care much. Just about everyone's happy to see him take a hit, even if no one thinks he's going to be off the streets for any real length of time. There's absolutely no interest—well, except from Kader and a few Finnigan goons—in finding this Miller character. He's already on his way to becoming a folk hero."

"Anyone connecting the Bigios to the job?"

"A few people are assuming it was them, just because they figure anytime the Finnigans take a hit, it's the Bigios' doing. But no one's got a hint of evidence of a connection."

Perfect. And to top it all off, X-Prime had cashed in his chips just before his staged death. The team had agreed in advance to evenly divide any gambling winnings, and the total for each runner came to significantly more than the original payment for the run. It was a complete, total, unvarnished success. *Damn, I'm good at this,* Bannickburn thought.

"Visitor," Jackie said.

"Who?"

"Shivers. Lurking around outside."

"Ah! Splendid. I'll go let him in."

Jackie's eyes finally focused on him. "The hell you will. You'll go out, greet him, and talk to him someplace else. Shivers doesn't come in here. You shouldn't have let him get this close."

"But he's the one who introduced me to Bailey, who hired me for this whole wonderful job! Surely that's enough to earn an invite inside."

"You'd think. But it isn't. Keep him out."

Bannickburn sighed. He'd pulled off the very public humiliation of a much-feared mobster, only to be pushed around by a short blonde. The world never stayed perfect for long.

Jimmy had his cycle, so they took it into Bellevue for a real breakfast, one that had meat that wasn't all fat. They laughed at the drones and wage slaves who scarfed down their food so they could get to work, and ate slowly and with relish. The fog in Bannickburn's brain was still there, but the food and fresh air seemed to help clear his head.

"I just wish I could've watched him die," Bannickburn was saying. "He seemed like an intrepid lad, and he really put gusto into his performance. I've never *seen* so many tics at a card table. So I'm sure that, when the opportunity came for him to die, he did it with a certain flair. He must have really sold that death. Of course, he'd taken the Cold Slab, so that could only help."

"Cold Slab? What's that?"

"It's new. Experimental. Simulates death."

Jimmy actually looked impressed. "Playing with experimental drugs, are we? That's big-league stuff. How did you get your hands on that?"

"Bailey obtained it for us. He seems to have excellent pharmaceutical connections," Bannickburn said, then wished he hadn't. Jimmy was a friend, of course, but people who didn't know details of an operation usually didn't know them for a reason. He'd battled this problem ever since his youth—when he was excited and happy, he talked, and often became more expansive than he should be.

Luckily, Jimmy didn't seem too interested in learning more about the drug. After a slight pause, he left the topic behind. "If I were you, I'd expect an invitation from Sottocapo Martel later today. He's a very fair man who likes to show his gratitude toward people who do good work for him. I'd keep your dinner plans open."

That should mean good bacon for breakfast and steak for dinner, Bannickburn thought. This was quickly shaping up as the perfect day, especially if he could round up a good lunch.

"Sounds like Kader never knew what hit him," Jimmy said.

Bannickburn nodded modestly. "Well, that was the plan."

"Still, he must have had some expectation, right? You don't do what he did without expecting something to come back around to you, right?"

"Yeah, I suppose."

"It's almost like he was trying to start another war. He had to know Kader would retaliate, and then they'd retaliate against us, and then everything blows up."

"That's why we kept the Bigios out of it."

"But he has to guess, right? After what he did?"

And then, finally, it hit Bannickburn. Without the brain cloud, it probably would have registered sooner. Jimmy was out of the loop. He didn't know what Kader had done, so he was fishing for information. Bannickburn had no idea why Jimmy shouldn't know what was going on, and he also had no idea why Jimmy wanted to find out. He hated to do this to his friend—without Jimmy, the run wouldn't have happened in the first place—but he had to close up.

"I don't know," Bannickburn said. "Tough to say what someone else is thinking."

"Sure. And I guess that what he did was sort of . . . surreptitious, right? Below board? So he wouldn't raise a whole lot of ire."

"I guess."

The conversation went that way through the rest of breakfast. Jimmy poked and prodded, and Bannickburn gave him nothing in return. At the end of the meal, a clearly frustrated Jimmy didn't even offer to pay. Fortunately, Bannickburn was feeling wealthy enough to pay for both of them.

When he returned to Jackie's, the invitation Shivers told him to expect had arrived. Sottocapo Martel wanted to extend his personal congratulations to Bannickburn that night at the Brigham Steakhouse. Unlike Shivers, Martel promised up front to pay.

"Don't go," Jackie said once Bannickburn reviewed the invitation. "You're on top. You're coming off of a success. This is the time to end it."

"Ah, my dear, but that would be rude. All the man did was invite me to dinner. A well-deserved dinner, I might add. He didn't tell me to crawl into his lair."

"He might as well have."

His reflexes begged him to make an argument, but when he thought of his breakfast with Jimmy, and the machinations between the different levels of the mob, he was beginning to give more heed to Jackie's warnings. He felt like his head was well above water, but he remembered what Jackie had said about the trickle of drops.

"Okay," he said in his most soothing voice. "Okay. Listen. I have to go. You *know* I have to go. Standing up a Bigio sottocapo is the kind of bad manners that can easily lead to broken fingers. So I'll go, and I will generously accept Martel's thanks, and if they even so much as dangle more work in front of me I will say that I am unavailable and they should look elsewhere. I will spend all evening, if necessary, politely disentangling myself from their association. Is that satisfactory?"

Jackie smiled in relief. "Quite."

"All right, then. Of course, I'll still be having the occasional drink with Jimmy and Quinn . . ."

Jackie shot him a look that made him throw both hands in the air. "But not until at least a month has passed," he finished.

He felt a pang of regret as soon as he said the words, since he was having too much fun to have it end. But there definitely was such a thing as getting in too deep with Bailey and his people, and he was perilously close to that level.

It was okay, he told himself. He'd managed to find one way to indulge his thirst for a little power. He could always find others.

16

Most of the project had gone so perfectly that it was a shame Bailey couldn't just sit back and bask in the glory of his success. Yet while his current project had gone well, an episode had occurred that endangered the future, and he couldn't have that. Sadly, he had to make another trip to Slidestream's office.

He'd obtained the chip earlier in the day. Better Than Life chips were easy for him to get—he regularly had drinks with Vanessa Yarl, a Bigio caporegime who helped get BTLs into the hands of desperately addicted users. Yarl had done a double take when he told her what kind of chip he wanted (he could practically hear her blinking rapidly over the telecom when he mentioned it), but she'd said she'd get it for him. All part of the perks of "family" life.

Kross was waiting for him when Bailey arrived at the building down the street. He'd sent the ork ahead because, had he just wandered over by himself, there was a good chance the man he was looking for would be hiding somewhere, and Bailey would have to spend time tracking him down. But with Kross at his disposal, he could skip over the boring part, do what he needed to do, and set up a fine anecdote for Kross to relate to Martel.

The small decker was doing his best to look relaxed

under Kross' glare. But he shifted in his chair roughly every fifteen seconds, so the illusion didn't work.

"Slide!" Bailey said cheerfully. "How are you? Hey, I wanted to congratulate you on a fine job last night. A *fine* job. Hacking into Gates security—that's top-quality work."

Slidestream sat up a little straighter. He snarled a bit at Kross, then made his face pleasant for Bailey. His confidence was on the rise.

"Of course, from what I understand—and correct me if I'm wrong, because I couldn't even hack my way into my own office—the trick on the Matrix isn't just getting in somewhere, it's *staying* somewhere. Since protocols change on the fly, specifically to keep people like you *out*, it's all too easy to get into someplace only to get kicked right back out. Do I have that right?"

Slidestream slowly melted back into his chair, his confidence ebbing again. "Yeah. Yeah, I guess."

"Oh, so you *know* about that problem?" Bailey said. "I wasn't sure. Because a strange thing happened while I was watching the show—my picture blacked out."

"Yeah, see, what happened was . . ."

"Now, I wouldn't be happy about losing my view under any circumstances, but there was this showdown. Did you see the showdown?"

"Well, I saw the beginning . . ."

"Right, right, of course, you saw the beginning. Kader, this Miller character, the card cheat, and a whole passel of Gates security. And I wondered, how are they going to deal with this situation. Did you wonder about that, Slide?"

"Yeah, I guess."

"Well, sadly, we're both left to wonder what happened. Sure, I could ask the people involved, but there's always the chance they'd lie. And why would they lie? Because when you have a bag of tricks, like this Mr. Miller seems to have, you don't like to let them out of the bag. But I wouldn't have to rely on Miller telling me the truth if I had *seen the fragging footage*. Do you understand what I'm saying?"

Slidestream understood too well. "It was only thirty-five seconds! Do you know what I was up against? The fact that I got in at all . . . do you know how many people could have done that? And kept you there as long as I did? And only lost thirty-five seconds? I pulled off a *miracle* for you!"

"You told me you could do it. And then you failed. I don't think there's much to discuss."

Kross recognized his cue. He stepped forward, seized Slidestream's arms, and pinned them behind his back.

"The problem here, Slide," Bailey said as he stepped forward, "is that since you don't seem to be a man of your word, you don't expect others to keep their promises. But I take a promise seriously, because a man is only as good as his bond. I have that right, don't I, Mr. Kross?"

Kross growled something that might have signified assent.

"Right. So the best way to look at this is as a demonstration of the importance of following through on your word." He paused briefly. "Don't look so concerned! Come on, give me a smile. Haven't you ever heard me talk about the glory of dying with a smile on your face? Give it a shot."

Bailey inserted the Black Death chip into Slidestream's head, and much unpleasant thrashing about and screaming ensued. Bailey checked his watch—really, there was no reason for Slidestream to drag this out. There was a lot more to do this evening.

Within a minute, he had removed the chip from Slidestream's jack and walked out the door, Kross just behind, holding his nose. Mouth agape, what had once been Slidestream sat still in his chair, smoke curling out from behind his eyeballs.

"When you tell Sottocapo Martel about our exploits of the evening, do you think you'll cast me as a charming rogue? Or will you just go for the ruthless enforcer type?"

Kross didn't rise to Bailey's baiting.

"I really hope you include the charming part. It's not just that I'm effective at what I do—it's that I do it with such *panache*."

Kross delivered the grunt Bailey had heard so many times.

"Well put."

Kross parked his cycle and almost ran into the Brigham to get away from Bailey.

Bailey smiled. Martel had sent him a fine companion—Bailey wouldn't know how to behave if he was working with someone he actually got along with.

Martel was, naturally, at his table, and Kross was already seated next to him as Bailey approached.

"Sirloin. Large one. Rare," Kross snapped at a passing waiter. Bailey had made the ork forget his normal veneer of manners—truly, this was a triumphant evening all around.

"Please. Sit," Martel said in his low rumble. Bailey obliged.

"I understand Mr. Bannickburn will be along shortly," Bailey said, and added a silent, fervent wish that this would turn out to be true. He wasn't relishing spending any time alone with Martel and his lackey.

Thankfully, Bannickburn arrived practically on Bailey's heels. Martel actually stood to greet him, extending his hand and taking Bannickburn's in a crushing grip. Bannickburn was far too seasoned to grimace at the pain.

"Mr. Bannickburn," Martel said. The water in the glasses on the table quivered at his voice. "You have our thanks." He sat.

"It was my pleasure," Bannickburn replied modestly.

"Mr. Bailey. Proceed," Martel said, returning his attention to his dinner.

"Right. Yes. Well, Robert, Mr. Martel would like me to convey his thanks, and that of his associates for your recent work. The job you did surpassed all reasonable expectations we could have placed on it."

"You're very kind," Bannickburn said.

"Not at all. And Mr. Martel wants you to be assured that he has not just noticed your success in this mission, but in the wide variety of projects given you. Calling you a valuable asset to this thing of ours is accurate, but seems inadequate—calling you our good friend seems more fitting."

Martel gave a slow nod of approval at Bailey's words.

"If there's any one thing the sottocapo would like to convey to you tonight," Bailey went on, "it is how valuable our friendship can be. I'm sure you understand that there are thousands, perhaps millions of people in the world who would enjoy having someone like the sottocapo as a friend, and these sorts are often quite aggressive in their efforts to gain the sottocapo's attention and, hopefully, his sympathies."

"Nuisances," Martel said, the word falling heavily off his tongue.

"You now have what all these people want," Bailey said. "It is our belief, of course, that you will live up to the trust we are putting in you by offering our hand in friendship—that you will honor the sottocapo as he honors you."

"Of course," said Bannickburn, who appeared bemused by the formality of Bailey's presentation.

"And that's the long and the short of it," Bailey said. "Did I cover everything, Alexei?"

Martel did not appear pleased at being addressed by his first name, but he grunted, and it sounded enough like "yup" for the others at the table to move on to other topics of conversation.

The next part of the evening had to appear spontaneous and casual, and that was the main reason Bailey was here. Kross could have served as Martel's mouthpiece just as easily as Bailey, but the light-conversation part of the evening might have proven more difficult for him (though he was surprisingly adept at social conversation for an ork). Bailey, though, was in his element, and he and Bannickburn swapped war stories for forty-five minutes—or, as Bailey measured time when eating with Sottocapo Martel, for a sirloin and two pork chops.

Then they hit a moment when Bannickburn appeared relaxed, even Kross seemed fairly mellow, and Martel was between courses. It was time to discuss the evening's true purpose.

Martel leaned on the table, and it screamed under his weight. The abrasive screech turned almost every head in the restaurant; most of them, once they realized who they were looking at, turned back.

Bannickburn, Bailey, and Kross, however, all kept their attention on Martel, because they knew that was what he wanted. He leaned forward slightly, and beneath his thick brow the two pinpoints of his eyes locked with Bannickburn's. Then he stood, slowly, unfolding his body until his entire frame, well over two meters and about a hundred and fifty kilos, towered over the table.

"Mr. Bannickburn," Martel rumbled. "Have a favor to ask you. Important—want you to consider it carefully."

Bannickburn fidgeted—the first time during the evening that he'd looked uncomfortable—but he held Martel's gaze. "I'm not sure I'd—" he began, but Martel had only paused to take a breath, not to allow Bannickburn to say anything. The sottocapo continued what was, for him, a long-winded speech.

"Mr. Bannickburn. I would appreciate it very much if you would get me a drink of water."

Bannickburn looked at Bailey, then at Kross, then at Bailey. Bailey was putting all his efforts into remaining expressionless. Kross looked similarly blank, but Bailey thought that that appearance came to the ork (hell, any ork) naturally.

Bannickburn looked again at Martel, who still loomed in front of him. "Water?" he said.

Martel nodded and held his position for precisely five seconds. Then he leaned back a little, wiped his hands, and thudded toward the men's room.

Bannickburn watched him go. "Water?" he said again.

Bailey stood. "Come with me, Robert," he said.

"Where are we going?"

"Kitchen."

"Martel wants water from the kitchen?"

"Just come on," Bailey said, and the two of them left Kross alone at the table.

Since Martel was at the Brigham so often, and Bailey worked under Martel, Bailey had needed, on many occasions, to have conversations in the restaurant's kitchen. It was a good place to talk, especially in Bailey's favorite spot—two stools near the door of the walk-in meat locker, right by the long wooden table where meat was cut. The slabs of beef hanging from their cold hooks on the other side of the open freezer door, the long, sharp knives wielded by cooks with wickedly quick hands, and the *whump-whump* sound of steel cleanly slicing muscle all worked together to give the appropriate ambiance to the types of conversations Bailey tended to have back here. He found the surroundings gave enough hints of death and dismemberment that he hardly ever needed to resort to threats of his own.

Nowadays, when he went into the kitchen, the busboys, waiters, and cooks just gave him a curt nod and went about their business. He was almost like another member of the staff. His boss regularly dropped over a hundred nuyen per night at the joint, keeping much of the staff employed, so they cut Bailey a lot of slack.

"Where's the sink?" Bannickburn asked. "Why are you sitting down?"

"You should sit down, too," Bailey said. "We need to have a brief chat."

"Do we? Last I checked, what *I* needed to do was procure a drink for Martel."

"That's what we need to talk about. It's not what you think. Sit down."

Bannickburn obediently perched on one of the tall wooden stools. A cook brought a quarter lamb out of the freezer and threw it on the table behind Bailey. The chef took out a knife and removed the leg with a single quick stroke, almost burying the blade in the wooden surface. Bailey suppressed a smile.

"Listen, Robert, you've just struck gold. I didn't know Martel would ask you to do this, but I hoped he would. This isn't just any old glass of water he wants you to get. This is a bottle. And it's not here. It's in Portland. In the hands of some associates of that . . . other family in town."

Bannickburn grasped the plot immediately. "The Finnigans have people in Tir Tairngire? And they've got a bottle of water, and Martel wants it?" He shook his head. "Why?"

"I'll be perfectly honest with you—I have no idea," Bailey said. "All I know is that this is something Martel's been obsessing about. For whatever reason, he's made getting this bottle of water into his own little Manhattan Project."

"He thinks the results will be that good?"

Bailey shrugged. "I guess."

"Why? What could a bottle of water do for him?"

"I told you, I don't know. And Sottocapo Martel is not the kind of person who takes kindly to lots of questions."

Bannickburn stood silently for a moment, watching the lamb on the table behind Bailey get sliced into eversmaller pieces. Finally he shook his head.

"I don't think so, Quinn. I don't think this one is for me."

"What do you mean it's not for you?" Bailey smiled and spread his arms wide. "It's the Tir! You're an elf! It's perfect for you!"

"I'm not especially fond of the Tirs."

"Even better! All the more reason to do this! Stick it to them!"

"I'd rather just avoid them."

Time for a different tack, Bailey thought. "Look, I told you how important this is to Martel. You can be sure that'll be reflected in what he pays you. It'll make what you took home from the Kader job look like chump change, and I'm including your side income from pick-pocketing and gambling when I say that."

That gave Bannickburn pause. Bailey watched happily as greed worked its way across the elf's features, raising his eyebrows, wrinkling his nose, pursing his lips. But then, inexplicably, the greed slipped away.

"If he's paying that much, it just means the job's that much more dangerous. I'm sorry, Quinn. I'm going to have to sit this one out."

Bailey sat on his stool silently for a moment, then nodded his head. "All right, Robert. All right. Your de-cision, right? Martel's not going to be happy, but he won't be homicidal, so that works out okay for you. Look, there will be other jobs. I'm sure of it. I'll be in touch." He stuck out his hand.

Bannickburn looked at it curiously. "Aren't we going back to dinner?" he asked.

"I am," Bailey said. "You're not. When I said Martel wouldn't be homicidal, that was more of an educated guess than a certainty. It would still be best if you weren't here when I tell him you've turned him down. You're going out the back and hurrying home."

"Okay. 'Night, Quinn."

" 'Night, Robert. Be seeing you."

17

Bannickburn had other friends. Not many, and they weren't the most quick-witted lads in the metroplex, but they were friends. It was high time, he decided, to spend time with them. One night had passed since his dinner with Martel, Bailey, and Kross, and he wanted to stay away from that group for at least a week or two. Shivers, too.

He was away from Bellevue, in a makeshift dice parlor called the Masterson that sat in a dried-up sewer pipe. The sound of dice bouncing off warped wooden tables echoed off the corrugated metal interior. The atmosphere was poor (and, when the air moved up from underground, quite rancid), the furnishings subpar at best, and the liquor one step up from kerosene. But there was usually a fair share of drunks and imbeciles who had stumbled onto a little cash and were ripe for the plucking by someone who knew how to throw dice.

Bannickburn had just finished relieving a one-eyed troll of a few shiny coins, and was spending them on a green liquor that looked and tasted like glass cleaner. At least it had a hint of lime. A dreadlocked ork named G-Dogg, whom Bannickburn had met through Jackie, sat next to him, not playing any games, just enjoying himself by watching Bannickburn pick his next victim. It helped that Bannickburn kept buying G-Dogg drinks.

"Is it the wrist?" G-Dogg asked.

"A little."

"Is it loaded dice?"

"Keep your voice down!" Bannickburn looked around rapidly to see if anyone was paying attention. It looked safe. "No, it's not," he said in a loud whisper. "Too much hassle to keep switching the real and the loaded dice back and forth."

"Is it magic? A focus?"

"No," Bannickburn scoffed. "I don't have magic to waste on trivial matters like that."

"Is it the way you drop it out of your palm?"

"A little."

"Why don't you just say what it *is?*" G-Dogg complained.

"That would be telling," Bannickburn said, with his most irritating, smug smile.

G-Dogg rolled his eyes. "Fine. I'm changing the subject. How's Jackie?"

"Fine. I guess."

"You guess?"

"Haven't seen her in a couple of days. She's been out. But last time I saw her, she was fine."

"And you and her? Are you and her fine?"

"Bloody hell, Guggenheim, is that any of your business?"

G-Dogg laughed—a short, quick bark. "That's not what the 'G' stands for. Nice try, though."

Bannickburn shrugged. "I gave it a shot. Will you tell me if I ever get it right?"

"Sure. Then I'll rip your arms off."

Bannickburn considered. "May not be worth it."

"I wouldn't think so."

G-Dogg smiled, but it quickly dropped as movement rippled through the Masterson. Door security at the gambling hall was nonexistent, so the patrons had learned to quickly respond to any possible threat that walked in. A serious threat—gun-toting gangers, revenge-minded thugs—made most of the patrons flee into the sewers. Minor threats just made them hide their cash to avoid looking like possible targets for the newcomer, which was what happened now. Cash, credsticks, and anything else with appraisable value disappeared into pockets, socks, pouches, or any other concealed places players could dream up. Bannickburn turned toward the hall's entrance to see what kind of threat had walked in.

It was a threat with floppy red hair, a black leather jacket, and a permanent sneer. It was Shivers.

"Gods almighty," Bannickburn whispered.

"What?" G-Dogg asked.

"Nothing. But you might want to run along now. I'm afraid the fun part of my evening is over."

"Really? Anything I can help with? I'll back you up if you need it."

"I know, G." G-Dogg's eagerness to help was both endearing and somewhat annoying. "But there's not much you can do in this one. You'd best not be involved."

G-Dogg nodded and took a few steps away from Bannickburn to give him a little privacy. Bannickburn knew the ork would keep an eye on him, which was reassuring.

Shivers paced slowly through the hall, scanning the players' faces, clearly looking for someone. Bannickburn was fairly certain who Shivers wanted to find, and since he had no reason to hide, he decided to keep on drinking his glass cleaner until Shivers found him.

When he did, a remarkable change happened. The sneer on Shivers' mouth almost disappeared. The angry furrow of his brow loosened. He almost looked like he *cared* about something. It was odd and more than a little unnerving.

Shivers walked quickly toward Bannickburn, apparently not wanting to make a scene by calling across the hall.

"Come on, Robert," he said as soon as he was within three meters of Bannickburn. "Let's go."

"Go? Where?"

"I don't know, wherever you want. Just pick some-place safe. I'll help you get there."

"Someplace safe? Why? What's going on?"

Shivers' eyes widened. "What do you mean, 'What's going on?' You don't know?"

"Don't know what?"

"People are looking for you, Robert. And not to buy you a drink, if you know what I'm saying."

"What people?" Bannickburn's voice rose in anger. "Martel? Bailey said he wouldn't be homicidal!"

Shivers' confusion only deepened. "Martel? No! Martel loves you after what you did at the casino. No, it's Kader."

"Kader?"

Shivers grabbed the elf's arm. "Come on. Let's get out of here. Then we'll talk."

He didn't want to take Shivers back to Jackie's—that could end his relationship with her then and there. He owed it to her to keep Shivers away. He tried to prod Shivers into suggesting a place, but apparently Shivers was reluctant to take a marked man to any of his safe places.

So that left the embarrassment that passed for Ban-nickburn's home. Part of him had wanted to abandon it as soon as Jackie said he could stay with her, but one thing he'd learned in his lifetime was that you can never accumulate too many safe places to crash. So he kept paying the minimal rent on his small room in Vico's Den, a storage facility that had been converted into liv-ing quarters. The "conversion" actually hadn't taken much effort—Vico took down the STORAGE FOR RENT sign, replaced it with an APARTMENTS FOR RENT sign, and that was that. The rooms were small, cold, with limited electricity and, of course, nothing resembling a datajack. But there were more than three hundred rooms in the entire facility, and few authorities or crime bosses had the patience to conduct a room-by-room search of the place—especially given the rough nature of the characters that lived in old storage buildings in the Barrens.

Bannickburn stooped to open the padlock, then pushed the door up. It opened with a rattle.

Shivers entered before he was invited in, taking in the matching mahogany buffet and coffee table and the twin tan wingback chairs. He focused particularly on the buffet.

"Is that a Morganton?" Shivers asked.

"Of course."

"Impressive. Where did the furniture come from?"

"Careful shopping and scavenging, my boy." In truth, the antiques represented Bannickburn's life savings. Since he couldn't put his money in a bank, he figured he might as well put it into functional form. Plus, it was much harder for people to walk off with a buffet than with a pile of cash.

Shivers and Bannickburn sat. Bannickburn would have offered to make tea, but his hot plate was broken. And he didn't have any tea.

"All right," he said. "What's this about Kader?"

"There are rumors going around about surveillance footage that's leaked out. Footage that links you to that Alex guy, shows you were in cahoots."

"Doesn't matter," Bannickburn replied quickly. "Kader doesn't know who I am. He only knows Miller."

"Well, that's the second part of the problem. Seems someone took a few pictures of you while you were being made up as Miller, and they plan to leak those to Kader."

"What?"

"Yeah, I know, it's incredible. But that's what's happening. Kader hasn't even seen any of this stuff yet, but he's on the warpath. He's issuing contracts on 'the guy with Alex in the surveillance footage.' And if he actually gets his hands on the footage . . ." Shivers shook his head, the front locks of his hair swaying gently. "Then you have real trouble."

"But this doesn't make any *sense*. Who would be taking pictures while I was getting made up?"

"I don't know, but it doesn't matter much, does it? The point is, you're in trouble. Lucky for you, I can help."

Then Bannickburn started to see. Slowly, everything started making more sense, and the bottom fell out of his stomach. He'd screwed this one up pretty good. The drops had been falling steadily, and he'd ignored them. And now he was about to go under.

"This is one of the things we specialize in," Shivers was saying. "Protection. We can take you in. Give you sanctuary from Kader. He doesn't want a mob war, either, so he's not going to come after you while we've got you. We can keep you safe."

Bannickburn nodded absently.

"We may be able to do more than that, even," Shivers said. "The footage isn't in Kader's hands yet. If we act quickly, we may be able to keep it that way. He'll still be mad, of course, but he won't have the proof he's looking for. That should help."

Of course he won't, Bannickburn thought. *He won't have it until you want him to, because you have it.* The only person who would have taken pictures when he was applying his disguises was someone looking for blackmail material for later. And there were plenty of Bigio people around when he was getting ready for the job.

"That's awfully generous of you," Bannickburn said aloud, trying not to let the anger show in his voice. "Go ahead and get the footage. Hold on to it. I approve."

Shivers sat silently in his chair. He ran his hand along the smooth upholstery. Then he just looked at Bannickburn, and smiled without warmth.

The two men stared silently at each other for a minute or two. Bannickburn was waiting for Shivers to go ahead and say what he was already thinking, to make the conditions more explicit. But, of course, Shivers didn't want that. It would work out best for Shivers if any ideas for what was going to happen next came straight from Bannickburn.

The elf wasn't worried about his safety yet. Sure, he knew at least five hit men living right here in this building, but the information Kader was acting on was too vague. For the moment, he was safe. He had no doubt that Shivers had inflated the danger so he could talk to Bannickburn alone.

But his relative safety was fragile. If he sent Shivers out of here unhappy, the situation would head downhill fast. Kader would probably have the footage in his hand, confirming Bannickburn's identity, within the hour.

He tried to wait Shivers out for another few minutes, but the mafioso remained resolutely silent. Finally, Bannickburn caved.

"You want me to come with you," he said.

"For your own good. Yeah."

"We'll just go to your house? Have a few drinks, then turn in?"

"My house isn't big enough or secure enough," Shivers said. "Sorry."

Bannickburn sighed. Shivers was going to make him guess every bit of what he was supposed to do.

He took another stab. "Bailey? I could stay with him."

"Bailey really doesn't like to have other people at his house." Shivers put a slight emphasis on the word "house." Bannickburn took that as a clue.

"His office, then. It seems pretty secure. He's got a nice couch in the reception area."

Shivers slapped his knee, putting on a show of approval. "Of *course*," he said with mock enthusiasm. "There's always some muscle there anyway. They could keep an eye on you. Bailey's office would be perfect."

Now for the part Bannickburn really didn't want to do. "It would be quite generous of Bailey to put me up there."

Shivers nodded gravely. "Yes. Yes it would."

"I'd like to repay his generosity, of course," Bannickburn said, then glanced around the storage unit. "Perhaps he'd like the buffet?"

Shivers didn't spare another glance for the buffet. "I'm sure he'd like it," he said. "But not for this particular favor."

"I could pay cash rent for the time I'm there."

Shivers shook his head gently.

"I could help out around the office."

Shivers cocked his head, pretending to think. "Hmmm. That might work. There might be a thing or two to do."

"I was thinking some secretarial work. Filing. Correspondence. That sort of thing."

"Think again."

All right, Bannickburn thought. *I know what they're after. I know what it'll take. All right.*

"Maybe I could go to the Tir for him."

Shivers stood up immediately. "About damn time you said it. Of course you could. Come on, let's go."

18

Bannickburn turned. He heard a leathery squeak. He almost drifted off again, but his shoulder was wedged underneath him at an uncomfortable angle.

This wasn't working. He rolled over onto his left side, and promptly got a face full of smooth leather. It pressed his nose flat and woke him up the rest of the way.

He sat up, rubbed his eyes, and looked around, trying to remember where he was. There was a large black desk. Behind the desk was a black chair, and on the chair was an ork leaning back with his feet on the desk. The ork wore a pinstriped gray suit with a white handkerchief. His feet were clad in enormous wingtips.

"Good morning," Kross said.

"Hello, Kross," Bannickburn said, stretching as he tried to remember why he was sleeping on someone's leather sofa.

Then it came to him, like a hangover when sunlight hits your eyes.

"I have good news for you," Kross said, though he didn't sound pleased to be delivering it.

"What's that?" Bannickburn said.

"Murson Kader has not yet managed to get his hands on the footage implicating you. As a result, his associates have told him to call off the hit he ordered, as the information in the contract is far too vague. For the moment, you're in the clear."

"What a surprise," Bannickburn said. "You work for an efficient organization."

Kross stood up, pulling on the lapels of his jacket to make them exactly even. "First, I don't work for the organization, I just often work *with* them. And second, yes, I work with an organization that knows how to get things done."

"Right." Bannickburn's voice sounded dead.

"I have another piece of good news for you," Kross said, sounding even more ill-tempered. "Sottocapo Martel has asked me to accompany you to Portland. I said I would."

Great, thought Bannickburn. *I get my own little spy to make the mission that much trickier.*

"I'm sure they'll love you in the Tir," he said aloud. "Immigration officials there are big fans of organized crime."

"I'm an ork," he said. "A meta. They'll like me more than they'd like the humans you surrounded yourself with on the Gates run."

Bannickburn snapped his fingers. "Right. Thanks for reminding me. They're the first matter of business today. Getting them on board."

"Why on earth do you need them?"

"I'm not going into the Tir alone." Bannickburn held up a hand before Kross could start to reply. "And I need more than you. Nothing personal."

The expression on Kross' face indicated that, despite Bannickburn's assurance, he thought it was quite personal indeed.

But then the ork shrugged. "Go ahead. Try to convince them. Not too many humans look forward to a visit to the Tir."

"I wasn't exactly looking forward to a visit to the Tir," Cayman said. "I got a nice haul—I can think of plenty of other places I'd rather spend it."

"This will be an even nicer haul," Bannickburn promised. "And an even better vacation."

The water of Pine Lake that lapped at the stones near their feet left a stain every time it receded, oil and mercury and substances better left unnamed forming a glistening trail on top of the rocks. A few residents of the Barrens had an ongoing contest to see who could survive the longest in the lake, with the current record of eighty-five seconds being held by a man with no fingers and toes who now spent his days in a small closet of the Body Mall rocking back and forth on his misshapen feet. Opinions differed as to whether he'd been that way before he set the record or not.

Bannickburn had talked to Spindle first. Then he talked to X-Prime, who had recovered completely from the dose of Cold Slab, and was back among the living. Both of them expressed interest in the money, disinterest in the Tir. Both of them left Bannickburn with the idea that if he could get the right team together, then maybe they'd consider going along, too. Bannickburn understood that Cayman would likely be a prime component of "the right team."

"I'm not looking for more at the moment," Cayman said. "The first mission's pay is plenty for the time being. You carry too much nuyen, you're just asking to get robbed."

"We can work that out. Jackie's quite adept at finding places to store money, even for poor SINless souls such as ourselves. The pay for this one's quite good—would buy you a fine vacation, indeed."

"Just doesn't sound like my kind of thing," Cayman said.

"But I need you," Bannickburn pressed. After the difficulty he had putting this team together in the first place, he'd be damned if he'd just let it fall by the wayside and start from scratch. "You sign on, I get Spindle and X-Prime, too. You're the key. If you're on, I've got all I need."

"Yeah, that's another thing. What do you need all

these people for? Spindle I can see, sure—you need a rigger to get you there and back, fine. But why me? You've got the ork for muscle already. And why Alex? You've seen pretty much the full range of the boy's limited skills, and it doesn't sound like you need them in the Tir. You go in, grab some water, get out. What do you need so many people for?"

Because I don't trust my bosses, Bannickburn thought. *Because I can't be sure if they're setting me up on this mission. Because if I don't trust them, I certainly can't trust their ork lackey to help me in a pinch.*

But he didn't say any of this. Telling Cayman that he was worried about a Mafia double cross would not be likely to persuade him to join in. He tried to think of something, anything to say to convince Cayman, but he had no real ideas.

Except one.

He exhaled for a long time, hoping maybe he could come up with another approach, hoping he wouldn't have to do what he'd just decided to do. But he had only the one idea, so Bannickburn reluctantly followed the path it laid out.

"You know I don't want to do the mission, right?" he said.

"So you've said."

"And I told you why I'm doing it anyway, right?

"The almighty persuasive powers of the mob. Yeah."

"What do you think happens if I fail on this?" Bannickburn asked.

"Your body ends up slowly floating toward the Pacific?"

"Yes, most likely. But what happens to you?"

Cayman furrowed his brow, and his mouth twisted in confusion. "To *me*? What would happen to me?"

"What do you think happens if I fail on this?"

"Mob ices you."

"Which one?"

Cayman looked puzzled. "Which one?" he repeated.

"Right. Which family?"

"Bailey's family. Bigios."

Bannickburn shook his head. "No. Since when did the Mafia get their own hands dirty on a job they could farm out to someone else? If I fail, all Bailey and Martel will do is turn over the footage of our activities at the casino. Then they'll let Kader and his Finnigan friends do the dirty work."

"Okay. So?"

"So they'll look at the footage carefully. They'll come after me, and anyone else they can implicate. They'll see you wheeling X-Prime out of the casino. They'll probably get footage of you with Prime the day before the run. They'll get me first, then they'll probably get Alex. Then you and Spindle. My neck's not the only one on the line here."

Cayman just glared. Bannickburn felt nauseous—he'd been angry when Shivers had blackmailed him into this job, and then he'd turned around and done the same thing to Cayman. Sometimes corruption was a slow creep, seeping from person to person. Other times it was a flash flood.

"I could handle it," Cayman finally said, fight burning in his eyes. "I've had plenty of people wanting to kill me. None of them have done it yet." He took a breath. "Prime couldn't, though. Kader would wave some fraggin' candy in his face and he'd follow him anywhere. They wouldn't ever find any *pieces* of the poor guy. So if this is the way it is, then I guess I'm coming with you."

Bannickburn fought the urge to let Cayman wriggle away, to acknowledge that this wasn't any way to start what could be a trying mission. But he needed help, and he didn't have time to find anyone else.

"Okay. Good. Thanks." Unsurprisingly, Cayman didn't say you're welcome.

The excitement of working for the mob had pretty much worn off. It hadn't helped Bannickburn that he'd just come from meeting with Twitch, Jackie's mage friend. The bastard had raised his prices on Bannickburn, gouging him mercilessly. He knew Bannickburn didn't have much choice. Bannickburn resolved, then and there, to stay away from other mages as much as possible. He'd find other ways.

Which brought him to his next errand. Bailey was, naturally, interested in seeing the mission succeed, so he'd put Bannickburn in touch with his best pharmacist. Bannickburn figured he'd come away with some valuable resources.

This was not the type of professional who put out a shingle and waited for business to show up. This was the sort of professional who sat behind an armored door flanked by two guards with big guns and clawed cyberlimbs. To get to the door, Bannickburn had entered an elevator in a one-hundred-fifty-year-old office building in Tacoma. He had to get into an elevator by himself—meaning he loitered awkwardly in the lobby as several unshaven, odiferous folks passed by him and gave him curious looks. Finally, when he had his chance, he jumped into an elevator car, let the door close and, as instructed, used his fingernail to rotate a keyhole that read BSMT ACCS. That got him down to the cellar.

Once there, he had to step gingerly past some commandingly large piles of rat droppings, through a narrow shuttered door wedged behind the building's boiler, and down a long corridor filled with echoing drops of water. Finally, the armored door was in front of him.

He smiled at the goons posted on either side of the door, but they gave no indication that they were aware of his presence. He shrugged and tapped on the narrow slot in the door.

He had to wait about a minute before the slot opened and a pair of bloodshot green eyes stared out at him. Or maybe they didn't—they didn't seem to actually focus on anything.

Bannickburn frowned at the eyes. He'd never liked the way red and green looked together.

"You Pharmley?"

"No. She's next door," the voice attached to the eyes said, then let out a long, high-pitched giggle.

Not a good sign, Bannickburn thought. Pharmacists who were too fond of their own product were not the most reliable chemists in the world.

Finally the woman stopped laughing at her own joke. "No, no, sorry. It's me. Yeah. I'm me. And you're what's-his-name, from Bailey. Banklebum. Balindrome. Blunderbuss."

"Yeah."

"You got money?"

Bannickburn waved a black credstick in front of the slot.

"Then you got me. What can I get for you?"

Bannickburn held a list in front of the slot. "These."

Two shaky fingers reached through the slot and pulled the list through. Pharmley went quiet, and Bannickburn saw her eyes looking down, doing her best to focus on what he'd written. Luckily, Bannickburn had been fore-warned and had written in large, clear print.

Still, it took quite a while for Pharmley to take in the whole list. Finally, she spoke. "Hey! Most of the things on this list are *illegal!*" Then she started to giggle again.

Bannickburn waited patiently, and finally Pharmley got serious.

"Okay, number one is no problem. There's a shortage of two—I'll have to ask for a little extra if you want that. Three, no can do. Just got trendy among some ork gangers, they're buying it faster than I can get it. Four, five six, sure, I can do for you, but you better know what you're doing with those because the side effects and af-tereffects are something wicked. Oh, and don't mix *any* of those. With *anything.*"

"Yeah, yeah."

"The rest of your list—what are you, dreaming? I haven't seen half of that stuff for most of a *decade.* And the other stuff is way too new and hot to be available to schlubs like you. But nice try."

"I figured I'd take a shot." Actually, getting five of the first six on his list was far better than he'd thought he'd be able to do. He'd be going into this run well equipped. Sure, he'd be about a tenth as powerful as he was at his prime, but the important thing was, he'd have a bigger bag of tricks available than he had *now*.

He hoped he wouldn't need it. He had a good team, he had some hopefully unsuspecting dupes just waiting to have a bottle of water snatched from them, and he had a quick way to get in and out. Piece of cake.

Except Bailey had threatened his life to get him to do this job. And was willing to pay him far more than he had for the Kader job. Bannickburn was still a relative novice in working with the mob, but he was pretty sure they didn't do those kinds of things for milk runs.

19

Appropriately, they would start their journey at Port Gamble. Across Puget Sound from Seattle, Port Gamble was Salish-Shidhe territory, but it was an easily overlooked town. Bremerton was bigger, Belfair got more traffic and lived richly off the proceeds from equipment seized at the checkpoint just to the south, but not much happened at Port Gamble. Not even gambling.

They took a ferry across the sound before dawn, once again taking advantage of Bailey's numerous contacts. The boat ride wasn't long, but there was at least enough time for the skipper, Bluebeard, to relate his tale of woe.

"I liked Bailey. I always considered him a pal. I still do, really—look at what he set me up with. There's this boat, and he sends lubbers like you to me lots of times, so I still make a living. But I was doing better, once. Quinn was just a little guy back then, barely got made, and he let me run with him. I'd do anything for him. He usually used me as eyes, running around, telling him what I saw, giving him the heads-up on danger. We got through plenty—once stole a pile of orichalcum out from under the nose of this ugly troll mage. Wouldn't have happened without me—I was the one that told Quinn when the stupid troll was getting drowsy.

"But then he took me out on a run once—three in the morning, just like now. And I wasn't on my game.

Yeah, I admit it. I screwed up. I was watching the perimeter while Bailey was working on a safe, and I let someone by. I saw his back, and he was heading for where Quinn was working, I tried to get there to warn him, but I was too slow. Guy put a bullet in poor Quinn's back. Good thing he was armored up.

"Well, a lot happened then, but we got away. I was just happy to be alive, but Quinn wasn't. Once we were safe, he turned on me, fast like a cobra. His thumb went for my eye. 'That's for not being watchful.' Then he whipped out his gun, made a line of shots just below my knee. 'That's for being slow.' 'Course, they had to cut the whole thing off right after.

"Yeah, I know I should be mad. But I done him wrong—don't he have a right to punish me for it? And look at how he treated me afterward. He saw me with my eye patch—couldn't afford a new eye—and with my prosthetic, a thing barely more than a peg leg, and he smiled that smile of his, and he said, 'You know what you look like now, Blue? You look like a pirate.' And he set me up with my boat then and there.

"So he's strict, yeah—I guess you could even say he's ruthless—but he takes care of his people, don't he?"

Yeah, Bannickburn thought. *He takes care of people, all right.* Bailey just couldn't resist using this pathetic old sailor as a sad object lesson—a way to slip in one more warning before Bannickburn and his team headed out.

The boat chugged along, churning up enough water that Bannickburn was convinced every border patrol boat in the Sound would be on their tail. But he kept a regular watch as he leaned on a rusty rail on the starboard side, and he saw no trace of any boats. The bright lights of Seattle dominated his vision, flashing and sparkling even at this distance. The city seemed to suck in light from everything around it, leaving it gleaming in the middle of a dark void. Bannickburn felt a strange sensation in his gut as he watched the lights shrink, and he realized that even though he'd only be gone for a day or so, he'd miss the city. He'd spent most of his time there living in a room meant for packing crates, not humans; he'd been quite poor and often hungry; and quality cigars were tough to find and even more difficult to afford. But he had started to like the fragging place anyway.

He decided he'd be better off looking at Port Gamble, ahead. Not that there was anything to see. A few lights cut through the darkness, but there were no headlights of moving traffic, no blinking signs in front of a restaurant or club. It looked phenomenally boring, which made it perfect.

Bluebeard followed Bannickburn's gaze. "We'll head a little west of the town. There's a beach, rocky, ramps right up to a little meadow. There's a dirt road there, kind of—not much, but a few worn, parallel tire tracks. Should be enough."

"Spindle tells me she can go over any surface except water and possibly lava. The road should be fine."

"Okay. Our approach will be pretty slow. I'll cut the engine and we'll drift in."

Bannickburn nodded. He'd get to spend about twenty minutes on a dark boat watching for Salish patrols as he drifted into a useless, mostly empty town. Ah, the glamorous life.

"Gun it," X-Prime said.

"Shut up," Spindle said.

"Gun it!"

"Can it!" she snapped.

"I want to *move!*" he whined.

Bannickburn cringed. He was sitting next to Spindle in the front of the van. On the bench behind him were Kross and Jackie, while X-Prime and Cayman occupied the back bench. If the ork didn't rip the kid's head off before they reached Shelton, it would be a minor miracle.

"If you don't shut up, I'm coming back there and helping the ork rip you in two," Cayman said. X-Prime went quiet, but Bannickburn glanced back and saw a

small smile tugging at one corner of his mouth. Bannickburn fervently hoped the younger man would find some
other way to amuse himself on the journey besides baiting Cayman.

The van crept over the loose stones, quietly moving
farther inland. The outside of the van was beautiful—a
black paint job that seemed to suck in light at nighttime,
moving across the land like a dark stain. During the day,
it reflected enough light to give the paint a greenish
tinge—it would blend in well in a forest or even tall
grass. At least, as well as a Land Rover van could blend
in anywhere. And Spindle assured Bannickburn that the
van's concealment abilities were more than skin deep,
with a fine set of electronic warfare devices that let it
see things far more often than anything could see it.

The unfortunate tradeoff for the high level of con-
cealability was the lack of windows. Plugged into her
vehicle with its many small cameras, Spindle had a full
range of vision, but the five passengers could only look
forward—unless they were content to eye the ripped upholstery of the van's interior.

The inside of the van was nowhere near as immaculate
as the outside. Spindle's chair was in fine shape, covered
in brown leather a shade lighter than the rest of the
seats. It clearly had been reupholstered recently, while
the other seats were left to rot. X-Prime kept shifting
on his bench to avoid being stabbed by a loose spring
beneath him.

There wasn't much to do inside the vehicle, and, despite X-Prime's whining, the van still crawled at about
thirteen kilometers per hour. Bannickburn decided it
was time for a distraction.

"All right," he announced. "I'm starting a pool. Fifty
nuyen for anyone who wants in. Person who makes the
best guess about why Martel wants a bottle of water
wins the pot. You can talk among yourselves, but you
can only make one official bet. When you're ready, hand
over your cash and make your wager. I'll keep track of

the winner." He waved his hand with a small royal flourish. "That's all."

Kross folded his arms and frowned, apparently not thrilled with the topic. The others in the van, though, seemed already deep in thought.

X-Prime snapped his fingers. "Tir Tairngire mountain spring water," he said. "Best tasting water in the world. Never exported. Who *wouldn't* want a bottle?"

"For what he's paying us?" Cayman scoffed. "Please."

"Blood of a flesh-form insect spirit," Jackie said. "Blood ritual drek. That's worth plenty of cash."

"Is that clear?" X-Prime said. "I thought bug blood was kind of white and milky."

"Maybe it's bug plasma," Jackie said.

"Ew, gross," X-Prime said.

"But possible," she said, and the others nodded slowly.

Bannickburn decided to throw out one of his own. "A sample of water from the Mediterranean. So Martel can uncork it and enjoy the pleasant aromas of southern Italy whenever he wants."

Everyone in the van—even Spindle, who was mostly wrapped up in driving—scoffed and jeered. Bannickburn just smiled.

"Maybe it's not the water he's after," Cayman suggested. "Maybe it's the bottle. Could be the base is a gemstone. Could even have a microchip embedded in it. Could be almost anything."

"I'm afraid we can't count 'almost anything' as an official guess," Bannickburn said. "Too vague."

X-Prime tapped his index fingers together, still working on a solution. "Okay, so we know how much it's worth to Martel. We figure if he thinks he can sell it, he'll get more than he's paying us. We don't know how much profit he's expecting, but we can make a reasonable guess. Twenty percent wouldn't be out of line for a retailer, but I'd expect Martel to be looking at getting at least a fifty percent markup."

Bannickburn shot a look at Cayman, and the big man, hunched awkwardly on his bench, shrugged. "Finances and accounting," he said. "You finally got the boy in an area he actually knows something about."

Jackie was looking at X-Prime thoughtfully, though she might have been looking past him to a piece of shredded gray fabric dangling from the ceiling.

"You may know the value Martel puts on it," she said slowly, "but I'll tell you something—pretty soon, the value of that bottle's going to go up."

"What do you mean?" Bannickburn asked.

Jackie flicked her eyes quickly toward Kross, a move so fast the ork didn't notice it. But Bannickburn did. *Right,* he thought. *Can't talk freely with the spy sitting right there.* It would have to wait.

Bannickburn let half an hour go by, to avoid raising Kross' suspicions. They skirted south by southwest on small roads, occasionally passing another car, but most of the time not seeing anyone. Just the way the route was supposed to be.

After he thought enough time had passed, Bannickburn stretched his arms and yawned.

"That's it," he said. "I can't nap while I'm upright like this. I want a bench. Who wants the front?"

Kross, Cayman, and X-Prime all shot their arms into the air. Cayman's calloused hand went up so fast it banged into the van's ceiling. A few pieces of disintegrated foam insulation drifted onto his head.

Bannickburn looked at X-Prime and Cayman. "The only way one of you can come up is if the other will let me rest my legs on him," he said.

The two men exchanged a glance, with Cayman looking particularly unhappy. Then they looked at Bannickburn and shook their heads.

"I guess the ork gets the front."

Bannickburn quickly settled in next to Jackie, resting his head on her shoulder, partly for comfort, partly to be able to talk quietly to her.

"Have I ever told you how much I admire those twin

pools of wonder that are known as your eyes?" he asked.

"Have I ever told you that you talk like a bad trid romance?" she returned.

"Ah, but how else am I to talk when confronted with the miracle, the glory that is *you*." Bannickburn continued on in this way for a time, doing his best to discourage Kross from any attempted eavesdropping. It seemed to work—after a good ten minutes, the ork was slumped in his seat, breathing evenly, either asleep or on the verge of it.

"Okay," Bannickburn said. "I think we can talk. How's the value of the bottle going to go up?"

"Who are we taking the bottle from?" she asked.

"Some Finnigans," Bannickburn replied. "Or at least, some people working for the Finnigans."

"Right. So we go in and take it from them, which means they no longer have it, even though they want it. And once we've got it, we're transporting it back to Seattle to other people who want it, but until we get there, haven't got it, either.

"We'll have a couple hours in the van," she continued, "and in that time we'll have something that the two most powerful mob families in Seattle want but don't have. I'd say that makes the value of that bottle go up considerably. Now, let's say we use our time wisely on the drive, and we talk with representatives from each family, and we tell them what's what."

Bannickburn saw it now. "We make it clear that we know both sides want it," he said. "We tell them that one family's going to get the bottle, the other isn't. We start a bidding war. We clean up."

"We might," Jackie agreed. "But there's a risk. We're doing this to try to keep the Mafia from killing you. We play the families off each other, we might just be giving them extra incentive to do away with you, and fast. A little extra cash is nice, but not that useful if we're dead."

"They won't kill us while we have the water," Bannickburn said confidently. "They won't want to risk losing it."

"And after we sell it to one or the other? Doesn't the loser come after us?"

Bannickburn chewed on his lower lip. "That could be a problem," he admitted.

"Yeah."

Bannickburn shifted his head a little, looking out the front window, watching the side of the road where black trees whizzed by in front of a black sky.

There had to be a way to turn this around, he thought. To get back in control of the situation.

"We need to know what the water is," he said. "Why it's important. When we know that, we may figure out the best way to use whatever it is. Get both families off our backs. But we'll need to know what it is before we get back to Seattle. Got any ideas on how we could get some analysis done on the fly?"

Jackie snorted quietly. "Of course. Been thinking of that since the moment you dragged me into this."

"Dragged? Didn't you volunteer?"

"For the fun part. Not for the running-into-the-lair-of-psychotic-elves part."

"Oh. Right. Well, the point is, you're thinking about it."

"Right."

"Good." He felt himself growing drowsy. Spindle was in complete control of the van, and Bannickburn wouldn't be needed until the Tir border—assuming they didn't run into unfriendly Salish authorities. But they could wake him up if they needed to. He could sleep now, and when he woke up, he could take the first steps toward getting his life back.

20

Poor Slidestream, Bailey thought. The boy really had done some nice work for him. Most of the equipment Bailey had on his desk—the stuff that allowed Bailey to keep track of the fifteen thousand things he needed to worry about at the moment—was from Slidestream. The kid had some real talent. Just no discipline.

Bailey wasn't the most rigorously disciplined person on the planet himself, but he knew how to get things done. He had to. Without any innate talents, aside from being a champion bulldrekker, he needed to compensate. Maybe that was why he'd been so harsh with poor Slidestream—he knew how much talent the boy had. If Bailey possessed that much ability, there'd be no telling how far he'd go with it, instead of scrambling for every little thing, spinning twelve plates at a time like some poor schlub he'd once seen on a terrible black-and-white 2-D video. People like Slidestream didn't realize what they had. They just coasted along, thinking everything in life would come to them as easily as their talent did.

Perhaps he should have recorded Slidestream's demise. It would make a fine cautionary tale on the dangers of sloppiness.

"Would you be inspired by a trideo of a man having his brain roasted from the inside?" he said.

Shivers didn't move. He sat in one of Bailey's thickly

padded chairs, right ankle on left knee, hands clasped near his stomach. He had been watching Bailey all night.

"Depends," Shivers said. "Inspired to get revenge on someone? Maybe. Inspired to go get some dinner? Probably not."

"Inspired to work harder," Bailey said. "To make more of yourself."

"You want to make a motivational trideo where a guy gets his brain cooked?" Shivers said. His expression remained blank, but his tone was heavily skeptical. "I don't know. Aztechnology might use it."

Bailey nodded. "That they might. That they might." Then he waved his hand. "Ah, it's no matter. I missed my opportunity to make such a recording, and probably won't have another in the near future. It's a shame, but there it is. Oh, well."

Bailey then slowly, exaggeratedly, turned his head to look at the clock on his desk. He did his best to make his eyes bug out like a cartoon character's. "My! Will you look at that! Did you have any idea it was getting so late? *I* certainly didn't. Time to turn in—or at least time to head out of the office and tie one on, don't you think?"

"Go ahead," Shivers said. "I think I'll just stay here. I'll be waiting when you get back."

Bailey sighed. It had been like this all night. Shivers had arrived six hours ago, towing along several well-armed, heavily scarred individuals who had made Bailey's receptionist ask to go home that very minute. Shivers' friends, as far as Bailey knew, had been camped out in the reception area ever since, keeping a close eye on Bailey's regular muscle. The two camps were ostensibly engaged in a standoff, each preventing the other from causing a problem, but the situation didn't seem overly tense—Bailey had heard them start rolling dice about three hours ago.

The interlopers served their purpose, though, by making sure Bailey couldn't forcibly eject Shivers. However friendly the standoff was, it was still an aggressive move by the younger man. Bailey had something Shivers wanted, and Shivers was willing to use the threat of violence (and, if it came to it, actual violence) to get it.

Over the course of the evening, Bailey had carefully reviewed the pros and cons of simply shooting Shivers in the head and being done with the whole situation, and so far the cons had won out. The biggest pros were that Bailey could finally leave his office, and the secrets he was trying to conceal would remain hidden. The cons were that Shivers' friends were likely to retaliate swiftly, and that Martel seemed to like Shivers and might not react well to Bailey simply offing him in a fit of pique. Besides, for all Shivers' icy manners, Bailey kind of liked him, too. He recognized a high level of skill and intelligence in the boy, even if Shivers didn't have the grace to laugh at Bailey's jokes.

So they were stuck here, together, with Bailey making constant remarks about Shivers leaving and Shivers deflecting them. Bailey desperately wanted to get about his business—to at least check on the progress of Kross and his cohort—but he couldn't as long as Shivers was there. He didn't want the merest hint of this particular mission drifting toward Shivers—he might like the boy, but that didn't keep him from seeing the predator in him.

"On second thought," Bailey said, "why go out when I can enjoy a fine meal here? I'll just put in a quick call to Rivelli's."

"Make mine veal parmesan," Shivers said.

"I don't recall inviting you to have dinner with me."

"No, you didn't. But if you don't order for me, I'll just call as soon as you're done and place my own order. Thought it would be more efficient to do it in one call instead of two."

Bailey sighed. This really was too much. The first thing he'd do tomorrow is change his security protocol—next time, Shivers would have to leave his friends outside the fragging building. The second thing he'd do tomorrow is work on a detailed plan for paying Shivers back for his insolence. Hopefully, by the end of the day tomorrow,

Bannickburn would be back, water in hand, and Bailey would be in Martel's good graces. That might give him more leeway to teach Shivers a lesson.

"I hope I'm not keeping you from getting things done," Shivers said after the food had been ordered. "If you're here so late, I imagine you have important things to do."

"I imagine I do," Bailey replied flatly. "Unfortunately, the things I'd most like to be doing are things that are best done without other people in the office."

"Really? Why's that?"

"Jimmy, please. Lots of people in the world can get away with acting stupid, but it's not convincing on you."

"Fair enough. It's like this, Quinn. I know you're working on something. I know it's something important to Martel. I want to know what it is, and I'm going to find out. One way or another."

"You are? God, I admire that sort of manly confidence. Are you dating anyone right now?"

"Shut up. Best thing you could do right now is tell me what you know. Not only do you get your office back, but you get me as a friend."

"A friend?" Bailey pouted. "But I wanted you to be so much *more* that that."

Shivers ignored him. "I could help you out. Make sure whatever's going on succeeds. Make sure Martel's impressed."

"Make sure you take plenty of credit for yourself," Bailey added.

"It's your choice. I'm going to find out, one way or another. And I'm ready to stay here all night, if I need to. Take the easy way out. Just tell me what's going on."

Bailey smiled. He didn't say anything. He just grinned. It had taken a long time, but the night had finally turned in his favor. It shouldn't have taken as long as it did, but times were busy—extra help wasn't always immediately available. But it had finally arrived.

The call to Rivelli's had been a ruse, Bailey's order part of a long-established code. The response on the other end told him that the help he needed was available. A mage had been dispatched—a mage who knew how to quickly and effectively put a group of people to sleep.

Part of Bailey wanted to point out to Shivers the clue that told him his mage had come through. But a bigger part of him wanted to smile irritatingly at Shivers until Shivers finally figured out what was going on. He deliberately pushed the corners of his mouth deeper into his cheeks, forming the smirk he'd first perfected in adolescence.

"What?" Shivers asked. Bailey didn't respond.

Shivers sat up straighter in his chair, planting both feet on the ground. He looked around the room cautiously, as if he expected a third party to leap out at him. Nothing happened. He looked back at Bailey; Bailey was careful to make sure his smirk appeared exactly the same.

"What?" Shivers asked. Again, Bailey didn't say anything, but he cocked his head slightly, as if listening for something.

Shivers caught on immediately. "Dice!" he said. He'd finally noticed the complete lack of sound from the reception area. He jumped to his feet and ran to the door, but froze before grabbing the knob. He turned slowly to Bailey.

"What happens if I open this door?"

Bailey furrowed his brow. "Hmmm . . . I believe you enter the reception area. If I remember correctly."

Shivers took a step back. "Get over here. Open the door."

Bailey leaned back in his chair, feeling happier than he had in hours. "James, you weren't in a position to give me any orders before, and you *really* aren't in such a position now. But, to show there are no hard feelings between us, I'll go ahead and open the door for you."

Bailey slowly sauntered over to the door, then pulled it open. His two thugs stood there, arms crossed, looking stern, but with their weapons holstered.

"You see, James? No one had any intention of hurting anyone. Stephen and Bruce there were just going to escort you out. That's all."

Behind them, the reception area was empty. There was no sign of Shivers' friends.

"Where did they go?" Shivers demanded. "What did you do to them?"

"Such accusations. It's late, James. Your friends were tired after a long night of gambling with Stephen and Bruce. I imagine they went somewhere to catch a few winks."

Shivers leaned closer to Bailey. "*Where* do you imagine they went?"

Bailey sighed. "I'm sure they were quite tired. It's possible they stumbled out the door of this building and fell right asleep in the nearby alley. If I were you, I would look for them there."

Shivers glared at Stephen and Bruce, then at Bailey. None of them seemed at all taken aback. Knowing he was outnumbered, Shivers stomped off. Bailey heard the echo of his footsteps until Shivers was down the stairs and out of the building.

He turned to Stephen and Bruce. "Thank you, gentlemen. Let's be sure to have a chat tomorrow about ways we can avoid having me held prisoner in my office for six hours while you play dice with my captors, hmmm?" Bailey smiled, knowing the two men would see right through his pleasant tones. They knew the meeting tomorrow would likely be quite painful for them. Most likely, neither of them would show, and Bailey wouldn't see either of them again. Which was probably the healthiest choice they could make.

Bailey went back into his office. By now, Shivers would have found his friends lying in an ungainly pile of ugly muscle. He'd find them quite unwakeable for at least three hours, by which time Bailey planned to be long gone. If this night had taught him anything, it was that he should do the rest of his work on this project from a more secure location.

He turned on his desktop screen for a quick look-see. The last he'd seen, Bannickburn's team had been approaching Bluebeard's ferry. *Good old Bluebeard*, Bailey thought. There was someone who, ever since the unpleasantness many years ago, had showed an extraordinary amount of discipline and loyalty. It was good to see someone learn from experience.

The tracking map showed that Bannickburn's team had made good progress and were approaching the Tir Tairngire border. *That should keep them amused*, he thought.

He wondered what they were doing in the van. Not much, he guessed. The euphoria of setting out on the journey had probably faded during the slow journey on Bluebeard's boat. Now they'd be impatient for action to start—until the really heavy fire came down, and they'd start wishing for inaction and boredom again.

He hoped Kross would call in soon. He felt better knowing what was going on, even though the whole run was pretty much out of his control. Getting regular reports made him *feel* like he was in control, and sometimes that was about as good as the real thing.

But if he was going to take a call from Kross, he needed to be somewhere else. Somewhere Shivers couldn't find him. He shut down his office terminal and scurried out the door.

After Bailey exited the building, he passed Shivers, who had found his lackeys. Bailey was inordinately pleased with the way Shivers' normally smooth red locks were hanging in his face, heavy with sweat, as Shivers tried to drag his motionless friends into the back of a pickup truck.

Bailey smiled and waved as he walked by. *It's always nice,* he thought, *when you can salvage a bad evening with a wonderful ending*.

21

The grass really was greener on the other side of the fence. The trees were taller, the blossoms brighter, and the water of the Columbia River, Bannickburn thought, was cleaner and cooler than any other river in the world.

The people across the border were, techically, his people. His elven brothers. He was supposed to have a kinship with them, or something. But they creeped him out—at least, the ones in the Tirs did. Their high degree of comfort with overly strong monarchs, their preference for their green meadows over the beauty of urban grime, their distance from the rest of the world all combined to make him want to stay well away from the Tirs whenever possible. So naturally, fate conspired to send him to this one.

Portland would be okay, though. It was a city. It was pretty open to foreign traffic. It had races in it besides elves. Sure, it had martial law, but that was the least that could be expected in a Tir.

The checkpoint before the bridge over the Columbia was, as expected, nearly empty of traffic at this time of the morning. As Spindle's van sped toward the gate, Bannickburn could see a number of lights starting to flash, and he could dimly hear the alarm bells that accompanied them. Their cargo—plenty of weapons, Jackie's deck, and a few other goodies—had already been detected. Hopefully, in a few moments none of that would matter.

Bannickburn had moved back to the front passenger seat, so the first thing the surprisingly amiable border guard saw when the van's window rolled down was two elves smiling at him.

"Welcome to Portland," the guard said. "I'm afraid our sensors have detected numerous restricted materials in your vehicle. I'm going to have to ask you to pull over to the right, to that small gray building. You'll be given further instructions there."

Pulling over to the inspection station would mean the discovery and likely confiscation of a number of precious goods. Peeling away from the gate without submitting to the inspection would mean an immediate hail of bullets flying into the van, along with a wreck-vehicle spell or two from the security mages. Neither option was attractive, which left them option number three.

Spindle smiled, which would have been quite charming, had Tir Tairngire border guards been susceptible to that sort of thing.

"That's not necessary," she said. She waved a credstick in front of the guard's face. "Just give this a quick scan, would you?"

The guard looked at the stick for five seconds before taking it and disappearing back into his little kiosk. Verification took barely longer than the time he'd spent staring at the item.

The upper half of the guard reappeared as he leaned out of the kiosk, credstick in his outstretched hand. "Thank you very much, ma'am," he said. "Proceed on your way."

Spindle nodded gratefully and drove ahead.

The credstick identified the bearer as a corporate security officer for Mustaffah Cartage, a small shipping business that moved precious cargo in heavily armored vehicles across Portland. Mustaffah Cartage was a small gem in the vast corporate treasury held by Kate Mustaf-

fah, and that was what helped Spindle's van get through
security—the Mustaffah name carried a lot of weight
in Portland.

The best thing about the ID, which Jackie had provided, was that it was entirely legitimate. Jackie had
picked it up two years ago—compensation from an elf
who was running out of resources to pay Jackie for certain favors, but who couldn't yet afford to do without
her services. Though of limited use—Mustaffah Cartage
only operated in Portland, so using the ID anyplace else
got you exactly nothing—Jackie had held onto the ID,
knowing that getting a free pass into Portland would
prove useful sometime. Bannickburn didn't have to turn
around to know that she had a cocky grin on her face.
There were few things she liked better than gliding past
tight security.

Once through the gate, they drove south past the airport. As far as Bannickburn could tell, Spindle was the
only living driver on the highway. Plenty of drone vans
trundled here and there, moving between the airport and
the numerous warehouses and industrial buildings that
surrounded it, but that was about all the traffic. They
passed windowless building after windowless building,
and before long came to the exit they wanted, which put
them right in the middle of the area that held plenty of
goods but few people.

As they drove by the massive warehouses, Bannickburn could almost feel the magic energy protecting the
merchandise inside. Thankfully, the bottle of water
wasn't behind any of those doors, so he wouldn't have
to figure out how to counter those particular spells.

Spindle led them east a little to the Maywood Park
neighborhood. With the nearby highway, airport, and
Columbia River, Maywood Park held more industry and
warehouses than anything else. It had a lonely feel, making it the ideal place for people like Bannickburn and
his team.

On the surface, the neighborhood looked harmless—
block after block of sturdy brick buildings. The occa-

sional windows were intact. He saw a few signs of neglect—tree roots buckling the sidewalks, ivy covering entire buildings, roofs that lost shingles every time the wind blew—but these were minor. It actually seemed far too nice, and Bannickburn began to think the stories he'd heard about the place were inaccurate. Or maybe they were in the wrong spot.

Spindle pulled her van to the side of the road and, with a sigh, turned it off.

"Ready for a break?" Bannickburn asked.

"No," she said flatly. "This is what I do. If I'm not doing this . . . well, it's what I'm comfortable doing."

"So it's a shame to have to stop," Bannickburn said. "Believe me, I understand."

He turned to the other four members of the team, all of whom were asleep. He thought about waking them all with a quick yell, but the only ones he needed at the moment were Kross and Cayman. He shook Kross, Kross shook Cayman, and the three of them walked out of the van.

"Keep an eye on things here," he said to Spindle as he walked away.

"Always," she said, and she stayed plugged into her van.

It was nice having Kross and Cayman walk behind him, and Bannickburn felt quite powerful. Kross was about the same height as Bannickburn, but carried an extra twenty-five kilos of muscle, while Cayman had at least an extra quarter meter of height. Having these two in tow made it clear that Bannickburn was someone to be reckoned with. Sure, once upon a time he hadn't needed any support to appear powerful or intimidating, but now he'd take what he could get.

They walked up to a yellow brick apartment building, one of the area's few residences. Up close, more wear was evident—the mortar between the bricks had disintegrated in many places, leaving gaping holes. An old buzzer system had once existed near the door, but the cover had been pulled off, most of the buttons removed,

and what few names were displayed probably belonged
to people who hadn't lived in the building for more than
a decade. The whole system was made obsolete by the
fact that the dented metal door wouldn't close enough
to lock.

Bannickburn shoved the door. It opened with a
screech and a scrape. He walked through, and suddenly
understood what he'd heard about the people who now
lived in Maywood Park. The smell of urine—some fresh,
some stale—assaulted his nose. A long fluorescent light
bulb swung uneasily in its fixture, buzzing as it flickered
on and off. Layer upon layer of graffiti covered any trace of
the hall's original paint. Farther down the hallway, an
obscenely large rat—a creature that could have held its
own against a bull terrier—scurried into the middle of
the corridor, stopped, gave them a good long stare, then
casually continued on its way. Should it get hungry, it
had a full complement of insects to choose from on the
building's walls and floors.

Kross stepped on one of the resident beetles. The loud
crunch echoed down the hall. His foot made an audible
slurp as he removed it from the floor. Bannickburn
cringed.

"Where are we supposed to be going?" he asked.

Cayman checked a piece of paper he was carrying—
before he fell asleep in the van, he had regaled Bannickburn with a long discourse on the untrustworthiness of
cyberdecks and all related electronic devices. "Second
floor," he said. "Number 216."

"Stairs better not be wooden," Kross grunted.
"They'll have been eaten by termites or burned for heat
long ago, and we'll have to fly up."

"We'll just grab the elf and throw him up," Cayman
said with a grin, and both of the bigger men smiled.
Bannickburn, who wasn't used to being the smallest in
a group, only managed a thin grin.

Thankfully, the stairs were concrete, and though badly
crumbled, they were still climbable. The three men ascended to the second floor.

Apartment 216 was the third door on their right. Bannickburn approached the door, then thought better of it and stepped back.

"I guess we shouldn't knock first," he said.

"Got that right," Cayman said. "You want to do the honors?" he asked Kross.

The ork responded by cocking his fist and slamming it into the door. The hinges held, but the wood shredded with a brittle crunch and fell in front of them. Kross and Cayman charged ahead, reducing the door to narrow, dry slats. Kross went right, Cayman left, while Bannickburn strolled in after them.

The apartment, such as it was, was a charred mess. Ragged, burned curtains dangled in front of open windows, dropping new pieces of black fabric with each gust of wind. There was no furniture.

"Here! Here!" Cayman yelled. Kross sprinted behind Bannickburn, and the elf turned to follow.

At the end of a short corridor was a small room, somewhat less damaged than the front room. The bare, water-stained mattress on the floor indicated that this was a bedroom. A woman with knobby knees poking out from under a long T-shirt huddled in a corner, apparently trying to back away from Cayman while clawing her eyes out.

"She's on something," Cayman said.

"You don't say," Bannickburn replied.

"Should I get her hands off her eyes?"

"Only if she needs to be able to see to tell us what we need."

"What are we supposed to get out of her, anyway? Coherence isn't her strong suit at the moment."

"We need to find out where Spargoyle is. Hold on." Bannickburn walked up to the bony woman and reached out toward her shoulder. She screamed, and he jerked his hand back.

"Where's Spargoyle?" he asked.

The woman gibbered, but didn't make any sound that seemed like language.

"Where's Spargoyle?" he asked again.

"Is that all you've got?" Kross asked.

"Do you have any other ideas?" Bannickburn shot back.

Kross thought. "Did we bring any useful pharmaceuticals?"

Bannickburn had, in fact, brought several useful drugs, but he hadn't revealed their existence to anyone else on the team. He was saving them for an emergency, and, at the moment, this didn't qualify.

He reached out his hand once more, but made sure not to come close enough to the woman to set her off again. "Come here," he said. "Come here, let me help you." The woman whimpered a little, but her gaze was fixed on Bannickburn's hand. "Come on," he said.

She reached out her own hand, tentative and shaking. Bannickburn remained steady.

She touched his hand, her grip cold and unsteady. Bannickburn gently closed his hand around hers, lifted her to her feet and led her forward a step or two. Then another. Finally, she was on the floor just in front of the mattress.

"Sit down," he said. She whimpered again, but listened. She sat.

Bannickburn squatted next to her. "Okay. You're doing fine. I just need to ask you one thing. Where's Spargoyle?"

The woman screamed again, the force of her voice sending Bannickburn stumbling backward. She leaped to her feet, turned, and ran to the corner of the room, bumping her head on the wall. Then she dropped into a crouch and huddled, trembling, in the corner.

For the first time, they saw the back of the shirt. Someone had written on it with a firm black marker. It said SPARGOYLE, 315 COMET TRAIL.

"I think we can find him at 315 Comet Trail," Bannickburn said.

"I guess Spargoyle wanted her to be able to find him," Kross said. "For some reason."

"Yeah," Cayman said as the three of them made their way out. "Too bad she put the shirt on backwards."

At least fifty people were in the room, but very few of them were actually *there*. Lights flashed, heavy bass shook the wooden floor, and the recorded voice of an ork howled unintelligible lyrics at a deafening volume, but none of it was really necessary. From narcotics to BTL chips to just plain alcohol, all the patrons of Club Morningstar had found something to erase their consciousness for a few hours. People lolled in chairs, staring at the walls, or at their hands, or at nothing at all.

They had traveled to the address on the T-shirt, only to find an old woman who was unable to speak without shouting. She had spent a good ten minutes running through an extensive list of unprintable insults before she calmed down long enough for them to tell her why they were there. Once they mentioned Spargoyle's name, she came up with an entirely new batch of scathing abuse, then told them he was probably at Club Morningstar. As soon as she said this, Bannickburn and his team slowly backed away from the woman and got the hell out of there.

And now they'd found the club. The good news was, if Spargoyle was here, he'd be easy to find, and would be in no condition to attempt to run away from them. The bad news was, if he was here, he most likely wouldn't be ready to speak coherently for an hour or two.

Bannickburn, still with Cayman and Kross in tow, approached the only reasonably sober person in the place—the bartender.

"What'll it be?" the bartender asked.

"I need to ask you something," Bannickburn said, screaming to be heard over the noise of thrash metal.

The bartender's glare hardened. "What'll it be?" he repeated.

Bannickburn sighed. *Oh well*, he thought. He'd add the cost of the drinks to the mission's expenses. "Guinness. A pint for each of us." Cayman and Kross smiled at Bannickburn's unexpected generosity and quickly dropped onto some bar stools. The seats wobbled precariously beneath them.

The bartender pulled the pints like an amateur, barely generating any froth on top. Bannickburn rolled his eyes, but was comforted by the fact that a nonfoamy Guinness was still a Guinness.

He took a long sip to assure the bartender he wasn't ordering drinks frivolously, then got back to his real reason for being there.

"Is Spargoyle here tonight?" he yelled.

"Who?" the bartender replied.

"Spargoyle!" Bannickburn screamed. He could feel his vocal cords shredding.

The bartender scratched his temple with his index finger, leaving a smudge of dirt on his head. Bannickburn looked distastefully at his ale, hoping the drink hadn't come in direct contact with any part of the bartender.

"He's been here tonight," the bartender said. "I seen him. But I don't know if he's still around."

"Okay. Thanks." He grabbed his pint, and motioned for the other two to follow him.

They wandered the club, looking for someone who fit the loose description they had of Spargoyle. It came from the old lady who had sent them to the club, something she screamed at them as they were backing away from her.

"Ugly son of a slitch!" she said. "Looks just like his name! Horned bastard." That was all they had to go on, but Bannickburn figured the "horned" part of the description would be enough.

It was. He was on the club's small second floor, slumped against a railing overlooking the main floor. As the old lady had said, he looked just like his name. Bannickburn guessed he had started life as a dwarf, but had gone through innumerable surgeries and procedures to get the look he wore today. His skin was stone gray (dermal sheath, most likely), he had two short horns protruding from his thick brow, and the black shorts he was wearing exposed thick, powerful gray legs. *He should be squatting on a ledge somewhere,* Bannickburn thought.

Spargoyle's eyes were open, but unfocused, with dilated pupils. His mouth opened and closed soundlessly—or at least, without making a sound that could be heard above the noise of the club.

Bannickburn walked up to him and put a hand on his shoulder. It felt hard and cold, like stone. Some pretty good equipment, he thought.

"Spargoyle!" he said, giving the shoulder a shake. "Hey, Spargoyle!"

He received no response. He glanced at Kross and Cayman. Both men slowly nodded. They knew what they needed to do.

If he'd known what Spargoyle had taken, Bannickburn could have been a little more precise in designing an antidote. But, most likely, the dwarf was enjoying the effects of a veritable cocktail of alcohol and numerous narcotics. They'd have to provide a more general cure.

They all agreed one dose of jazz wasn't going to do it—that would probably only take the edge off the other drugs Spargoyle had taken, leaving him comfortable and sleepy. Bannickburn hated to use this much of his stash in a single dose, and there was, of course, the risk that they could explode the dwarf's heart. But this was the path most likely to give them the reward they wanted, and Bannickburn couldn't bring himself to care too much about Spargoyle anyway.

X-Prime had drawn the short straw, so he got to administer the jazz poppers. Cayman and Kross had spread Spargoyle on the sidewalk, and the gray man lay there, blending in with the pavement fairly well. X-Prime knelt next to him, maneuvering the inhalers.

"His mouth's strong, and his jaw's like a steel trap," X-Prime complained. "I can't get them in."

"Do one after the other, idiot," snapped Cayman.

"Will that have the same effect?"

"Yeah, unless it takes you two fragging hours to put the second dose in."

"All right, all right. Here goes."

X-Prime placed the first popper in the dwarf's mouth and squeezed the inhaler. The reaction was almost immediate. Spargoyle remained unconscious, but he started twitching around. His head bobbed back and forth, and X-Prime had trouble getting the second popper placed.

"I knew I should've done both at the same time," X-Prime muttered.

"For hell's sake," Cayman said. He stepped forward, grabbed Spargoyle's large, heavy head between his steaklike palms, and held him still. "Do it!"

X-Prime squeezed the second popper, then took a few steps back.

"Okay," he said. "Show should start in a few seconds. Or he'll die. Either way, something will happen."

Bannickburn watched Spargoyle carefully. The dwarf had stopped twitching with the second dose of jazz. He exhaled, air seeping from him like he was a leaky tire. Then he lay still as stone. His lungs didn't fill, his chest didn't rise. The team members exchanged worried glances, and Bannickburn took a step forward.

With a whoosh, Spargoyle inhaled. Then exhaled. Then his breaths came more and more rapidly, a rasp growing louder in his throat. He blinked once, then several more times. His eyes focused and his head moved, back and forth, back and forth, looking around, trying to take in his surroundings. His shoulders twitched, banging against the sidewalk with solid thuds.

"Wha-wha-wha-wha-what?" Spargoyle said.

He sat up, his head still pivoting this way and that. He put his palms on the ground, and his arms trembled from the mere effort of supporting him.

"Hey, Spargoyle," Bannickburn said. "What's going on?"

"I don't . . . I . . . I don't . . . What's happening?" Spargoyle said. "I feel . . . I feel . . ."

"Weird?" Bannickburn said.

"Nauseous?" X-Prime said.

Spargoyle leaped to his feet. "Good! I—I—I feel good!" He did a small jig on the sidewalk, and his stone shoes made him sound like a tap dancer. "Whoa! No hangover at *all*! This is *great*!" Then he stopped dancing. "Who are you guys?"

"We're the guys who made you feel good," Bannickburn said. "I'm Miller."

Suddenly Spargoyle put his guard up, knowing that strangers generally don't do nice things for no reason. He tried to set his mouth in a hard line, but the effect of the Jazz they'd given him was too strong. His entire face kept twitching as if bees were crawling on him.

"What do you want?" Spargoyle said.

Cayman was keeping a careful eye on Bannickburn's left side, while Kross watched the right. That left Bannickburn free to talk.

"We hear you've got some stuff coming in. Bound for Seattle."

The dwarf shrugged with a sound like the grinding of a millstone. "I got lots of stuff going to Seattle."

"Of course you do. This is a small shipment. A single bottle. For a guy named Yeti." Yeti, according to Bailey, was the guy tagged to pick up the bottle for the Finnigans.

Spargoyle's eyes jumped here and there, but mostly he tried to focus them on Bannickburn. He leaned forward. "The bottle?" he said. "Do you have it? Did you hear about it? Where is it?" This was another effect of the jazz—Spargoyle couldn't speak cautiously if he tried. The words just spilled out as soon as they occurred to him.

"I thought your job was to know where it is. You didn't lose it, did you?"

"No! No, I never lost it! I never got it! It never came

to me!" His face, still twitching, edged gradually to an expression of dismay. "Oh, no. Oh, man. You guys are Finnigan guys, aren't you? From Yeti? Oh, man. Okay, I know, I know, I'm not supposed to know this is a Finnigan job, but I know, okay? O'Malley doesn't have the lightest touch in the world, right? And now the stupid bottle's late, and I don't have it, and you've come to break my fingers." His eyes widened. "Or kill me. Fragging drek! You're going to kill me, aren't you? Over a bottle of water! What the hell is it about a bottle of water! It's not my fault! I never found the guy! Never saw him! And I looked, okay? I tried to find them when they didn't show up, but I didn't. But I tried, okay? What more could I do?"

Spargoyle had given Bannickburn a role to play, and it was a role that made Spargoyle nervous and defensive. Bannickburn saw no reason why he shouldn't run with it.

"Is that what you were doing in the club where we found you?" he said. "Looking for the bottle?"

"Yeah! Of course . . ." Spargoyle's voice trailed off as he realized that argument wouldn't hold much water. "Okay. Okay. I'm going to level with you guys. I wasn't looking for them in the club. I went there to unwind, all right? But I'd been looking. I'd been *really* looking. Don't I get some time to rest? You want me looking twenty-four hours a day? That's impossible! I need, you know, some time to do my thing."

"Uh-huh," Bannickburn said. He looked over his right shoulder. "Hey, Kross!" They had a fake name all worked out for him, but Bannickburn decided not to use it, for no better reason than he liked to irritate the ork. "What do you think? A broken finger for every hour off the job? Or would we run out of digits too fast?"

"His dermal sheath might make it tricky," Kross said. "But I'd be happy to give it a try."

"Hey, hey, hey, no need for that, okay?" Spargoyle said. "Maybe you could break them, maybe you couldn't, but why bother to find out? We're all on the same side here, aren't we? I want to get the water to

Yeti, and you do, too. Let's find the water, all right? Then you can punish me all you want, if you still think I need it, okay?"

The jazz was definitely having an effect on Spargoyle, but Bannickburn guessed that wasn't the only explanation for his behavior. He was a genuinely nervous, weaselly little fake gargoyle. Maybe that was the reason for all the modifications—if he could *look* scary, then he might not actually have to *be* scary.

"All right," Bannickburn said magnanimously. "I can give you a little more time. Why don't you tell me what you did when the water didn't show up?"

Spargoyle looked around nervously. "When it didn't show up? Okay. Um. What I did. Well, the first thing I did is, I sat down, and I said 'Where's the fragging water?' And I thought for a while about what might have happened to it, and I came up with a lot of good ideas of where it might have gone and stuff."

Spargoyle continued this way for a while, making it clear that he had, in fact, done just about nothing to find the missing shipment. Bannickburn shook his head. The Finnigans must be desperate for any foothold they could get in the Tir if this was the kind of guy they worked with.

22

Spargoyle had a few names, and a few other vague ideas about who might be involved in getting the water to him. They followed every lead the dwarf gave them, and every one turned up dead. And all had died from the same cause—Portland police came after them, the suspect ran, and the police gunned—or, in some cases, fireballed—them down. The Finnigans' operation was being wiped clean.

None of this, of course, did much for Spargoyle's sense of well-being. The dwarf became increasingly agitated with each newly discovered death.

They found the last one—a withered, narc-addicted elf named SquidInk—only half an hour after the police had found him. They only got close enough to see the flashing lights and beacons marking the crime scene; Spargoyle had used his cybereyes to confirm that SquidInk was indeed the victim lying in the middle of the area, and then the four men quickly departed.

"Oh, man," Spargoyle said as he sat in Spindle's van. "Oh man oh man."

They'd dosed him three hours ago. The jazz had long worn off, and Spargoyle was deep in a post-high funk. But even if he'd still been riding high, all the deaths they'd discovered would be making him nervous.

"They're gonna come after me." The dwarf's voice was flat, lifeless, more in keeping with his stony face. "They're getting everyone connected with this. Oh, man."

"Well, at least you know that if the police come for you, you probably shouldn't run," Cayman said jovially. "Just let them take you."

"I don't stand a chance either way," Spargoyle replied.

Bannickburn had long ago stopped paying attention to Spargoyle's complaints, instead keeping his mind on the task at hand. "Everyone connected with the bottle is dead. But we haven't found the bottle. Which means either the police have it, or it never made it into the city. Since the police are still chasing people down, I'd guess they don't have it."

"Right. It's not here." Something like hope glimmered deep in Spargoyle's eyes. "That means I can't be blamed for not having it, right? It never came into the fragging city, and I don't have a visa to get into the rest of the Tir. Whoever didn't bring it in—it's their fault."

"Fine," said Bannickburn. "Sure. I absolve you of all responsibility." He waved at Spargoyle in a vaguely crosslike pattern. "Go away now."

"How long do you think he's got before the police catch up to him?" Cayman asked as he watched Spargoyle plod away.

"Fifteen to twenty minutes," Bannickburn said. "We'd better get some separation between him and us."

"He's the only living connection to the water," Kross said as the three men hurried back to Spindle's van. "And he knows nothing. How are we going to find the water if it's still in the Tir?"

"From the police. I'm sure they've been gathering information as they go."

"And they'll share that with us?"

"Not willingly, no," Bannickburn said. "But it's information, and it's on record somewhere. That, I'm pretty sure we can find."

"Then how do we get into the Tir to find the damn bottle?" Cayman asked.

"I'm still working on that."

Bannickburn stood at a gate in the south part of the wall, where I-205 met the Clackamas River. While Jackie had looked into what the Portland police knew, he had been poring over any available maps and descriptions of the Portland Wall that he could find. All his analysis led to two conclusions—first, trying to scale the wall was a fool's errand. Maybe it could be done, but attempting to spoof security at one of the gates seemed like the best way to get to the other side. The second conclusion was that anyone trying to spoof security should do it at the gate with the least protection in the city, which was where he stood now.

Of course, when it came to gates leading from Portland to the rest of the Tir, saying one gate had thinner security than the other was a little bit like saying one megacorp was less greedy than another. Even the most altruistic megacorp is far greedier than an average six-year-old, just as the gate in the Portland Wall with the least security still had enough guards to outnumber the total armed forces of certain small nations. So Bannickburn walked toward the gate with exaggerated care.

"The most I can give you is fifteen minutes," Jackie whispered in his ear. "Or thereabouts."

He raised a small microphone to his mouth. "If that's all I've got, that's what I'll use," he said.

"What's the line look like for those heading into the Tir?"

"Small line. Two people right now," he said. Since a main highway entered the Tir at this gate, most of the traffic was vehicular. A single line to the side was for pedestrians—those who wanted to walk through the wall without enduring the detailed vehicle scans that often made the wait interminable. Bannickburn headed for this line.

"Wait until there's only one person waiting. Then get in line and let me know you're there."

"How am I going to get far enough away in fifteen minutes?"

"It'll probably only be ten once they actually send you through."

"How am I going to get far enough away in *ten* minutes?"

"That's a good question," Jackie said. "Guess you'll be relying on your wits." She paused. "Been nice knowing you."

"Thanks. You'll make sure the water doesn't sneak into the city while I'm away, won't you?"

"Of course." Then her voice sounded almost serious. "Come back safe."

"Bloody well right I will," he said, then noticed that there was only one person in the pedestrian line. "It's time," he said, and walked forward.

Bannickburn's team didn't have the time or money to invest in enough fake identification to fool Tir border guards, who were notoriously difficult to dupe. Instead, their plans hinged on Jackie—she would have to interfere enough with the checkpoint's decks so that they let Bannickburn's relatively poor fake through.

Anything she did wouldn't last long. The Tir's systems were too strong, too filled with layers of redundancy, to stay hoodwinked for long. Hundreds of slave utilities, constantly monitoring system performance, would notice the oddity of Jackie's intrusion soon enough. They'd shut down any blocks she'd put up, review what she'd done while mucking around in the system, and make any needed corrections—like red-flagging Bannickburn's ID as a fake and sending an alarm to Tir security that an intruder was loose and needed to be tracked down. Then the fun would really start.

He wouldn't be going in without resources, of course. His survival might depend on knowing the right times to use the items he carried with him. But compared to

the numbers and power of the Tir Tairngire Defense
Force, his resources seemed like little more than a few
bits of string and a piece of chewing gum.

There was one more complication. Much as he'd like
to steer completely clear of the TDF, he had the same
objective they did. Jackie had pulled some information
from the Portland police about where they suspected the
bottle of water was. The TDF had the same info, and
would likely be heading toward the same place as Bannickburn. They were on an inevitable collision course—
unless Bannickburn could get there first. Since he was
on foot, he had doubts about that.

He approached the border guard, exuding the same
arrogance as the elves he had observed. The man
scanned him for weapons, which was why he hadn't
bothered carrying any. A chem sniffer checked for ex-
plosives or other dangerous chemicals, but thankfully it
wasn't looking for the kind of chemicals Bannickburn
had—the kind that were dangerous mainly to himself.
Bannickburn curtly answered the litany of questions,
submitted to a retinal scan, then waited for Jackie's fake
results to appear to the guard.

It only took seconds. "All right, Mr. Cummerbund.
Proceed."

"Thank you," Bannickburn said, brushing quickly by
the guard. *Good old Cummerbund,* he thought. He'd
been using variants of that identity for over a quarter of
a century, and it had never let him down.

He suppressed the urge to use all of his defensive
measures at once—ingest every drug he was carrying,
activate every focus—but that would probably stop his
heart and alert any half-awake defense officer (especially
any watching the astral plane) to his presence. Instead,
he settled on a simple plan of action—he jumped into
one of the cabs waiting on the other side of the gate.

He checked his chrono when he got in. He had maybe
seven minutes until Jackie's block broke down and he
became a wanted man. He could get just outside Glad-

stone, to the end of the urban electrical grid and the taxi's range, before the alert came out. Hopefully.

Traffic was light in the Portland suburbs. Most people with business in the city lived in the city to avoid the bother of passing the wall every day. And most Tir citizens without business in Portland chose not to live anywhere near the city, leaving the suburbs sparsely populated.

The cab took him five kilometers before Bannickburn's seven minutes ran out. From that instant, he was on edge. That, naturally, was the moment his driver decided to strike up a conversation.

"You sure you just want to go to the edge of town?" she said. The driver was a female ork, crammed into the driver's seat, and hunching over the steering wheel. "Plenty of places I could take you where you could get a car. Drive wherever you want. I leave you at the edge of the grid, you'll just be walking."

"I'll be fine," Bannickburn said.

"Really? Mind if I ask where you're going? What you're doing?"

Bannickburn pulled his chin up a little and let arrogance fill his voice. "As a matter of fact, I *do* mind."

The driver, unfortunately, had spent too much time among elves to be put off by haughtiness.

"Oooo—secret stuff! Is it government-secret? Business-secret? Wait, I know—magic-secret! You're doing research!"

"Secret-secret," Bannickburn said, anxious to end the conversation.

Thankfully, the driver was put off. The rest of the ride was quiet, leaving Bannickburn free to watch covertly for the security forces that undoubtedly had been alerted to his presence by now.

At the end of the grid, Bannickburn stepped out of the cab and threw the driver as normal a tip as he could, so he wouldn't be memorable. He waved, and then headed north to the Clackamas River.

Now it was time to break out some of his resources. First thing was the narcs. He wasn't happy about having to spend two of his jazz poppers on Spargoyle, but he still had a few left. He squeezed one into his mouth and felt the instant rush moving from his heart to his legs and arms to the tips of his fingers and toes. He started to run, keeping a pace significantly faster than he could maintain without the drugs, but probably much slower than anything the TDF was using.

The police's most recent intelligence said the Finnigan associates with the water were planning to head down the Clackamas toward the Willamette. What they'd do then was anybody's guess, but passing through the gate at the Clackamas River Bridge seemed to make the most sense. Hopefully, Bannickburn was traveling the exact same route the Finnigans were going to take, only in reverse. With any luck, he'd run right into them—and both of them would manage to stay clear of the TDF.

Bannickburn thought the logical thing for the smugglers to do would be to stick close to the Clackamas, maybe even sail on top of it, until they came near the gate. He didn't expect to find them within sight of the river—it would be too obvious, the TDF would be watching the water closely. While studying the maps, Bannickburn had come up with what he thought their real plan might be, and he based his route on that.

About seven kilometers east of its merge with the Willamette, the Clackamas took a turn to the north. It ran that way for almost two kilometers, made a short jog west, then headed back south, only turning west again at a spot less than a kilometer due west of where it turned in the first place. If Bannickburn were on the run and headed west, he'd get the hell off the river when it made that first big turn north, and he'd make a beeline for the Willamette, a distance of about seven kilometers over land. The trees and hills there would provide a lot better cover than the open water.

He didn't think he had much time. The urgency Bailey had conveyed—he'd practically pushed Bannickburn out of Seattle once Bannickburn finally accepted the mission—indicated that the Finnigans should be making their way out of the Tir at any time. In fact, they had been supposed to meet with Spargoyle days ago. Something had clearly held the Finnigans up, but Bannickburn couldn't believe they were that far from their goal, assuming they'd lived this long.

He ran almost northeast, staying on top of the hills and bluffs near the river, watching left, watching right, practically swiveling his head three hundred and sixty degrees, so he could keep an eye on everything around him. His legs kept churning, the jazz making anything less than a dead sprint feel sluggish. He'd already traveled more than a kilometer, and was making excellent time.

Back in ancient times, probably before the disintegration of the old U.S. of A., this area had been more developed. Trees sprang up all around him now, but the ground seemed as much concrete as dirt, old foundations that were slow to return to nature. Occasionally, he saw other remains left by the former inhabitants—an old tire, a corner of a reflective green sign, unidentifiable rusted metal—but there weren't many of these. The elves kept their nation clean, and these items were likely only visible because the rain and tree roots had worked to uncover them from the dirt grave that had housed them for many decades.

To his left, the Clackamas hurried on, slowly narrowing and quickening as Bannickburn moved farther from the Willamette. The gurgling water would have sounded soothing, except it was too often drowned out by the blood rushing in Bannickburn's ears.

Only a kilometer to go. He felt like he had enough energy to run for days, but in an hour or so that would change completely, and he'd be little more than a limp rag. Unless, of course, he dug back into his narc stash to keep himself going a little longer.

A feather tickled across his brain. He recognized what it was instantly, and felt nauseous. Someone was reach-

ing out with magic—looking for him, or someone else,
but *looking*. And they'd spotted him.

This would have been easier in the old days. In the
old days—

Who the frag cares, Bannickburn's brain shouted at
him in fury. *This is now, not then. Figure out a way to
survive with what you have.*

He stopped in his tracks, took a deep breath, and
looked around. *Let those damn elven eyes do some work.*
He couldn't see a trace of any intelligent life nearby.

Could be a lot of things. Could be a mage with invisibility. Could be someone detecting him at a long range.
But Bannickburn had gotten caught up on the latest Tir
security procedures, and he knew their first line of attack
in a situation like this, which was to send out the spirits.
The denisens of Tir had plenty of spirits at their disposal,
and they were reliable if single-minded and unimagina-
tive. Give them a job and they'd usually do it—that, and
nothing more. Bannickburn knew the TDF didn't have
much information about him. Right now, all the spirits
would be looking for was an elf fugitive. So Bannickburn
would transform himself into an elf who belonged here.

He thought the thoughts of a Tir elf. He pondered the
glories of nature, the evils of those who despoil it, the
fact that he was likely superior to ninety-nine percent of
the intelligent life on earth because he was so damn
enlightened. He made himself feel at home here, in his
element, beside a river he'd walked next to thousands
of times because it soothed his soul.

The feathered fingers tapped in his mind for a few
more seconds, then flitted away. He'd been seen, it was
clear, but whatever saw him was leaving him alone. The
spirit, if that's what it was, hadn't seen a fugitive. It had
seen a Tir native.

The thought that he'd passed as a native (even though
he'd only fooled a simple spirit) made Bannickburn feel
both triumphant and disgusted. The last thing he wanted
to be was one of *them*. He let his distaste for the Tir
and the urgency of his mission come back into his head.

Then his legs, which had started trembling from the strain of not moving while under the influence of jazz, carried him off again.

Ahead of him, slightly to his right, sprang an opportunity: A hilltop, higher than the surrounding area, with a small rocky outcropping that would serve as a good lookout point. Maybe he could finally spot what he was looking for.

He climbed the hill. The outcropping was well situated, near enough to trees and bushes that he could jump back into shelter if necessary, but open enough to give him a view of the area for several kilometers. He reached into his backpack for a nice, mundane piece of equipment—a pair of binoculars. He set them to their highest level of magnification and started scanning.

The good news was, he didn't see anyone who looked like they were following him. The bad news was, he didn't see anyone who looked like they might be his quarry.

He had some loose descriptions of the smugglers from the Portland police. There were three to five people in the gang, all elves except for one ork. They were pros—you don't penetrate the Tir with amateurs—and so were probably older and not flashy. So Bannickburn was looking for a group of average, ordinary-looking folks staying off roads and running for their lives. He figured he'd know them when he saw them.

The distant sound of rotors drew his attention. Time to move back a little.

The noise came closer, and Bannickburn caught a few glimpses of an autogyro flying low and coming closer. Sleek, black, and shiny, it reflected sunlight back at Bannickburn no matter which way it turned. It seemed to be a series of hard facets, and it was heading straight for him.

He was carrying a jammer in his backpack, and he thought this might be the time to use it, to keep the gyro from spotting him. Trouble was, sometimes the noise from a jammer was different enough from regular white noise that a team with decent equipment could detect the existence of the countermeasure. He was probably better off as a lone person on the ground, especially if he could find a thick pile of leaves to duck under.

His feet slid on loose dirt as he sidestepped down the hill, listening to the approaching craft. He scanned the ground, looking for roots or rocks, then glanced up to the sky, wondering just how close the autogyro was going to get. It sounded like it should almost be overhead. Then he saw what he was looking for—a pile of leaves stacked in a small hole. Bannickburn dove in, hoped for the best, and waited.

The autogyro passed overhead. It was so low that Bannickburn could easily read the craft's identification number. He watched it go, and for one brief, welcome moment it didn't reflect sunlight back in his face. Then it passed on, and he was watching its tail.

He started to take a deep, relieved breath when the autogyro stopped and hovered. It held steady for a while, looking, looking, looking.

Then it left as quickly as it had come.

He sat up a little, and leaves rustled as they fell away from him. The autogyro was looking somewhere else. They were close to him, but not quite close enough. Which meant one of two things—either they were looking for him and didn't quite know where he was, or they were looking for someone else.

That second possibility was the one that interested Bannickburn, since he had a pretty good idea who that someone else would be. His mind raced. How would the Finnigans react to the autogyro? They might hide, like Bannickburn, but that was likely only if they were on foot, and Bannickburn didn't figure they were. If they had wheels, they'd keep an eye on the autogyro and stay away from it. They'd be skirting to the south right about now.

Bannickburn moved, running to the hill's south face. If the autogyro was in the right place, Bannickburn probably only had one shot at this, and it would be coming up extremely quickly.

The autogyro had seen enough and it headed north. The smugglers would have a moment to breathe, and how they used that moment would decide how successful Bannickburn was going to be.

He sprinted down the south face of the hill at full speed, hopping over rocks, skidding every other step, but staying upright. The jazz, thankfully, was still working, and it felt almost like invisible hands on his back, shoving him forward.

He found a path, maybe three-quarters of the way down, that had been invisible from the hilltop. Not as wide as a road, certainly not paved, but still clear of plants and rocks. This was probably how the smugglers hoped to get to the river, and this was where the TDF autogyro was looking for them. For the moment, then, the smugglers were somewhere else. But hopefully they'd come back here.

Bannickburn took out his binoculars again—not looking behind at all, focusing a little to the south of the general direction the autogyro had been traveling.

There! In the trees, movement. It was slow, probably a full kilometer away. They were off-road, trying to get back on. If they got back before Bannickburn caught up to them, they'd be gone, and he'd have lost them.

He dashed forward, trying to get a look at the smugglers as he ran, but the lenses bounced too much. He couldn't fix on them, couldn't see what kind of vehicle they had.

He was getting closer, three-quarters of a kilometer, then half. They would've heard him by now except they had an engine rumbling, some kind of motorbike. Too loud to be an Offroader—maybe a Growler.

Time for a stealthy approach. He'd resisted using this next toy—it would send all sorts of flares into the astral plane—but he was also longing for it like nothing else he carried. It was a small vial of mercury, specially mined near an astral rift in Wales. He'd bought it from

Twist, and half the fun of using it would be the thought of inflicting a little drain on the pompous weasel. And a small astral flare in a place like the Tir wasn't likely to draw much attention. He grabbed the vial, triggered it with a small rub, and vanished.

He felt nothing. He couldn't see any part of himself, but he felt nothing. How could he feel nothing? This was his life's blood! He was back in the game, using magic again—couldn't he feel at least one damn thing?

But he didn't. That part of him was cut off for good. He got the effect of the spell, but the *feel* of the magic— the exhilaration, as well as the drain—belonged to Twist. That bastard.

Even while his bitterness distracted him, the jazz kept him running toward the people on the cycle. He could see them now. There were only two—one sitting on the bike, the other walking alongside. The one on foot only had to jog to keep up with the bike, since the driver was being overly cautious of the roots and rocks on the forest floor.

They'd never see him, hopefully never know he was coming. He scanned his targets, looking for obvious weapons, then saw one on the jogger. He wore a gun on his left hip. Bannickburn couldn't make out what kind, but it was still a lot better than anything he had. His first job was to take that weapon.

They finally heard him when he got close, the pounding footsteps in the woods cutting through the sound of their engine. They looked frantically for the source of the noise—finally saw the line of crushed leaves and broken twigs that showed Bannickburn's trail—but it was too late. Bannickburn caught the jogging man with a quick left to the solar plexus. As the man doubled over, Bannickburn yanked the gun from his hip holster. It was a light pistol, but it would do. The guy on the motorcycle had his own gun out, whirling around, looking for Bannickburn, but unable to pin down his location. Bannickburn got off three running shots before the motorcycle driver could draw a bead. Unfortunately, they all missed.

The driver traced the sound of Bannickburn's shots and unloaded a few rounds of his own. But he'd been so focused on tracking Bannickburn's sounds that he'd forgotten to pay attention to his friend, who abruptly straightened up just as the driver fired.

A round caught the man in the cheek, and the exit wound turned half of his head into pulp. He spun around, and fell limply to the ground. The motorcycle driver cursed and gunned his engine. The bad forest-floor traction threw his front wheel to his left and nearly spilled him to the dirt. He recovered, and now Bannickburn was in trouble—if the motorcycle got up to speed, Bannickburn would have no way to catch him.

But at least now he could take a set shot. He squared himself, braced his right arm with his left hand, and smoothly fired four times. The driver slumped and fell before he could get the cycle into second gear.

Bannickburn ran to it. The engine was still running, which was all he needed. He would be ready to go after he checked one crucial thing. On a hunch, he reached under the cycle's seat, found a latch, pulled, and lifted.

He found a black cloth, thick like a towel. He quickly unwrapped the bundle, and there it was. Blue glass, with an oval label that read HEART SPRINGS WATER, with a picture of a mountain stream, which, Bannickburn thought absently, really wasn't a spring. He rewrapped the bottle, closed the seat, hopped on the motorcycle, and was off.

He felt every bump in the forest floor beneath him, and stood as he drove to let his legs absorb the shock. He couldn't go full speed, but he could get it up to thirty or so—fast enough to leave the two bodies behind him.

Then there was the path, and he was on it. He gunned the motorcycle to near one hundred, not caring who saw him, because he hoped to outrun any pursuit.

He flew southeast, aiming for the Cascade Highway. That would get him back to 205 just south of the bridge. Then he just had to figure a way to get back into Portland, and then out the north side. Piece of cake.

He hit the highway at full speed. He could get to the wall in about a minute, and he hoped the TDF wouldn't be able to set up a decent roadblock in that amount of time, since they hopefully didn't know where the water was. If anyone had followed him on the flight to the highway, though, he'd be in trouble, since the Tir had plenty of vehicles at their disposal that were faster than the Growler.

He glanced at his instrument panel. It looked like a bare-bones model, but it had a scanner. He tuned it to Spindle's frequency.

"Where are you?" he said.

"Between the highway and the wall," she said immediately. "Haven't seen anything yet."

"I've got the bottle. Get on the highway, north of the bridge. Don't call any attention to yourself. I'll be there soon."

"I can't just sit on the highway waiting for you. Other cars won't like that."

"Right. Okay, go about a kilometer north, then get on the highway and move south. Don't go too fast. I'm on a bike. Look for me, I'll find you."

"Got it."

Bannickburn checked his mirrors, and didn't see anything that looked like security. So far, it looked like no one knew he had the bottle. That should be enough to get him to the gate safely. After that . . . well, he had a minute to plan.

He threw the gun he'd lifted from the Finnigans away, and it skittered across the highway. It was more hindrance than help—something that would set off too many alarms at the gate.

There wasn't much of a line at the gate, with only a few trucks ahead of him. He knew he was already under the influence of various detectors and sniffers, but he guessed the one chemical of note that he had, whatever the water was, was sealed tightly enough to avoid detection. He could feel the touch of magical detection on him, which was good. He was counting on there being plenty of magic in the area.

When the truck ahead of him pulled through the gate, Bannickburn moved his cycle ahead very slowly. A security official waited ahead, ready for a full scan and identity confirmation. Bannickburn grinned insolently at the man, and kept the motorcycle chugging forward.

"Stop here," the guard said. Bannickburn just smiled and slowly drove on.

"Sir, the law requires—"

The guard was interrupted by a loud rev of the cycle's engine. Bannickburn jerked the handlebars to the left as the tires squealed, and he left a stripe of black that veered off sharply. The guard drew his weapon, and turned to fire, only to be blocked by his own kiosk.

The guard triggered an alarm, and ran around the kiosk. The motorcycle sat there, engine purring gently, with no rider in sight. The guard arrived too late to see the seat of the motorcycle ease shut by itself.

The guard slowly walked forward, machine gun held steady. He came within five meters of the cycle when the engine roared again and the cycle sprang ahead.

The guard fired a burst into the cycle, and surrounding emplacements leveled blast after blast of bullets and arcane energy at it. The Growler traveled no more than twenty-five meters forward before it came to a final stop, engine smoking, tires ruptured, frame bent and broken in several places.

The guard walked cautiously toward it. As he approached, he saw plenty of gasoline and oil on the pavement, but no blood. He knew exactly what that meant.

He ran back to his kiosk. Bannickburn, jogging invisibly on the left side of the highway, was pretty sure what order was coming next—an order to cease all magical activities, including any active detect spells. That would clear up the astral plane around the gate, so anyone using something like, say, an invisibility spell, would stick out like a sore thumb. In a matter of seconds, he'd be plainly visible to security.

But he didn't have to wait that long. Spindle's van rolled toward him. He ran so it was between him and the gate, then he deactivated his focus and jumped in the van. Spindle wheeled it around and drove away from the gate.

The Portland police knew something was amiss, but they didn't know quite what. And Bannickburn's timing had been perfect, slipping into the van just before any security would have noticed the astral signature of his spell. So when the van arrived back at the gate out of the city, no one had been alerted to look for it. Spindle showed her Mustaffah Cartage ID again, and the van, with its precious bottle of water sitting wrapped in a towel and deposited gently inside an iron box, casually drove out of town.

23

Stupid fragging water hadn't even made it into Portland. Bailey would have felt contemptuous of the kind of people the Finnigans had working for them down there, but, then, the people Bailey himself sent had done even worse. Until now. Kross had managed to sneak in one last call, saying they were about to meet Bannickburn and get out of town. Kross said he was pretty sure Bannickburn had the water.

Bailey had gotten lucky. The collapse of Cabel's mission should have doomed him. The Finnigan people should have had enough time to get the water out. But they'd screwed up, been stuck in the Tir for whatever reason, and Bailey had been able to get another team down there. He didn't like relying on luck, but he'd be damned if he wouldn't take it when it was available.

Now Bailey had to wait. Kross probably wouldn't get a chance to phone in again, which was fine—they should just make a straight shot back to Seattle. He could follow their progress on his terminal, but watching a small dot crawl across a map grew old very quickly.

So Bailey had to find other ways to occupy his time, which was probably for the best since he had a backlog of tasks to accomplish. At the top of the list was making sure he would use the bottle of water wisely once it arrived.

He placed a few calls, pulled a few strings, and before he knew it his receptionist's voice came over the intercom. "There's a Willie Snowmaker here to see you."

The receptionist sounded echoey, which wasn't surprising, since she was talking from a steel desk in the middle of an enormous, empty metal airplane hangar. Bailey's office was through a door hidden by a stack of metal drums. This was his secure office, where he went when he didn't want people finding him. Only people he trusted were allowed in it. Snowmaker was one of those people.

"Send him in," he said.

Snowmaker, all 1.3 meters of him, strolled in, an ebony cane on his arm and an equally dark derby on his head. His charcoal gray suit was pinstriped, his hair was slicked back, and his blue eyes twinkled like he'd just heard an excellent joke. Bailey always enjoyed it when he could get Snowmaker to drop by for a visit.

"Mr. Bailey," Snowmaker said in a voice that strived for upper class but couldn't shake its Brooklyn origins. "A distinct pleasure, as always. Am I here for business or personal reasons today?"

"Business, of course," Bailey replied. "Much as I respect your line of work, the hazards of indulging in your product are too great." Bailey always found his diction becoming more formal in Snowmaker's presence.

"Of course, of course. No matter—you send enough customers to my network to qualify as three of my top ten clients. The fact that you don't indulge has little impact on my bottom line."

"I'm thrilled to hear that." Bailey suddenly remembered something from his last conversation with Snowmaker. "Did that voodoo situation ever work itself out?"

Snowmaker smiled. "Why yes, thank you for asking. As it turned out, the bocor in question was disassembling the doll into its component parts each night, which made it somewhat more difficult to find. However, find it we did, and we then dealt with the bocor appropriately."

Bailey was interested to know what Snowmaker considered "appropriate," but the etiquette of the situation unfortunately demanded that the specifics of the punishment go undiscussed.

"I'm glad to hear it's taken care of," Bailey said. "I hope your health continues to improve."

"You're quite kind," Snowmaker replied. He sat with his legs crossed, hands in front of him resting on top of his cane. His feet dangled a good thirty centimeters above the ground, but it didn't seem to bother Snowmaker in the least. "Now, I know you're a busy man, and the message I received seemed to indicate this was a matter of some urgency. With what can I assist you?"

Bailey had to tread cautiously now. At the moment, only a handful of people knew exactly what the water bottle project was about, and Bailey was determined to keep it that way. Snowmaker would need some info if he was going to answer Bailey's questions, but the goal would be to give him as little as possible.

"I have a product," Bailey said. "A product that's your kind of thing, but a little different. I need to know if you can handle it."

"Well, Mr. Bailey, my first inclination is to say yes, I can handle it, as I feel my distribution network can handle anything put into it. However, the fact that you're asking would seem to indicate that this is an unusual request. Perhaps if you provide more information about the nature of the substance in question, I could give you a more detailed reply."

Snowmaker was fishing. The best-case scenario was that he was digging for information simply because he needed it to answer the question, but in Bailey's experience that was almost never the case. Everyone always wanted to know more than they should.

The best thing to do at the moment was to pretend he didn't have the information Snowmaker wanted. Hopefully that would throw him off the scent.

He spread his hands. "This is the problem I have. The product is something that's filtered down to me, and everyone's quite careful about what they tell me. So I

barely know anything about what's going on—all I know
is, I was supposed to talk to you and share what little
I know."

"That makes things somewhat more difficult," Snowmaker said. "Perhaps instead of worrying about what we
don't know, we should discuss what we *do* know."

The man was focused—Bailey had to give him that.
"Here's what I know—the customer base for this substance will be different than your usual users. They
won't be buying the substance to use on themselves;
they'll be buying doses for others."

"I assume you do not mean they will be buying the
substance as gifts," Snowmaker said dryly.

"Quite right," Bailey said with a grin.

"Would it be similar to a poison, then?"

"Somewhat."

"Then we have no impediments," Snowmaker said
grandly. "Poison is part of our normal distribution channels. I would simply take your substance and introduce
it to that same customer base. I'm sure we'd find takers
for your product, assuming it is of any quality."

"Okay," Bailey said, not wishing to present any hints
as to what he thought about the quality of the substance.
Now for the tricky part. "There's a very real chance that
some customers might get it into their heads to use the
substance on your people."

Snowmaker widened his eyes. "Kill their own suppliers? That seems remarkably shortsighted."

Bailey shifted uncomfortably in his chair. "No, no,
that's not it. The substance wouldn't kill them. But it
could make their lives . . . interesting."

Now Snowmaker was really intrigued. His posture remained firm, but there was no concealing the predatory
interest in his eyes. " 'Interesting'? How do you mean?"

Bailey shook his head, hoping he looked exasperated.
"I wish I knew. Like I said, the people running this show
haven't really bothered to tell me. Let me give you their
exact words, then you can try to figure out what to make

of it. They said, 'Snowmaker needs to make sure his people steer very clear of the substance, or we could end up giving a lot of it away, and not even know it.'"

Snowmaker slowly lowered his chin onto the top of his cane, his eyes glazing as he lost himself in thought. Bailey had started writing that sentence this morning, then rewritten it, then edited it a few times, then thrown out what he had and tried again. He hoped the final version gave out just enough information and not a bit more.

Snowmaker was still trying to puzzle it out. Eventually, he either gave up trying to guess what was happening, or actually *did* figure it out, and then put on a show of befuddlement.

"I don't believe this should present any significant difficulty," he said. "As you are aware, many of my people on the street conduct business at a healthy remove from their clients, separated from them by steel doors and the like. When this . . . whatever it is comes on the market, I shall simply strongly advise them to include such precautions in the course of their normal business."

"Fine. That should work out." Bailey stood. "I appreciate you coming by, Mr. Snowmaker."

Snowmaker adroitly hopped to his feet. "My pleasure." He turned to leave, then stopped. "When this product becomes available, do you, perhaps, have an estimate of what sort of sales I should be expecting?"

"FTP," Bailey said. Faster than production—the gold standard in the narc trade. High demand and low supply that would allow Snowmaker to indulge in the kind of price hikes he generally only dreamed about.

Snowmaker almost rubbed his hands together greedily, but caught himself. "Excellent. Quite excellent." He grinned, revealing the sharp, pointed teeth that he had used on several occasions to rip out the throat of a treacherous underling. "I'll be ready, Mr. Bailey. You can count on me."

Bailey just nodded and watched Snowmaker go. The

distribution questions were dealt with, at least in principle. Now all he had to do was make sure the bottle made it safely to him.

He checked in on the tracking map. They'd progressed almost two millimeters since Snowmaker arrived. Bailey sighed. He really needed to stop looking at that. He'd just assume that everything was safe and sound, and that he was mere hours from becoming Sottocapo Martel's new favorite lieutenant.

The phone on his desk buzzed harshly, and at the same time a red light blinked rapidly. That would be a call on the secure line. Bailey prepared to talk in his serious voice.

"This is Bailey," he said after picking up the handset.

"Bailey? This is GreenJeans. We've got trouble."

GreenJeans was one of Bailey's prized possessions, a smooth-talking young woman who had at least six members of the Finnigan family convinced that they were a mere hairsbreadth away from bedding her. It would only take one more little gift, or one more piece of information, they thought, until she finally caved. That she could delay gratification among a group of men whose whole business was founded on the idea of instant gratification was a constant source of amazement to Bailey.

GreenJeans then said the last words Bailey wanted to hear from her.

"Someone here knows about your van."

"What?" Bailey leaped to his feet reflexively. *Nobody* was supposed to know about the van. Even GreenJeans, who knew the van existed, had no idea why it was important. And now someone in the Finnigan family knew? "Are you sure?"

"Quite. I was just talking to Reggie Riko, and he was trying to prove how big his balls are. He said he was leaving, hunting down a few elves in a van on their way from Portland to Seattle. Sounded like your guys to me."

"Frag it all to hell!" Bailey swore. "When did you talk to him?"

"Just fifteen minutes ago. But he jumped into an SUV when we were done talking, so he's already on the way."

"Hell. All right. Thanks, Green." He hung up while running out the door.

"Lock up!" he yelled to his receptionist as he ran by her. Then he looked at Stella and Stewart, Stephen and Bruce's replacements. They had spent the whole day crouching behind the metal drums that hid his office. "You two, with me."

He'd need more people. He'd make a few calls from his car, see who was on wheels already and could make a quick run south. He didn't need a full army, but if he knew the Finnigans, he'd need more than a couple of cars if he was going to head off the ambush headed toward his precious bottle of water.

24

The first trick had been getting a few drops of water from the bottle without Kross noticing. Jackie was impressed at how quick on his feet Bannickburn had been to make that happen. They pulled him into the van, gasping, and he collapsed in the front seat, doubled over like he had severe stomach cramps. He asked Jackie for a drink of water. She passed him a bottle. Still hunched over, he labored to take a sip in between breaths. When he passed the bottle back to her, he gave her the bottle first, then the cap. He squeezed her hand, briefly, when he gave her the cap, and she had understood immediately. This was the cap to the bottle he'd just smuggled out. It was turned upside-down, so it held a few drops of the water from Bannickburn's bottle. That was her sample.

The next part was easier. Once Kross had settled into his seat and wasn't paying attention to much of anything (and Bannickburn, coming down from the drugs he'd taken, had fallen into an unshakeable slumber), she dumped the drops into a chemical analyzer she'd brought along for exactly this purpose. A few lights flashed, the machinery inside did its business, and soon a list of chemicals was spread out on the analyzer's small display. As she flipped through the results of the analysis, she found all sorts of interesting information—what chemicals were in the water (and there certainly were more there than hydrogen and oxygen), how the various elements were bonded together, and even the expected boiling and freezing point of the substance. What she didn't find, unfortunately, was any indication of what the hell the stuff actually *was*.

But she had the data, and if there was anything she knew, it was how to handle data. She transferred the results to her deck, then jacked in using the van's satellite hookup. Since everyone expected her to be doing that anyway, no one paid any attention to her actions.

She felt almost embarrassed by what she was about to do. She wasn't going to do anything illegal. She wasn't going to break into anything. It was a humiliatingly simple action.

Then she brightened. If she went through conventional channels, she could be waiting hours to get the analysis she needed. Plus, there'd be a series of difficult questions about why she was requesting just what she was requesting. No, this was something best done through the gray market, if not the black. She felt a little better.

She zipped to an innocuous brown rectangle in a low-rent, low-security node. The door to the building she was looking for was a simple black opening—whatever money had been spent here hadn't gone to appearances.

She passed through the doorway, and found herself in a waiting room. Four other icons were there—a man with at least a dozen metal studs in his face, a burly man with a slim, elegant horse head, a green blob wearing a brown leather jacket and a fedora, and a four-foot-tall owl flipping through a magazine with its talons. A nurse in a starched white uniform sat behind a metal desk, and Jackie's inner alarms went off as soon as she saw her. The nurse looked petite and even a little frail, but she was also a powerful piece of IC. Jackie resolved to stay on her good side.

"Hello. I'm here to see Dr. Strangehooves."

"Yes," the nurse said in a voice as pinched as her face. "Do you have an appointment?"

"Does *anyone* here have an appointment?" Jackie snapped, but backtracked as she saw the nurse's face pucker in anger. "That is to say, no, I don't, but I have a matter of some urgency."

"I see. Unfortunately, so does everyone else here. Unless I can be persuaded that your matter is more serious than theirs, you'll have to wait."

Jackie knew how this game was played, and she didn't waste any time describing the situation to the nurse. Instead, she held her right hand in front of the nurse's face. There was a number on it, followed by a nuyen symbol. It looked like it had been scrawled there in black marker.

"It's this serious," she said.

"You *claim* it's that serious," the nurse amended. "But I don't see evidence of that yet."

Jackie transferred the money to the good doctor, and the nurse abruptly changed. The older woman was gone, replaced by a tall, narrow-waisted man with long blond hair and dimples. *Now* that's *customer service*, Jackie thought.

"Please go right through the door," the nurse said in a seductive baritone. "The doctor will see you immediately."

Jackie resisted the urge to tickle the nurse's chin as she walked by him, remembering that he might be cute, but he was still IC with a temper.

Strangehooves was waiting for her in one of his lab rooms. The place held nothing more than two chairs—Strangehooves would call in equipment as needed. He stood on all fours, a few strands of hay dangling from his mouth as he chewed, his goat's beard wagging slowly back and forth. He was a fine specimen, clear-eyed with a healthy, smooth gray coat. His stethoscope hung just in front of his chest.

When he saw her, he easily rose to stand on his hind legs and walked smoothly toward her. "Ms. Ozone," he said in his goatish bray. "What can I do for you?"

"Chem job. I've got all the stats on something, but I don't know what it is. I hoped you could help me out."

"Mmmm. Do we know anything about the nature of this 'something'?"

"The mob's interested in it."

"Wonderful. I always enjoying treading the same ground they stomp. What do you have for me?"

"Data. Pure data. You have a safe place for it?"

"Of course," Strangehooves said. A brown side table with a small black plastic box appeared next to him. "Just send it right here."

Jackie executed the necessary commands to put the data into the box. She added two tags to it—one would prevent the data from being copied, the other would destroy it in an hour. She liked Strangehooves, but that didn't mean she trusted him.

He clip-clopped over to the box, and put one of his forehooves on it. He stood stock-still for a good two minutes.

He frowned, an oddly natural expression for a goat. "It doesn't match anything in my database, and my database is considerably large. Where did you happen upon this?"

"I'm not at liberty to say," Jackie said delicately.

"Of course not." Strangehooves stood motionless again. Jackie hoped he wasn't leaving this icon empty while he was zipping around somewhere else and having fun.

Apparently he wasn't—when he moved again, he had made some progress. "This is quite interesting," he said. "I don't have an exact match, but I've managed to find some chemicals with a few similarities. Are you familiar with Zeta-Imp Chem's recent neurochemical research?"

"Of course! Who isn't?"

He paused. "Are you lying?"

"Yes."

"Right. Well, without bothering you with detail, they've been looking into chemical mental enhancements—pills that lead to better memory and the like."

"Haven't they ever heard of skillsofts?"

"They believe there's a market for people who want to improve their minds without having chips inserted in their brains."

Jackie tilted her head to one side. "They may be on to something."

"There are some interesting similarities, but . . ." He stroked his beard with a hoof. "Would you allow me a few moments away?"

"If you think you'll find something, knock yourself out."

"Thank you. I should return shortly. In the meantime, please entertain yourself."

And the room was full. A trideo player sat next to a full cabinet of flicks. Stacks of books and magazines lined the walls. Four men in red-and-white checked blazers appeared in the middle of the room, each holding an instrument and standing unnaturally still.

She turned to the band. "How about 'Black Barrel Baby'?" she asked. The men didn't move. "The Trina and the Toxic Trio version."

The men came to life. The lead singer sang in a high, aggressive female voice, while the others stood calmly, but still managed to thrash away at their instruments. All in all, a fine and somewhat surreal jukebox.

She ran through five more tunes before the doctor reappeared, his hooves over his ears. "Stop that racket, please," he said, and the band immediately obeyed. Then, in a blink, all the entertainment was gone. "I apologize for the extra time I took," he said, "but I needed to confirm a thing or two. I'm afraid I don't have anything conclusive, but I managed to make some interesting comparisons to some ZIC prototypes."

"You got data on ZIC prototypes?" Jackie asked, then whistled in amazement. "Can I have it?"

"No. The chemical you possess bears certain similarities, along with some key differences. I think I can say with near certainty that this chemical would work upon the memory section of the brain, most likely upon short-term memory. What it would do, I cannot tell—the makeup is too foreign."

She smiled. Strangehooves might not know what she had, but she did. Knowing where the bottle came from, it didn't take a genius to figure out what was in it. She'd actually suspected it for a while. Too bad she hadn't wanted to tip off Kross, or she would have made a bet a while ago and won the pool.

"Thank you, Doctor," she said, and Strangehooves beamed. He loved it when people called him by the title he didn't actually possess. "I hope you don't mind if I don't go through the formalities of checking out."

"Not at all," the goat said.

Jackie's icon vanished as she jacked out.

The bottle held a dissolved sample of the drug called Laés, which completely erased about twelve hours of memories from anyone who took it. It all made sense now. Once Bailey obtained the bottle, Jackie was sure he'd ship it off to the best labs willing to work for the mob to analyze the structure of the drug and see if there was any way they could manufacture it. If they could . . . was there any criminal alive who couldn't think of a million uses for a drug that erases twelves hours of memories? And it wasn't just criminals. Cheating husbands, employees who wanted to slip away from the boss for a day, children looking for a little free time away from their parents—there was no limit to the market for this product. No wonder Martel seemed so generous on the payments for the mission. If you took his eventual profits into account, he was actually getting a tremendous bargain.

Well, that bargain wouldn't last. She was more convinced than ever that they had a hot potato on their hands, and the two mob families would enter a healthy bidding war to get the bottle into their possession and away from their opponents. The team was going to clean up. Now all she had to do was let Bannickburn know what she had learned without alerting Kross.

"What's this?" Spindle said. Jackie jumped slightly at

the sound of her voice—the elf almost never spoke when jacked in to her vehicle.

"Something's coming," she said.

Bannickburn blinked sleepily, clearly fighting against the extreme weight of his eyelids. "What?" was the only word he managed to say.

"Six vehicles. Southbound. Tightly packed."

Bannickburn opened his mouth a couple of times, but nothing more than a grunt emerged. Jackie spoke up instead. "Just some convoy or another. Not something we have to worry about."

"They're in the northbound lanes. Heading south, right toward us. Nothing between them and us."

That was enough to give Bannickburn a little extra energy. "Go off-road, get around them, then keep going north. We'll outrun them."

"Van's not going to outrun anything," Spindle said. "Not them. They're faster."

"Just get on the other side of them!" Bannickburn repeated grumpily. "We'll go from there."

Jackie assumed that Spindle's silence meant she'd do her best. Jackie looked out the front window and saw the sunlight reflecting off the southbound cars heading toward them. With each second, it looked less and less like they were there by mistake.

Spindle waited as long as she could, then swerved. The back wheels of the van skidded as she shot off the road onto a grassy shoulder. Six vehicles—two motorcycles, four coupes—turned to give chase, carefully avoiding each other as they swerved around. Spindle made it back on the road before they turned around, and she gunned the van ahead.

There were no rear windows in the van. Now only Spindle knew how the pursuers were doing. Only she knew how soon they'd catch up.

25

"**G**et off the highway," Bannickburn said. "We've got no chance here, no way to keep ahead of them. Take the next exit."

He had no idea where the next exit was—the presence of regular, reliable road signs was not one of the Salish-Shidhe Council's strong suits. All he could hope was that it would come soon enough.

The van's engine sounded a sustained roar as Spindle kept it at full throttle. The noise enveloped Bannickburn's throbbing head, seeming ready to crush it. He tried to shake the feeling off, knowing he needed to concentrate, but narc aftereffects were never easy to get rid of.

Five loud clangs came from the back of the van, one after the other. Five metal slugs had embedded themselves in the rear doors.

"I don't have much in the way of rear guns," Spindle said, "so I reinforced the back doors. They can hold up to a lot more than that."

Bannickburn would have found that reassuring, except that he was sure the pursuers would be firing many more rounds in the next few minutes.

Sure enough, four more slugs hit the back. Still no exit ramp ahead. No more grassy shoulder, either, just concrete barriers on either side of the highway.

A loud engine roar, even louder than the van's—probably a motorcycle—sounded along the passenger side. Bannickburn wished the van had side windows so he could see what the frag was going on. Then four thuds hit the side of the van, one of them leaving a dent visible from the inside, and Bannickburn swiftly reconsidered his desire for windows.

"Hold on," Spindle said, then jerked the van viciously to the right. The top of the vehicle leaned dangerously, and the two tires still on the ground squealed. The noise from the motorcycle abruptly decreased, then fell behind them.

"Didn't get him," Spindle grunted. "Scared him, though." She gave the vehicle gas again, and the van did its best to respond.

Behind Bannickburn, Kross had two handguns on his lap. One of them looked like it could stop a charging elephant in its tracks. The other one was bigger. The ork looked up.

"Rope," he said.

"Got it," X-Prime said, reaching into the back of the van. He pulled out a sturdy nylon rope.

"I need a loop around my waist, then the other end tied to the seat. You know knots?" Kross asked.

"Sure! When I was a boy, I was a—" X-Prime stopped short, seeing that Cayman was preparing some severe mockery for what he was about to reveal. "Never mind what I was," he said. "I just learned a lot of knots is all."

He quickly had Kross secured. The ork looked at Cayman. "You and the kid need to man the door. Think you can pull it closed at this speed?"

"Do you think you could eat an entire infant at one sitting?" Cayman shot back.

Kross scowled. "Hardly any orks do that, you know." Cayman only grinned in response, while X-Prime looked relieved that his mentor had found a new target.

Kross looked at Spindle. "Let me know when someone's coming up on the right again. And please don't swerve while I'm leaning out the door."

Spindle nodded curtly.

More gunfire peppered the back of the car as they sped along, but Spindle's armor held up. Bannickburn tried to come up with a useful activity for himself, but watching for an exit seemed like the only thing he could do at the moment.

"Someone coming on the right," Spindle said. "Cycle."

Kross smiled. "I hear him." He gave his rope a quick test yank, then readied a gun in each hand.

Now Bannickburn could hear it, too. Quieter than the first cycle, closing quickly.

"Now," Kross said.

Cayman pulled down the latch and the door slid open. Wind swirled around the gap, and Kross leaned forward into the gale. He leveled his guns at the cycle rider. Bannickburn could see the rider's eyes widen behind his wraparound shades. Their pursuer had a gun of his own, but he'd been aiming at the tires. He couldn't swing it around in time.

Kross fired both guns. One bullet caught the rider in the shoulder. A moist splotch appeared on his thick black jersey, making him drop his gun. The second shattered his sunglasses and buried itself in his face.

The front wheel of the cycle bucked and the back end flipped in the air. The lifeless rider was catapulted forward, flying at least fifteen meters before skidding on the pavement. His motorcycle followed him, sending up a shower of sparks as it dragged along the ground, eventually hitting its former rider and rolling over him before both came to a stop.

"Close it," Kross said. Cayman and Alex heaved forward, pushing the door closed. Kross wore a satisfied smirk. "One down. They'll be a little more careful about sneaking up on that side."

Bannickburn pointed. "Exit ahead!"

Spindle nodded, but didn't change her speed or make any motion toward the ramp. Bannickburn thought about pointing out the exit again, but then saw her clenched, sweating brow, and decided she had enough to concentrate on.

"Everyone sit down and buckle up," she said through gritted teeth. The back of the van was rattled by as many as ten more shots. Dents in the rear doors appeared on the inside.

The van sped ahead and the ramp drew closer, half a kilometer away, then a quarter. Still Spindle streaked down the middle of the highway.

They were almost even with the ramp when she made her move. She slammed on the brakes as hard as she could. Every passenger hurtled forward, safety straps digging into their bodies. Four cars and a motorcycle whizzed by, not able to react in time to Spindle's maneuver.

She veered to the right, nearly rolling the van, then gunned the throttle again and they sped toward the exit ramp.

They only had a few moments before their pursuers got turned around. They needed to make use of the time, and avoid any interference from local traffic.

The exit ramp ended at a road running east and west. Spindle ignored the stop sign and blasted onto the street, turning west, heading under the highway. Bannickburn didn't see any other vehicles around. The terrain here was fairly barren—no trees, a few spots of brown grass, an ample supply of weeds, and plenty of dirt.

"Where the hell are we?" he asked.

"Longview," Jackie said. "Cross had a factory near here once. They put so much heavy metal in the water that toxic spirits from miles around came by. This was a playground for them. Drove all the residents away. The Salish have gotten the toxics out, but the place is still a dump. Might be a few decades before it becomes habitable."

Bannickburn looked at her quizzically. "How do you know this?"

She pointed to the datajack still in her head. "Old friends at Cross. I've taken the liberty of having them keep any Salish cops away from here for a while."

"I love a team member who shows initiative," Bannickburn said. "Call up some overhead photos. See if there's anything nearby that can give us cover."

"Already done," she said. "Most everything near here's been razed, but there's a subdivision a bit to the northwest—Summerdale Glen. No one's gotten around to tearing those houses down yet. There're a few streets running through there that could help us out."

"Get the directions to Spindle," he said.

Electrons flowed this way and that around the van, then Spindle nodded. "Got it. Let's run around first, though. Keep 'em guessing."

"Go ahead," Bannickburn said.

A dirt road headed to the south, wandering through some tall weeds. Spindle shot into it, as if hoping the weeds might provide some concealment, but Bannickburn could see they weren't tall enough. Still, he didn't know how close the pursuers had gotten since they left the highway. Maybe this would shake them.

Gunfire sounded, and again the back was hammered by bullets. Apparently they hadn't shaken anyone.

"What's back there?" Kross demanded. "Cycle or car?"

"Car," Spindle said.

"Good," Kross said. "Bigger target. I'm going out."

He hurled the door open and leaned out as far as he could, his legs shaking under him. He fired his guns, three rounds from each, yelling above the wind as the bullets sped off.

Then the car behind them fired. Bullets whizzed by the ork, one skimming off the side of the van in a shower of sparks. Kross ducked.

Just then, Spindle hit a bump in the dirt road. The

impact sent an already unbalanced Kross off his feet. He fell toward the ground.

Cayman reached out, catching Kross around the waist, then gave a heave, and pulled the ork back into the van. Cayman fell back, Kross landing on top of him.

Kross stood quickly. Blood ran in a thin rivulet through the canyons of his face—the bullet that had skimmed the van must have taken a piece of him, too. He was snarling, but he didn't forget his manners.

"Thanks," he said to Cayman as he stood, leaned out the door again, and unleashed a torrent of shots.

He screamed. Bannickburn whirled around, convinced the ork had been hit. But Kross remained on his feet, looking strong, raising his arms over his head.

"Take that, you bastard!" Kross yelled, then pulled himself back into the van. Cayman slid the door closed.

"That'll hold 'em for a while," he said. "They were single file, and I took out the lead one. They'll have to get around him, and if one of them gets close again, I'll take him out, too. We'll be okay as long as we can keep them strung out behind us."

Right then, the dirt road ended. Suddenly they were on broad pavement, a street four lanes wide. There still were no other vehicles in sight besides their pursuers.

"Find a narrower road!" Bannickburn yelled.

"I can't! This must've been a downtown," Spindle said. "All the roads are wide. Here they come!"

Kross swore and stood again. Cayman had the door open immediately, and the ork leaned out once more, leveling his handguns. But he didn't fire.

"What's going on?" Bannickburn called.

"They're staying on the other side!" Kross yelled back. "I can't get a shot off."

"Get back in!" Spindle said. "I've gotta swerve."

Kross obeyed, jumping back to his seat. Spindle took the van to the left, banging into one of their pursuers with a jolt. Tires screeched outside.

"Everyone down!" Spindle screamed, just before a flurry of bullets struck the left side of the van. A dozen rounds, then two dozen, then more walloped the vehicle. Spindle swerved this way and that, but the pursuers finally had the position they wanted and they kept on blasting. Daylight showed through one bullet hole, then two, then three. Jackie and X-Prime, sitting on the driver's side of the van, squirmed to the right, trying to get away from the deadly fire.

The bullets kept coming. When one gunman paused to reload, the others kept on firing. The side of the van would be nothing more than Swiss cheese in a moment.

"What?" Spindle said. Bannickburn looked around, not sure what she was responding to. "Bailey!" she said, reacting to a voice only she could hear. "Holy drek, what are you—? Never mind, just help us!"

There was a distant boom outside, followed by an explosion that rattled through the van's sides.

"He got that one!" Spindle crowed.

"What's going on?" Bannickburn asked.

"It's Bailey," Spindle said. "He came down with half a dozen cars. They've got the Finnigans on the run."

"Finnigans?"

"He said that's who our pursuers were."

Of course, thought Bannickburn. *Only makes sense.* He eased back into his seat, relaxing every part of himself except his arms, which clutched the bottle of water.

"Let's get going back north," he said. "Quinn should take care of our friends. Get us out of here."

"Amen," Spindle said. Wind whistled through the bullet holes on the left side as the van shuddered forward.

They kept going for about five kilometers. Bannickburn was content to stay away from the highway and travel back roads as long as they could. Stay away from possible reinforcements.

Something in the road ahead caught his eye. "What's that? That glint?"

"Hold on," Spindle said. Bannickburn waited while she tried to get a good reading on what he had seen.

"More cars," she said. "Four of them. Sitting in the middle of the road."

"Is anyone in them? Are they running?"

"I can't tell."

"See if you can call them on the radio."

Spindle tried frequency after frequency without receiving a response. She shrugged. "Either there's no one there, or they're not hearing me, or they're ignoring me."

Bannickburn squinted at the cars sitting ahead. They were blocking the entire road. His instincts told him this was not a good thing.

"What's happening behind us?" he asked

"Finnigans know they're outnumbered, so they're trying not to engage Bailey, but they also don't want to let us get away. They're just kind of dancing around back there. We've got more than a kilometer on them."

"Okay. If we've got some room, let's slow down before we get too close to these guys."

Spindle obediently cut her speed. Bannickburn did not take his eyes off the cars ahead of him, waiting to see if they moved. They looked like muscle cars in four different shades—red, black, yellow, blue. Their headlights were round, their front grilles thrusting forward like the prows of ship's, their windshields tinted. All four faced the van and did nothing.

Bannickburn decided he definitely didn't like this. "Turn around," he said.

"There're Finnigans back there," Spindle reminded him.

At that moment, the headlights of all four cars suddenly came on, and Bannickburn could hear four engines roar to life.

"Turn *around*!" he yelled.

Spindle didn't need any more convincing. She threw the van into a skid, made a quick U-turn, and headed south.

"They're coming after us," she reported. Bannickburn was not at all surprised.

He looked ahead and saw Bailey's car. Bailey was in a black Mercedes, most likely as heavily armored as a tank. It even had a retractable gun turret where most cars had a sunroof. The rooftop guns were blazing now, firing randomly at the Finnigans skittering around him. Three smaller cars and a motorcycle orbited Bailey's Mercedes like small satellites, occasionally making a run at a Finnigan, only to pull back close.

"I thought Bailey had six vehicles," Bannickburn said.

"He lost a motorcycle early on," Spindle replied.

That meant they had six vehicles total—a motorcycle, a van that had taken plenty of abuse, three small sports cars, and Bailey's Mercedes. The Finnigans had a motorcycle, three sedans, and the four muscle cars behind them. Six versus eight. *Not good*, Bannickburn thought.

Bullets flew into the back of the van, causing Bannickburn to jump. "They caught up to us?" he asked.

"They're fast," Spindle replied. "Bailey, we've got trouble back here."

As soon as Spindle said this, the Mercedes jumped forward, its turret turning to face front, moving to engage the muscle cars.

"Bailey says to follow him once he passes us," Spindle says.

"Do it," Bannickburn said. The van was already turning as the Mercedes raced by.

Bailey's car was flanked by two of his flunkies' sports cars. Muzzle flashes came from each car, but the only rounds that made contact bounced harmlessly off the muscle cars' windshields.

"Nice cars," X-Prime said admiringly from the back.

"Who *are* these guys?" Bannickburn asked. No one replied.

Bailey's car cruised ahead, and did what the bullets couldn't—parting the muscle cars, whose drivers didn't want to collide with the Mercedes' sheer bulk. They bent around after Bailey's cars and the van passed through. Now Bannickburn, Bailey, and company were heading north with eight pursuers at their backs.

Bannickburn could only look ahead, blind to what was happening behind him. Two of Bailey's cars dropped back to engage the pursuers, disappearing from Bannick-burn's view. He wished he had Spindle's perspective on the battle.

"Here they come!" she said. Bannickburn assumed she meant this as a warning for the others to brace themselves.

Gunfire erupted all around, though mostly to the rear. Tires screeched, people outside screamed, and the road continued to rumble underneath. The van shimmied back and forth, weaving, serpentining, hoping to avoid the terrible number of bullets coming from the rear.

There was a loud report, then another. The back of the van sagged and its speed dropped.

"I've lost my two rear tires!" Spindle yelled. "I can't run!" She sounded like her own legs had been cut off.

Jackie pointed ahead. "Summerdale Glen!" she yelled.

Sure enough, in the middle of the weeds and dirt rose what had to be four dozen houses, packed close together, all of them identical. All of them shelter.

"Get there!" Bannickburn yelled. "Tell Bailey what we're doing so he can keep them off us until we get there. Everyone get a gun and load up."

X-Prime passed the guns and ammo around. Loading was difficult, as the van's bare rear rims passed every little bump in the road into the frame, jolting everyone. Behind them, Bannickburn could hear the sound of engines passing back and forth, trying to keep the pursuers away from the hobbled van. At least once Bannickburn heard the unmistakable crunch of metal on metal, followed by glass shattering and metal folding as a car rolled. He had no idea who it was.

Then the homes loomed ahead. Their doors and windows were boarded, chimneys crumbled, siding loose in many spots. All of them were tan with brown shutters, all of them stood in front of weedy patches that had once been manicured lawns.

The streets in the subdivision were narrow. Bannickburn scanned the houses, not exactly sure what he was looking for. Then he saw it.

"There! Past the bend, on the outside! See that house? With the garage door a little open?"

"Yeah," Spindle said.

"That's our new home. Run there as fast as you can, then slam on the brakes." He looked at the rest of his team, and the large submachine gun resting in Cayman's arms caught his eyes. "Nice," he said. Then he made assignments, hoping he wasn't sentencing his team members to death.

The van came around the turn. Most of the other cars had turned down other streets and were skirmishing with each other, but Spindle reported two cars behind them. Bannickburn took a deep breath, then crowded around the sliding door with Jackie, Kross, Cayman, and X-Prime.

Spindle swerved to the left side of the street, then hit the brakes, while the others leaned forward, to keep from falling to the back of the van. The pursuers, having seen this trick before, were ready for it. They didn't race past, but instead began slowing to trap the van.

The van stopped, the door slid open, and five people holding seven guns between them let loose with everything they had. The interior of the car nearest them filled with red mist. The other car, realizing it was outgunned, squealed off.

"Go!" Bannickburn yelled. They raced across the street and, one by one, slid under the open garage door. Spindle came last, casting sad glances at her battered van as she ran.

"Dammit," she kept saying. "Dammit."

"They'll leave it alone now," Bannickburn said. "It's not holding what they want anymore."

"They've already done enough," Spindle said. "You better have an extra gun for me."

Bannickburn just smiled as Spindle gracefully passed under the garage door. Then, feeling considerably more clumsy, Bannickburn followed.

"Find the basement," Bannickburn said, and followed his team into their impromptu headquarters—an abandoned, polluted suburban home in Salish territory.

Bannickburn tried to remember when working for Bailey had been fun, but it seemed to be in the distant past.

26

The sun was setting when X-Prime crept out the back door. He felt like a kid again, sneaking out to play kick the can with the neighborhood kids (he'd been a very mild child—sneaking out to do something like smoke a cigarette or grope a girl would never have occurred to him). Except this time, if he got caught, the consequences would be a little stiffer than getting grounded.

Behind him, he heard Cayman putting the metal sheet they'd found in the basement back into place. It would be secured pretty well—if X-Prime came back in a hurry, pursued by unfriendlies, he'd end up standing in front of the door as he waited for Cayman or someone else to open it. What that meant was, unlike kick the can, if anyone chased him, he wouldn't have a safe base to run back to.

He kept his head below the level of the backyard fence—tricky, since years of neglect had left gaping holes—stepping through the weeds and over the mounds of dirt that made up the yard, walking quickly to the back. Once there, he scrambled over the fence and out of the development.

On the other side of the fence, there was nothing but more weeds, broken pavement, and rats and squirrels.

He was out of Summerdale Glen, though, and that made him feel a little safer.

He'd been given three jobs. The first was to get some idea where the Finnigans and the muscle-car drivers were. The second was to figure out who was in the muscle cars and what they wanted. The third was not to get killed.

X-Prime had hoped, when he'd been briefed, that the last job would be a bit of a higher priority, but that didn't seem to be the case. But it was his own top priority.

He ran around the perimeter to the east, heading back to the road they'd taken into the development. He checked the houses he passed, looking for any traces of light inside—or, more obviously, for cars parked in front of them. He didn't see anything on this side of the development.

They'd already found Bailey. Spindle had snuck out and lifted the radio from her van, bringing it into the house. They'd talked briefly to Bailey, keeping exchanges short and changing frequencies often in case their enemies were listening. As it turned out, the outer arc around the development was called Windswept Lane (the tall metal poles with their purple street signs had remained standing and legible, despite the ruin that had fallen on the area). Bannickburn's team was at number 403, while Bailey wasn't too far away, a block west and a block south, at 209 Carnation Drive. Bailey didn't know where the Finnigans and the others were holed up, but he thought they were somewhere to the west of him.

So, at the eastern entrance to the development, X-Prime was probably as far from the others as he could get. He considered staying there and letting all the others shoot it out, but he felt too exposed in the evening air. And while he didn't know the others that well, he couldn't let Cayman and Spindle go down without firing at least a few shots in their defense. He moved on.

He walked west along the main road of the development, peering over fences, seeing nothing. He passed six houses, and was almost at the other end of the development, when he heard whistling. He froze, then squatted low, his Colt cocked and ready in his right hand. He looked around and didn't see anyone. The whistling was coming from ahead of him.

He stepped carefully, then stepped again. The whistling didn't change, didn't give a hint that the whistler knew someone was drawing closer. X-Prime listened for movement, but only heard the song. It was "I Still Haven't Found What I'm Looking For," an old Irish gospel song. X-Prime took another step.

The whistling stopped. X-Prime dropped to one knee, gun leveled. No one came into sight.

"If you're going to walk that slow, this is going to take all night." The voice came from around the corner, inflected with a light Dublin accent. "Maybe I should take a few steps. Meet you halfway."

"Don't move," X-Prime commanded.

"Please," the voice said with heavy mockery. "If I wanted to kill you, you'd have died about three houses back. I whistled so you'd finally notice me, after I'd been shadowing you from the other side of the houses. Now just come here and talk like a civilized person."

"I don't think so," X-Prime said.

A heavy sigh traveled around the corner. "Lord. Life is so difficult when we can't trust one another. Here's what I'm going to do. I'll put myself on the ground and crawl forward. You can tell me to stop crawling anytime you want, and come over and inspect me to make sure I'm neutered enough for your taste. All right?"

X-Prime aimed his gun a little lower. "Okay. Crawl."

He heard the person around the corner drop to the ground, then crawl across the dirt. A hand came around the fence first, followed by a head topped with light red hair combed into a curve that flopped down on the left side.

"Stop right there," he ordered. The man obeyed. "Drop down on your belly, hands spread out."

"Lord," the man said again, but complied.

X-Prime approached slowly, keeping an eye peeled for any associates of the man on the ground. He didn't see anyone. He kept the gun steady on the man's head.

X-Prime made a wide circle around him, keeping out of reach of the man's hands, then stepped forward quickly, putting his foot on the man's arm.

"Ow," the man said.

"Shut up," X-Prime said. He patted him down thoroughly and didn't find anything. Not even a knife.

"Okay. You can sit up. You can either put your hands behind your head or sit on them."

The man sat up and put his hands under him. "I suppose this is more comfortable," he said. "But the rocks here are unmercifully sharp."

"Pity," X-Prime said. "What do you want?"

"First, to introduce myself. My name is James Shivers."

X-Prime nodded. He remembered hearing the name.

"Okay," X-Prime said.

"Second, I want you to go back to your house and tell Mr. Bannickburn that I'm here, and I want his bottle. Mr. Kader and I are here to make sure it leaves in our hands, not yours."

Kader? X-Prime thought. *Kader's here?* That couldn't be good.

"You're lucky I found you before Kader did," Shivers said. "As it turns out, he watched a rather disconcerting video a few hours ago, and it's gotten his blood up. I was there when he saw it. It wasn't pleasant to see him vent his anger. Particularly against you and Mr. Bannickburn. I'm not sure he really cares about your precious water bottle—just having the two of you dead would be satisfaction enough."

"I'm sure," X-Prime said. He thought he did an exemplary job of keeping any trace of nervousness from his voice.

"Tell Bannickburn and Bailey that they're outnumbered. They can't get away. The easiest thing is just to hand over the water."

"And if we hand over the water, Kader will just let us walk out of here?" X-Prime said.

"I can talk him into that, yeah. Or at least, the money we plan on making from the bottle will do the convincing. You have my word that if you turn over the bottle, you'll leave unharmed."

"Why bother with sending a message?" X-Prime asked. "If your numbers are superior, why not just storm us?"

"Manners. It's fitting that your people know who they're dealing with." Then he shrugged. "And while all of you would die if we stormed you, some of us would, too, and that some of us might include me. It's something I'd like to avoid if possible." Then he stared at X-Prime, a cold glint in his eye despite his awkward posture on the ground. "But if that's what we need to do, we'll do it. In six hours."

"And why shouldn't I just shoot you right now and make the numbers more even?"

Up the street, a pair of round headlights flashed on, and an engine roared to life. The car had been in a garage and must have just rolled out.

"Nothing," Shivers said. "You could kill me easily. Then all you have to do is outrun a Mustang and you'll be fine."

X-Prime looked warily at the headlights. He might have only six hours left to live, but that was six hours more than he'd have if he took out Shivers. He knew what he had to do, but he didn't lower his gun.

"All right. I'll deliver your message," X-Prime said, then slowly backed away, keeping the gun leveled at Shivers' head.

Shivers watched him go, his smirk piercing the night. "Good to meet you, Alex. Tell your bosses you're a fine employee."

X-Prime lowered the gun and squeezed the trigger. The bullet hit the ground in front of Shivers, sending dirt into his face. Shivers jerked his head backward.

"Don't push your luck," X-Prime said. Then a thought

struck him. "You're working with Kader now? I thought you were with the Bigios."

"I work for myself," Shivers said. "Now and always."

"Then why should I take your word for anything?"

Shivers might have smiled, but X-Prime was now too far away to see him clearly. "Because that's all you have."

X-Prime considered this, and decided Shivers was right. He kept his gun aimed at Shivers for a few more steps, then turned and walked east into the increasing darkness.

"Shivers?" Bannickburn said. "Shivers is here? What's he *doing* here?"

"He wants the water bottle," X-Prime said. "Like everyone else here."

"But he's on *our* side!"

X-Prime shrugged. "Apparently he's not."

Bannickburn felt like he'd been kicked in the stomach. His supposed best friend in this strange bleeding land was preparing to kill him. And now, no matter what he did, he was dead. If he didn't turn the water over, Kader and Shivers would kill him. If he gave the water to the Finnigans, Martel would most likely kill him when he got back to Seattle. Of course, he could always turn over the bottle and never go back to Seattle, but he didn't feel inclined to run again. And Martel would not easily give up on finding him.

Only one solution came to mind—take the fight to them before they brought it to him. Unfortunately, that was the same strategy he'd used in the Stinklands so long ago, and it hadn't worked out too well.

He was in a dank, spider-filled basement. Puddles of moldy water sat here and there, and Bannickburn was certain the air, and now his lungs, had become filled with the same mold. He sat on a wooden stool with uneven legs. Jackie and Cayman sat on a board suspended between two cinder blocks. Kross was left to alternate between sitting on the floor or standing; with the suit he was wearing, he generally chose to stand. Spindle was upstairs, keeping watch. X-Prime was pacing back and forth in front of Bannickburn.

It wasn't much of a hideout, its chief advantage being that there was no good way to fire a bullet into it. In six hours, though, Kader and Shivers would make an attempt, and if they managed to trap them in their headquarters, Bannickburn and his team would quickly be butchered. In short, the basement was of limited utility. Bannickburn's time here would best be spent dreaming up a way to get out quickly. He got Bailey on the radio, and briefed him on the message from Shivers.

"That filthy, slimy, whore-born pustule on a monkey's ass," Bailey said. "That little piece of excrement buried in maggots and weevils. That . . . that . . . absolute *pisser*."

"I understand," Bannickburn said. "And I agree. But what now?"

"What *now?* We fraggin' rip him *limb from limb!* We plant his fraggin' head three feet underground, and come back next year, and see if there's a new batch of traitors growing here. We *kill* him!"

"May not be that easy."

"Right." Bailey took a breath. "A plan. We need a plan."

"Maybe shouldn't be discussed over the radio. In case they're listening."

"Tough for us to get out," Bailey countered. "They got a couple cars running up and down our street, keeping us pinned inside."

"Okay. Let me think for a few minutes."

Bannickburn flicked off the radio. "We need a plan," he said, then he sat and thought. He looked at the other members of the team. Each of them started to say something, then stopped, instantly seeing a hole in whatever plan they were about to present.

Bannickburn rolled his eyes. "You're all tremendously helpful. Okay. Here's the first thing we do."

27

The house at 301 Carnation Drive burned. It had smoked for about half an hour, then the Molotov cocktails Bailey's people had thrown in (while they dashed between the cars that kept zipping up and down Violet Cove) finally pushed the house beyond smoldering and into full-scale burning. The wind pushed the smoke west, hopefully into the faces of Kader, Shivers, and their men.

Then X-Prime and Cayman came out. X-Prime carried the large sheet of metal that, until recently, had been protecting the back door of their hideout. Cayman carried one of the prizes of his weapon collection, an Ingram SuperMach. Under covering fire from Bailey's people, Cayman and X-Prime made it into the front yard of a house just north of Bailey's hideout. The decrepit fence, combined with X-Prime's metal sheet, would, they hoped, give them enough protection until the bigger guns and grenade launchers came out.

The yellow Mustang rounded the corner, heading south. The driver watched the fire to his right more than the dark fence to his left, so he didn't see Cayman when he leaped up and sprayed forty rounds into the car. Crawling along, the car didn't squeal or skid when the driver was hit; instead, it kept creeping ahead, getting slower and slower, until it came to a stop at the intersection of Violet Cove and Carnation Drive. No one got out of the car—Cayman had hit the driver and the gunman both.

They didn't have to wait long for retaliation. Two more Mustangs, the blue and the black, sped east on Carnation Drive, pushing smoke away from them as their engines roared. The occupants of the cars fired constantly, the bullets going right where the triggermen were looking, smartlinks guiding their aim. They peppered Bailey's house, and the fence that had hidden Cayman and X-Prime, with dozens of rounds. Cayman and X-Prime had already moved on, knowing the return blow would be heavier than anything their modest shield could handle.

That was the end of the watchfulness of the previous few hours, the simmering hostility. Cayman's shots commenced open warfare that would continue until one side or another surrendered or died.

Bailey left his headquarters before the fire across the street was set. The moment they put their plan together, Bailey had known what his role was going to be, and he accepted it with relish. It wasn't quite accurate to say he'd completely forgotten about the bottle of water, but he now had more pressing matters on his mind.

He walked low through the backyard of the house where he'd been hiding, scrambled over a few fences (and through one—he found a spot so rotten he just punched his way through), and ended up on the northeast corner of the block that sheltered his people.

Bannickburn was holed up in a house across the street from him—it was easily identified by the bullet-riddled van in front of it. He didn't want to be this far east—a house or two to the west should be the ideal spot.

He found the perfect location at 411 Windswept Lane. An entire panel of the backyard fence had fallen away, opening to the barren land beyond. There was a tree, one of the few still standing in the neighborhood, no more than twenty feet from the gap. A few of its branches were dead, but a cluster of leaves about three meters off the ground would provide him the necessary concealment. He scampered up the tree.

Behind him, the burning house glowed orange, while the smoke drifted slowly northwest. Gunshots clattered—first one long burst, then a more steady exchange of gunfire. People were dying behind him— maybe Kader's people, maybe Bannickburn's people, maybe his own people. He didn't care much. The one person he wanted dead was, he was pretty sure, still alive. In a few minutes, he planned on taking care of that.

The night breeze was enough to blow the smoke in the right direction, but not enough to rustle the leaves in Bailey's tree, which was good. Nothing interfered with his perception of surrounding sounds.

He saw Jimmy before he heard him. It was only a quick glimpse—a head with a black watch cap, darting above the fence before ducking back down—but it was enough. He didn't see Jimmy's red hair, or any other identifiable traits, but he knew who it was. He knew Jimmy well enough to know that as soon as the fighting broke out in the middle of the development, Jimmy would use the chaos as a distraction while he snuck off and got the water. He hadn't, Bailey admitted to himself, known Jimmy well enough to know that he'd turn traitor, but he had a pretty good grasp of Shivers' tactics in a fight.

He wouldn't get a great shot off. Shivers was too smart to linger in front of the gap in the fence for very long. Bailey's finger would have to be squeezing the trigger before he saw Jimmy again.

Now he heard it—soft footfalls on the lightly crunching dirt. He caught occasional dark glimpses of Jimmy between fence slats, but never enough to take a shot.

The footfalls stopped. Bailey estimated that Jimmy was a mere two meters away from the gap. He grabbed his right wrist with his left hand, steadying his shooting arm.

He waited maybe twenty seconds. Then came three

quick, loud steps, then silence. Then Shivers flew across the gap, a full meter above the ground, diving, preparing to roll.

Bailey squeezed the trigger as soon as he heard the last step. He was gratified to see Jimmy's flying body—he'd guessed right again. Jimmy didn't just roll across the ground, since that would be too obvious. He had clearly hoped the elevated dive would be more unexpected. Unfortunately for him, it wasn't.

Bailey heard a grunt right after the pop of his gun. He smiled, then scrambled down from the tree. His hiding place had served its purpose—now, his presence revealed, he'd be a sitting duck if he stayed up there.

Jimmy was scrambling on the other side of the fence, either looking for some kind of defensive position or writhing in pain. Bailey fervently hoped it was the latter, but he took no chances. Dropping from the tree, he landed in a crouch, gun pointed toward the noise, in case Jimmy felt like sticking any part of himself above the fence.

He didn't. The scrambling stopped, replaced by quick, even steps. Jimmy was on his feet and running.

Bailey dashed after him, running through the gap in the fence, and firing a second shot at the fleeing shadow. He glanced down at the ground as he ran over it and thought he saw a trace of reflective wetness—Jimmy's blood, further polluting this foul patch of earth.

The fence line gradually arced to the right, and as it turned Jimmy gained some degree of concealment. Bailey continued after him in a mad dash as long as he could see at least a trace of his foe, but when Shivers managed to disappear from him completely, Bailey slowed. Now all bets were off—Jimmy could have climbed the fence, could be doubling back, could be hiding in a hole in the ground. Bailey couldn't charge headlong anymore.

He couldn't just sneak ahead, either. Too predictable. If he continued along the fence while Jimmy maneuvered out of his sight, he'd invite an ambush. Sooner or later, Jimmy would jump out at him. Bailey had to be unpredictable.

The most concealment and the best hiding places lay to his right, in the backyards of the houses. So he didn't go that way. He dropped to his belly and crawled out into the dirt and weeds.

Progress was slow, especially since he stopped every few seconds to look and listen. He worried that Jimmy had just taken off, abandoned his pursuer to go after the water. But that wasn't Jimmy's style, especially if Bailey had marked him with a bullet. Shivers would want to hunt him down before continuing on, not leaving any loose ends. Besides, if he went after the water, he'd be in for a surprise—Bannickburn had left the safety of his house by now. The place should be empty, except maybe for the ork waiting to greet interlopers.

He saw a movement on the other side of the fence to his left, in the backyard where Bannickburn had been staying. Jimmy was moving slowly, looking for his assailant somewhere, but not spotting him.

Here I am, Bailey thought. He made sure his cartridge was full of ammo, then leveled his gun and fired four rounds through the fence.

Another scramble ahead of him. Jimmy was running toward the house. Panicked, maybe; wounded, hopefully. Bailey might have a small window of time to finish him off.

He got to his feet and charged forward, firing a few more rounds where the first four had gone, adding holes to the already innumerable pockmarks in the gray wood surface. It should be weak enough now, he thought.

He put his arms over his head and crashed through the fence, splinters tearing at his hands. He didn't care. He lowered his arms in time to see a surprised Jimmy in front of him, trying to get his gun around. Bailey fired a few more rounds.

Jimmy went down, but he wasn't motionless. He was rolling like a log toward Bailey. Bailey lowered his aim and took another shot, but it fell short—he'd been expecting Jimmy to keep moving, but the man had stopped.

Jimmy got a shot off, catching Bailey in his right forearm. Bailey dropped his gun. *Oops,* he thought. *Better pick that up.*

He went flat on the ground as a second shot from Jimmy whizzed over his head. Then more shots came, aimed at the ground, and Bailey had to roll to stay away from them. He hadn't gotten his hand on his gun.

He wouldn't last long this way, unarmed and on the ground. Jimmy must be leveling his killing shot right now.

There was a report, and Bailey waited for death to finally round him up. When he didn't feel any new pain, he looked up.

Jimmy was spinning to the ground, one hand clasped to his cheek. Bailey could see a gun barrel sticking out between the boards over the back doorway. *Must be Kross,* Bailey thought. *Good ork.*

Unfortunately, Kross couldn't see through the door well enough to let loose a killing shot. Then a clatter of gunfire echoed from the front of the house, and the ork bellowed. The gun barrel disappeared, and Bailey was left alone with Jimmy.

He couldn't see his gun—it was buried in the weeds and dirt. But he could see Jimmy, who was starting to realize he'd only been grazed in the cheek. Bailey charged.

His left shoulder hit Jimmy in the gut, sending the man's arms flying out. Shivers lost his grip on his gun. Now they were evenly matched.

Jimmy fell back on the broken concrete that had once been a small patio. If he was surprised to see who his assailant was, he didn't show it. He let his backside absorb the impact of his fall, swinging his arms around to pummel Bailey. The blow on Bailey's wounded right arm was particularly painful.

Bailey pulled Jimmy closer to him, then brought his knee up. It met its intended target, and Jimmy folded at the waist, gasping. Bailey loosened his grip enough to put a few blows into Jimmy's kidneys.

Jimmy heaved, managing to roll both himself and Bailey. They turned, once, twice, three times, each one trying to stop when he was on top. After the third roll, Bailey managed to stop himself, digging a knee into the dirt, rocks cutting through to his flesh. He pushed up on his hands, and had a clear view of Jimmy's face. He punched once, twice, three times. Jimmy wasn't putting up his guard. Bailey had a clear target.

Wait, he thought vaguely as he pummeled his underling. *He's not putting up his guard for a reason. I'm forgetting something. . . .*

Jimmy's right arm moved up, and ice entered Bailey's side. He sagged suddenly, uncontrollably. It didn't really hurt, but the feeling seemed to drain him.

Then Jimmy the Shiv took his flat metal knife out of Bailey's side and plunged it into his chest.

Bailey fell back in slow motion. He heard Jimmy cough a few times and heard his own wheezing breaths. He looked up at the stars, suddenly enchanted. *I didn't know there were stars out tonight. Look how bright they are.*

He grasped the knife in his chest. It was piercing all sorts of things that had no business being touched by dirty metal. He could try, maybe, to pull it out, but at this point it would be a pretty meaningless gesture.

Jimmy had gotten to his feet, and stood over Bailey. His face was blank. He didn't say anything, but he didn't really have to. There was nothing to explain.

Bailey's breath was shallower, more painful now. He tried to talk, but only a whispered rasp came out. "Jimmy," he said. "Jimmy."

Jimmy only arched an eyebrow in response.

"I've been . . . I've been . . . doing this a long time. Made a lot of money. Kept some of it. Cash. Hid it, just for me. For when . . . for when . . . I retire. You . . . might as well have it. Money shouldn't just . . . shouldn't just sit in the ground."

The familiar bored expression made its way onto Jimmy's face, but he didn't walk away.

"I'll tell . . . tell you where to find it. Come here. Come closer. I can . . . can barely talk."

Jimmy looked one way, then the other, then shrugged. He moved closer, dropping to one knee just to Bailey's left.

With all the strength he had left, and at the cost of a considerable load of pain, Bailey reared up and spat blood in Jimmy's face.

"Stupid bastard," he said, in his normal, full voice. "I don't have any money saved anywhere. I spent it all on clothes and women. A lot better than giving it to the moron that killed me, don't you think?" Then he laughed. It hurt terribly, but he couldn't care less. He just laughed, while Jimmy shook his head.

He laughed until a spasm racked his body, forcing air out of his lungs once and for all. His body settled into the ground, and Quinn Bailey died with a smile on his face, just like he always said he would.

28

This was the plan. Bailey's men, with help from X-Prime and Cayman, would cause a disruption in the middle of the development. Bailey would track down and eliminate Shivers. Jackie and Spindle would try to find a vehicle or two that worked well enough to get them back to Seattle. Kross would stay at the house, hoping to ambush any enemies who came looking for them. And Bannickburn would stay on the move, away from the action, keeping the bottle of water safe.

He kept telling himself that his role was important. After all, he was guarding the bottle of water, the reason for all this fuss. But he was out of the action. He should have been on the front line, blowing up entire *houses,* not cowering in the back, sneaking from empty house to empty house. It was embarrassing.

Of course, with the protection they'd given him, he damn well better stay away from trouble. All the real firepower had gone to the people in the thick of things, while he was left with a lousy Colt Asp and its measly six bullets in the cylinder. Sure, he had a box of extra ammo, but quick reloading was not his forte. He certainly didn't want to have to do it in the middle of a firefight.

At least he had some extra resources at his disposal. He'd carefully selected a useful substance or two to in-

gest before he left his hideout. No jazz this time—he
didn't know how long he'd be wandering about, and he
couldn't afford to crash while the battle was still going
on. The Welsh mercury focus was constantly in his hand,
and he'd been invisible since the moment he left his
house. That didn't mean he didn't have to be cautious—
he might be invisible to regular eyes, but technology
could still draw a bead on him. He kept low, walked
quietly, and looked for other houses he might be able
to duck into for shelter. When he had a spare moment,
he pried some boards loose from a couple of houses so
he could dash into them if necessary.

The sun had completely set, and the only light came
from the stars and the burning house to the west of
Bannickburn. That worked against him—the low light
didn't affect how easily he could be spotted, since he
was invisible, but it kept him from easily seeing anyone
approaching him.

Gunfire sounded near the burning house, interspersed
with the occasional louder pops of bigger guns, or possibly grenades. The body count had to be mounting out
there—Bannickburn could only hope it was the right
bodies.

He found a couple of places where he could sit for a
few moments—the well of a basement window behind
one house, a small spot behind a collapsed porch roof
in front of another—but he never stayed put for long.
No hiding place was so good that he couldn't be spotted
if he just sat there.

He wasn't sure how he was supposed to know when
things were over, so he could stop darting back and
forth. The end of gunfire might be an indication, but he
wouldn't be sure which side had won, and he couldn't
just go blundering ahead. If he saw Jackie and Spindle
cruising by in some car, that would be a very good sign.
He could jump in the car and get out of here. Beyond
those signs, though, he wasn't sure what he was supposed to do except wait for a friendly face to save him.

He stayed mostly on Windswept Lane, running north

and south, near the spot where they'd entered the development. Occasionally he ducked down a street called Serenity Place, but each time he took a step in that direction, the sound of gunfire immediately became louder. He never stayed down that street for long.

He was walking away from Serenity Place, back to the relative safety of Windswept Lane, when a voice stopped him in his tracks.

"Robert Lionel Bannickburn," the voice said in a dead rasp. The orange glow from the west reflected off the smooth metal on the head of the man standing in the middle of the street. His skeletal grin was clearly visible.

It was pretty clear how Kader had spotted him—he probably had infrared vision in his cybereye—but Bannickburn had no idea how the man had snuck up on him like that. He considered dropping his invisibility so he could focus fully on Kader, but there could be other Finnigans around who didn't see him as clearly as Kader did. He kept himself concealed.

"I know everything," Kader said in his flat voice. "I know who you are. I know what you did to me at Gates. I even know what's in that bottle in your hands." Bannickburn didn't know how Kader could know that—Jackie had only just found out, and only recently shared the news with him. "And if I know all this," Kader continued, "you should know that there's no way I can let you out of here alive."

Kader had a gun in his right hand, a big one: an Eichiro Hatamoto—a shotgun reworked into a big handgun. He could have pulled the trigger before he had spoken, and easily taken Bannickburn out.

But the blast from the Hamamoto would be too big. Kader couldn't just put a bullet in Bannickburn's head; the round from the Hatamoto would hit him everywhere, and could very well put a hole in the precious bottle of water. At least Bannickburn knew where Kader's priorities were—the potential income from the bottle trumped, for now, Kader's desire for fast and brutal revenge. That was something, he thought. Whatever else he did, he had to hold on to the bottle.

In fact, Bannickburn realized he had the advantage. Kader didn't want to shoot him, but he had no problem shooting Kader. He aimed his gun and fired.

Kader moved with lightning speed. *Dammit,* Bannickburn thought helplessly as he watched his shot go wide. Wired reflexes to go with Kader's cyberarm. *Can't be much human left in that body.*

Kader charged toward Bannickburn's right side, closing fast. Bannickburn unleashed a second wild shot, then dashed to his left. Whatever was going to happen, he didn't want it to happen in the open street, where he'd be too easy for Kader's henchmen to find.

There was a house to his left, at the corner of Windswept and Serenity, with a window devoid of glass on the south side. Bannickburn had taken a few of the boards out, and he'd be able to get in there easily if he could stay ahead of Kader.

He couldn't. Kader hit him from behind, slamming into him like a train running over a penny. Bannickburn was flattened.

He dropped his gun, clutching both hands around the bottle of water as he fell. He cradled it as gently as he could as his arms skidded across the dirt yard. If he'd been on the street, the bottle might have burst open, but the dirt, though it scraped Bannickburn through his clothes, provided just enough cushion to keep the bottle whole.

Kader was on top of him, ready to pummel Bannickburn's sides, when he paused. Bannickburn had a guess what the cause of the hesitation might be, but he didn't stop to think about it. He scrambled ahead, out of Kader's reach, and dashed toward the window.

He was almost inside when Kader caught him again, hands firmly grasping his ankle. Kader gave a twist, wrenching Bannickburn's lower leg, and something in his knee popped. But then, once again, Kader's grip briefly loosened, and Bannickburn scrambled inside.

Kader followed, walking cautiously, his movements not as fluid as before. His gun hung at his side, and the red glare of his artificial eye was like a laser cutting into Bannickburn. Kader took two steps back, carefully placed his gun by the window, and flexed his hands (which, when it came to his right cyberarm, was completely unnecessary), then strode forward to get the job done by hand.

Bannickburn backed away slowly. There was no way he could hold his own in a hand-to-hand fight with Kader. All he could hope to do was hold on long enough.

The floorboards groaned beneath Kader's feet as he drew closer. Bannickburn only had about two meters between himself and the back wall, and he didn't want to get pinned there. He had to move soon.

Kader put his right foot forward, and Bannickburn darted. He leaned down low, his knees barely above the ground, reaching for Kader's leg, but the mafioso was too fast. His right arm swung around, hitting Bannickburn in the back of the head with an impact like a wrecking ball. Bannickburn saw stars, but he kept his legs moving, kept his arm outstretched, and he brushed Kader's legs as he flew by. The force of Kader's blow seemed to double Bannickburn's speed, and soon he was across the room, hitting the wall and stopping. In front of him, a mere three meters away, was Kader's gun.

He feinted toward the gun, but Kader wasn't stupid—he'd moved toward the weapon as soon as Bannickburn had passed him. Bannickburn wouldn't be able to reach it in time. Kader flinched as Bannickburn made his initial move, then Bannickburn changed direction, running toward Kader's right side.

He didn't want to get too close, since the blow from the cyberarm still rang in his head, but he needed to get another touch in. He brushed his hand against Kader's chest, then passed him like a bull running by a matador.

He turned again, breathing heavily. Kader was lumbering toward him, but his speed had decreased. The metal half of Kader's face remained, naturally, unchanged, but the left side showed a hint of confusion. He knew something was happening, but he didn't know what yet.

Bannickburn knew he couldn't let too much time go between touches, or the effect would wear off before it became strong enough. He was going to get pounded again, but he had to be aggressive.

He spread his legs into a wide stance, bent forward, holding his left hand out while his right arm cradled the bottle of water. Kader didn't bother to assume any kind of posture, but instead just walked forward to pound the daylights out of Bannickburn.

Bannickburn made another charge, hoping to brush by lightly again, but Kader wasn't having any of it. He didn't seem as quick as he had been outside, but he was fast enough. As Bannickburn reached out, Kader pivoted, raised his cyberarm, and brought it down like an ax, chopping into Bannickburn's back. The elf fell hard, right arm tucked under him protecting the water.

Kader quickly followed his blow with a kick, a solid blow to Bannickburn's ribs. Then he aimed a foot at Bannickburn's head. Bannickburn raised his hand defensively, trying to jerk his head back, and at least kept the foot from hitting his skull. It made solid contact with his hand, though, and it felt like the steel toe of Kader's boot passed right through his palm.

Bannickburn rolled, pain shooting through his head, knee, hand, and a few other parts that had been hit in all his scrambling around. Kader was slow to catch him, giving Bannickburn two full rolls, but then he was there. Another kick came to Bannickburn's midsection, then Kader moved down to work with his hands. His first move was to take the water. Bannickburn tried to clutch it, but Kader easily slipped it from his grasp. He carefully placed it behind him, then turned back to Bannickburn and went to work.

Left to the kidneys. Right to the stomach. Left to the jaw. Bannickburn's senses reeled, his arms flailed, hop-

ing to make any sort of contact with Kader. He touched
his arm, brushed his leg, but made no real impact.

Kader, oddly enough, seemed to be tiring. He stopped
raining blows on Bannickburn for a moment, looking at
his left arm with a puzzled expression. He looked like
he wanted to take a step forward, but his feet didn't
come off the ground, and he had to drag them. Then he
shrugged and aimed another blow.

It was another one to the face, near the temple. Bannickburn was down for the count. His vision went black.

He wasn't out for long. He'd been unconscious plenty
of times, and usually had a pretty good feel for how long
it took him to wake back up. This time, it didn't feel
like much more than a minute.

He wasn't being hit. That should have been a blessed
relief, but all it really did was give his existing cuts,
bruises, and other damage a chance to make their presence known. He hurt plenty, but nothing vital felt like
it had been too badly damaged. If he lay still for another
minute or two—maybe twenty—he might be able to
move again.

He didn't have twenty minutes. He started looking
around.

Kader lay next to him in an odd tripod shape. The
last punch had done the job—his body had completely
frozen as he followed through on the blow. Left stiff, his
unbalanced body had tilted forward until his head came
to rest on the ground, his torso oddly pivoted from the
punch he had thrown.

Bannickburn scooted to a sitting position and managed to see Kader's left eye. It was alive and alert, puzzled and panicked.

"Witch's Moss," Bannickburn said, speaking through
a mouthful of blood. He spat, and continued. "Every
time I touched you, and you touched me, you got a little
slower. Until this happened."

He pushed himself backward until he was sitting
against the cracked plaster wall of the room, then contemplated what to do. His first instinct was to kill Kader.

That would be the easiest thing to do. He could shoot him with the Hatamoto, or just keep touching him until the Witch's Moss froze his lungs. After all, that's what Kader would do to him—that's what Kader had been about to do until the Witch's Moss kicked in. So there were plenty of good reasons to finish him off.

Then Bannickburn sighed. The day he started doing something simply because he could was the day he finally gave up on who he once had been. He might as well go and get all cybered up, like Kader, because killing a man in cold blood, even an enemy like Kader, would mean giving up on ever being Robert Lionel Bannickburn, combat mage of legend, again.

He spied the water bottle behind the odd tripod that was Kader, and suddenly had an idea. He wasn't going to take it anywhere or try to use it to bargain with anyone. He'd had enough of the mob. Kader came after him to get the water. Shivers betrayed him to get the bottle. No Mafia family would put up with him getting them into a bidding war over it. They'd just keep coming to kill him, and take it for themselves.

Best to be rid of it. Especially since he had the perfect receptacle for it in front of him.

He heaved himself to his feet and limped forward. He gave Kader a quick shove, and the mafioso rolled onto his side. Bannickburn thought he heard him grunt.

After some pushing and straining, he managed to get Kader in a sort of sitting position— his head against the wall, his back awkwardly sloping down to the floor. Bannickburn waited a few minutes until he saw one of Kader's fingers twitch, then figured he could touch him again without killing him.

He pried open Kader's mouth, then shuffled over to the water bottle. Kader watched him carefully, and Bannickburn could see the realization in his eyes. They hardened with murderous intent, but Bannickburn didn't care. Soon most of this evening wouldn't even be a memory.

He poured some of the water down Kader's throat.

Reflexes took over in Kader's body, and he swallowed, pushing the water into his stomach. Then Bannickburn poured some more. Then more. Then the bottle was empty.

He didn't stay to watch Kader's eyes, because he didn't want to take a chance that Kader would see him after the drug was administered, and remember him. He wished he could have watched, though, to see the memory of the past twelve hours drain away. Kader's knowledge of the contents of the bottle, of the identity of the man who had conned him at the Gates Casino, even of Bannickburn's name, would all drift away. Of course, for all Bannickburn knew, Shivers would just go ahead and tell everything to Kader again, but, with any luck, Shivers was dead. For now, at least, Kader's vendetta would be forgotten.

Bannickburn shuffled outside, taking Kader's Hatamoto with him. As he staggered through the yard, the blue Mustang pulled up next to him. Bannickburn tried to raise Kader's gun, but his arms had no life. The driver's-side window lowered, and Bannickburn waited for a gun barrel to emerge.

Instead, he saw Spindle. "Get in here! Now!"

Bannickburn might have smiled, but he couldn't really tell through all the swelling on his face. He moved as fast as he could, which felt slightly faster than an infant's crawl.

Spindle stepped out of the car, moved her seat up, then pushed Bannickburn into the car when he reached the door. He fell onto the back seat and lay still.

"Robert?" It was Jackie's voice. He turned his head to see her concerned face peering back at him over the passenger seat.

"Hi," he said.

"Where's the water?"

He might have smiled again. "Gone."

"Does Kader have it?"

He would have laughed if it hadn't felt like knives

were stabbing his lungs. "Kind of." He coughed. "The others?"

"Bailey's dead," she said. She didn't sound too sad. "Cayman, X-Prime, and Kross are in a car that one of Bailey's guys is driving. That guy and the motorcycle driver are the only ones of Bailey's people that survived."

"Kader's? Jimmy's?"

"We haven't seen Jimmy," Jackie said. "Maybe Bailey got him before he checked out. There are a couple other thugs running around, but not too many vehicles for them. I don't think we'll have much pursuit."

Bannickburn had some more questions, but they'd have to wait. The soothing rumble of tires on concrete, combined with his exhaustion and pain, sent him into unconsciousness.

29

In most of life, at least in Bannickburn's experience, not being able to use your arms caused considerable difficulty and inconvenience. There was one circumstance, though, when it didn't work out all that badly—when you had a beautiful young lady to wait on you.

"Jackie? Would you be so kind as to help me with a sip of water?"

Jackie rolled her eyes. "This is what I get for not having straws in the house." She walked over to him and held a cup to his lips. He smiled gratefully.

Thanks to the Witch's Moss, he couldn't move his arms. And thanks to the thick tape over his broken ribs, he couldn't move his torso. His sprained knee kept him from walking, and the blows to his head kept him from keeping his eyes open for too long and letting in painful light. All he was suited for today was lying still and being served by Jackie. He could do that.

He knew he had to enjoy this respite while it lasted. Before long, both Kader and Martel might be looking for his hide. He'd have to be mobile soon. Just not now.

"Uh-oh," Jackie said. Bannickburn opened his eyes. Trouble might be coming immediately.

"Kross is outside."

Bannickburn lunged forward, then settled back into

his reclined position as pain shot through his body. "What's he doing?"

"Nothing. Leaning against a wall. Looking at his fingernails. Just waiting."

Bannickburn sighed. "Would you mind wheeling me out?"

"Not at all," Jackie said.

With her help, he moved from the couch to a wheeled armchair. She pushed him through one of her convoluted entrance paths out to the street.

Kross watched them approach. He showed no hint that he'd been in a firefight the day before. His gray suit pants were finely creased, his tie was perfectly knotted, and he looked calm and relaxed. Bannickburn hated him more than ever.

"Mr. Bannickburn," Kross said. "Caporegime Shivers would like a word with you."

"Caporegime?" Bannickburn asked.

Kross nodded.

"Well. Good for him. Tell him that I respectfully decline his invitation."

"I'm afraid that's not an option," Kross said casually.

"I'm not in much shape for a journey anywhere, and I'm not anxious to be anywhere alone with Shivers. You remember what he did to us, don't you?"

Kross nonchalantly waved his hand. "I was mostly along as an observer. I didn't take his actions personally."

Bannickburn whistled. "*Damn,* they must pay you well. Blind loyalty like that doesn't come cheap."

Kross dropped his casual posture, and stood stiffly in front of Bannickburn.

"You're not in a good position to be making any insults," he said coldly.

"Right. Habits are hard to break. Anyway, tell your boss I said congratulations and go to hell."

A cold voice sounded from behind Bannickburn. "You don't want me angry with you, do you, Robert?"

Jackie and Bannickburn both whirled, furious. "You little—" Bannickburn started.

Shivers raised his hands appeasingly. "Robert, Robert, please." he said. "Let's not start on unpleasant footing. We're not enemies."

"Really?" Jackie said. "Your attempt to ambush and kill us kind of left another impression."

"Business is business," Shivers said. He, unlike Kross, bore some marks from the previous night. His arm was in a sling, he had a bandage over his cheek, and he moved his torso awkwardly. "The water bottle was business. I was sent down to correct a situation that my superiors thought was unstable."

"You were *sent* down?" Bannickburn said. "By Martel?"

"Of course. Not many other people knew about it."

"Why did Martel send you? We had it under control."

"That's not what Sottocapo Martel thought. He became quite worried when he heard Kader had received leaked information about the mission, as well as about your identity. He believed Bailey had been careless with information, so he sent me to ensure things were done correctly."

"You were sent to *counteract* Kader? But you *sided* with him!"

Shivers just shrugged. "Seemingly," he said.

Bannickburn shook his head, wondering. But then he thought about everything he had seen, everything Jimmy had done, and what he knew about the man. And it started to make sense.

"You leaked the information about me to Kader," Bannickburn said slowly. "I know Martel had it. You put him on Bailey's tail. Then, when Martel found out what happened, he blamed Bailey instead of you, and sent you to save the day."

Shivers smirked. "Which I did. I kept the water out of Kader's hands and kept you, our precious operative, alive."

"You had nothing to do with either of those things!"

"That may be your story. Martel's heard quite a different account, and that's now what he believes."

"And for your heroism, he promoted you to caporegime."

"That seems to be the case."

"So you set Bailey up. Either way, he was screwed—either Kader or Martel would get him. And no matter what happened, you'd fill Martel's head with lies that made you look good. As long as you survived, of course."

"That's something I'm good at."

"Why? Why go after Bailey?"

"Because he wasn't as funny as he thought he was," Shivers said bluntly. "And I could do his job better than him."

Bannickburn could only shake his head. He couldn't believe he'd dived into this snake pit and survived.

"So why are you here?" he asked. "To gloat?"

"Not at all," Shivers said. "To work out an agreement."

"Which is?"

"You never try to tell Martel about what you think is true. Allow him to believe what he believes right now."

"And what do I get in return?"

"You remain, in Murson Kader's mind, a forgotten man. The evidence implicating you in the Gates con is buried. No one, including me, will have cause to hunt you down and kill you."

Well, no one I've dealt with recently, Bannickburn thought. Then he nodded wearily. "Fine. But Kader's still going to be looking for revenge."

"I don't think so. He received a very kind letter from the Gates Casino, apologizing for the mishap of the other night. They've invited him back as a regular customer."

Bannickburn gaped. "And how did you manage *that?*"

"Ah, Robert," Shivers said. "That would be telling. Be well." He motioned to Kross, and the two of them walked away.

Bannickburn finally remembered to close his mouth, which had been hanging open, when they were out of sight. Then he dropped his chin to his chest.

"My dear," he said, "you have earned the right to say 'I told you so' repeatedly over the next year or so."

"Don't think I won't take advantage of it," she said. "Come on, let's go back inside."

Jackie wheeled Bannickburn back toward the warehouse. He sat still, a blanket on his lap, feeling pain when the chair so much as bumped over a pebble. He felt like an old man.

A thought struck him as they traveled back to her doss.

"That chemical analysis you did," he said. "How long did it take?"

She shrugged. "Not long. A few minutes at most."

"And that gave you the chemical composition of the Laés?"

"Yeah. Why?"

"When the Finnigan people picked up the water in the Tir," he said. "Wouldn't that be the first thing they did? So they'd have the data no matter what?"

Her eyes widened a little. "Yeah. Probably."

"Could they have sent the data to Seattle?"

"I don't know. Maybe. But Tir networks are tough to crack. They might not have been able to send out the data. And when you left The Finnigan toughs lying in the woods after you took the bottle, that might have been the end of any data they had."

"You said 'might' a couple of times," Bannickburn said. "That leaves the possibility that they got the data out."

Jackie tilted her head. "It's possible."

"So everything we did to keep the bottle out of Finnigan hands . . ."

She patted his shoulder. "Shhh. This isn't the time to think about it. Shivers told you no one's coming to kill you for the time being. That should be enough."

He supposed it was. He sat back in the chair. The

conversation had taken what little energy he had, and he was ready to sleep for another day or so. He closed his eyes, and immediately started drifting away.

As he crept toward dreaming, he remembered the fight last night. He thought of the look in Kader's eyes when he felt the first traces of paralysis, then eventually became frozen—the slow drops of each touch from Bannickburn gathering into an unstoppable wave of rigidity. He hadn't understood what was happening to him, and beneath his cold metal face he must have felt traces of fear.

Bannickburn hadn't scared anyone big and powerful like that in a long, long time. It almost made the whole mess worthwhile.

Acknowledgements

While the arrogant side of me is tempted to claim that no one helped me, and that all credit (or blame) is due to me, the honest side compels me to mention the many people who have helped me in assorted ways.

- My mother and father, through their prodigious book collections and their bedtime stories, made a lifetime reader out of me. Plus, they did lots of other nice things that I don't have space to list. Suffice it to say, they deserve the top spot on this particular list.
- I should also mention my two brothers and six sisters, mainly because I like them and they're good people. In my family, what I just said qualifies as incredibly mushy.
- I don't think I could have dreamed up an editor as supportive as Sharon Turner Mulvihill. Even when she was calling for a total rewrite of this thing or the other, she was encouraging and upbeat. We fragile-ego types appreciate that.
- Having Mike Mulvihill's vast body of Shadowrun knowledge to draw upon was tremendously helpful. Five years ago, when I first talked to him about maybe writing Shadowrun stuff, he was open and generous with what he knew, and that happened

again with this book. He's never made me feel bad about all the things I don't know.

- A few years ago, when Randall Bills was skipping town after FASA closed, he dumped a whole pile of Shadowrun sourcebooks on me. They proved incredibly useful in writing this. Plus, Randall's pretty much a god to me, so his name must be invoked.

- I should also mention that when I wandered to FASA's booth at GenCon years back and told them I might be writing Shadowrun stuff, Dan Grendell loaded me down with some key books that helped me learn the ways of the Shadowrun universe. Thanks, Flake!

- Rob Boyle of FanPro let me be involved in sourcebook production in a few different ways in the past year, which helped immerse me more and more in the universe. That helped.

- After writing two Crimson Skies™ novels for FASA, Donna Ippolito encouraged me to look into their other properties, to see which one I might like to write about. I told her that Shadowrun sounded like a lot of fun to me, and though it took a while, I finally got to write a Shadowrun novel. And it was just as fun as I thought it would be.

- To everyone who read *The Scorpion Jar*: you're all beautiful people! And I'd like to especially acknowledge Meredith Everton, who said she enjoyed it even though politics aren't her thing. I hope this one will be more up her alley.

- And finally, my little family—my wife, Kathy, and son, Finn. Words can't express, so I'll keep trying to show you guys how I feel in other ways.

About the Author

Along with writing this book, Jason M. Hardy hopes to someday direct and choreograph *Shadowrun: The Musical,* which would be the first Broadway show since *Oklahoma!* to feature a singing troll. His previous work includes the MechWarrior®: Dark Age™ novel *The Scorpion Jar,* stories on the BattleCorps Web site (www.battlecorps.com), an original roleplaying game setting called *The Labyrinth of Oversoul,* and at least one completely unpublishable novel that he wrote a decade ago, and that he hopes none of you ever see.

He lives in Chicago with his wife and son.

STEPHEN KENSON

SHADOWRUN BOOK #1: BORN TO RUN

Earth, 2063. Long-dormant magical forces have reawakened, and the creatures of mankind's legends and nightmares have come out of hiding. Megacorporations act as the new world superpowers, and the dregs of society fight for their own power. Sliding through the cracks in between are shadowrunners—underworld professionals who will do anything for a profit, and anything it takes to get the job done.

Kellan Colt has come to Seattle to make a name for herself. But her first run proves that in her line of work, there's no such thing as a sure thing, and that in her world, there is only one law—survival.

0-451-46058-8

Available wherever books are sold or at penguin.com

STEPHEN KENSON

SHADOWRUN BOOK #2: POISON AGENDAS

Earth, 2063. Shadowrunner Kellan Colt
thinks she's ready to strike out on her own
when she discovers the location of a secret
cache of military weaponry—right in the heart
of the supernatural creature-infested
Awakened wilderness.

0-451-46063-4

**Available wherever books are sold or at
penguin.com**

STEPHEN KENSON

SHADOWRUN BOOK #3:
FALLEN ANGLES

Kellan Colt has come far in her magical
training. But she still doesn't know the truth
about her shadowrunner mother or the secrets
of the amulet she possessed. Troubled by
disturbing dreams, Kellan is drawn into the
paranoid elven homeland of Tir Tairngire
where she must unravel the most difficult
riddle of all: who can she really trust
in the shadows?

0-451-46076-6

**Available wherever books are sold or at
penguin.com**

Penguin Group (USA) Online

What will you be reading tomorrow?

Tom Clancy, Patricia Cornwell, W.E.B. Griffin,
Nora Roberts, William Gibson, Robin Cook,
Brian Jacques, Catherine Coulter, Stephen King,
Dean Koontz, Ken Follett, Clive Cussler,
Eric Jerome Dickey, John Sandford,
Terry McMillan, Sue Monk Kidd, Amy Tan,
John Berendt…

You'll find them all at
penguin.com

*Read excerpts and newsletters,
find tour schedules and reading group guides,
and enter contests.*

Subscribe to Penguin Group (USA) newsletters
and get an exclusive inside look
at exciting new titles and the authors you love
long before everyone else does.

PENGUIN GROUP (USA)
us.penguingroup.com